RUTA SEPETYS

OUT
of the
EASY

*For Mom,
who always put her children first*

PENGUIN BOOKS
An imprint of Penguin Random House LLC, New York

First published in the United States of America by Philomel Books,
a division of Penguin Young Readers Group, 2013
Published by Speak, an imprint of Penguin Group (USA), 2014
Published by Penguin Books, an imprint of Penguin Random House LLC, 2020

Copyright © 2013 by Ruta Sepetys
The Fountains of Silence teaser text copyright © 2019 by Ruta Sepetys

Penguin supports copyright. Copyright fuels creativity, encourages diverse voices, promotes free speech, and creates a vibrant culture. Thank you for buying an authorized edition of this book and for complying with copyright laws by not reproducing, scanning, or distributing any part of it in any form without permission. You are supporting writers and allowing Penguin to continue to publish books for every reader.

Penguin Books & colophon are registered trademarks of Penguin Books Limited.

Visit us online at penguinrandomhouse.com

THE LIBRARY OF CONGRESS HAS CATALOGED THE PHILOMEL BOOKS EDITION AS FOLLOWS:
Sepetys, Ruta.
Out of the Easy / Ruta Sepetys.
p. cm.
Summary: Josie, the seventeen-year-old daughter of a French Quarter prostitute, is striving to escape 1950 New Orleans and enroll at prestigious Smith College when she becomes entangled in a murder investigation.
ISBN 978-0-399-25692-9 (hardcover)
[1. Conduct of life—Fiction. 2. Prostitution—Fiction. 3. Murder—Fiction.
4. Mothers and daughters—Fiction. 5. New Orleans (La.)—History—20th century—Fiction.
6. Mystery and detective stories.] I. Title.
PZ7.S47957Out 2013
[Fic]—dc23
2012016062

Penguin Books ISBN 9780147508430

Edited by Tamra Tuller. Design by Semadar Megged.

Printed in the United States of America

19th Printing

Praise for

OUT *of the* EASY

"A satisfying novel, bringing to life the midcentury French Quarter . . . Sepetys writes with rawness and palpable emotional unease." —*The New York Times Book Review* (Editors' Choice)

"A haunting peek at the life of a teenage girl in 1950s New Orleans."
—*Entertainment Weekly*

"Sepetys's latest is full of transporting writing, drawing you into a past that is fully reconstructed by her superb imagination."
—*The Boston Globe*

"Street-smart, literary, and compassionate . . . Atmospheric and assured . . . nicely paced novel." —*The Wall Street Journal*

"Unforgettable." —*Toronto Star*

★ "With a rich and realistic setting, a compelling and entertaining first-person narration, a colorful cast of memorable characters and an intriguing storyline, this is a surefire winner. Immensely satisfying." —*Kirkus Reviews*, STARRED REVIEW

★ "[A]nother taut and charged historical novel . . . Sepetys has also built a stellar cast. Readers will find Josie irresistible from the get-go and will devour the sultry mix of mystery, historical detail, and romance." —*Publishers Weekly*, STARRED REVIEW

★ "A Dickensian array of characters; the mystique, ambience, and language of the French Quarter; a suspenseful, action-packed story. With dramatic and contextual flair, Sepetys introduces teens to another memorable heroine."
—*School Library Journal*, STARRED REVIEW

"A page-turner that noir romance fans will gobble up. The legions of fans that Sepetys earned with her best-selling debut novel will all be lining up for this." —*Booklist*

"This suspenseful novel . . . proves Sepetys's extraordinary versatility as a storyteller." —*Shelf Awareness*

ALSO BY RUTA SEPETYS

The Fountains of Silence

Salt to the Sea

Between Shades of Gray

There is no excellent beauty that hath not some strangeness in the proportion.

—Sir Francis Bacon

ONE

My mother's a prostitute. Not the filthy, streetwalking kind. She's actually quite pretty, fairly well spoken, and has lovely clothes. But she sleeps with men for money or gifts, and according to the dictionary, that makes her a prostitute.

She started working in 1940 when I was seven, the year we moved from Detroit to New Orleans. We took a cab from the train station straight to a fancy hotel on St. Charles Avenue. Mother met a man from Tuscaloosa in the lobby while having a drink. She introduced me as her niece and told the man she was delivering me to her sister. She winked at me constantly and whispered that she'd buy me a doll if I just played along and waited for her. I slept alone in the lobby that night, dreaming of my new doll. The next morning, Mother checked us in to our own big room with tall windows and small round soaps that smelled like lemon. She received a green velvet box with a strand of pearls from the man from Tuscaloosa.

"Josie, this town is going to treat us just fine," said Mother, standing topless in front of the mirror, admiring her new pearls.

The next day, a Negro driver named Cokie arrived at the hotel. Mother had received an invitation to visit someone important in the Quarter. She made me take a bath and insisted I put on a nice dress. She even put a ribbon in my hair. I looked silly, but I didn't say anything to Mother. I just smiled and nodded.

"Now, Josie, you aren't to say a thing. I've been hoping Willie would call for me, and I don't need you messing things up with your stubbornness. Don't speak unless you're spoken to. And for gosh sakes, don't start that humming. It's spooky when you do that. If you're good, I'll buy you something real special."

"Like a doll?" I said, hoping to jog her memory.

"Sure, hon, would you like a doll?" she said, finishing her sweep of lipstick and kissing the air in front of the mirror.

Cokie and I hit it off right away. He drove an old taxicab painted a foggy gray. If you looked close, you could see the ghost of taxi lettering on the door. He gave me a couple Mary Jane candies and a wink that said, "Hang in there, kiddo." Cokie whistled through the gaps in his teeth as he drove us to Willie's in his taxicab. I hummed along, hoping the molasses from the Mary Jane might yank out a tooth. That was the second night we were in New Orleans.

We pulled to a stop on Conti Street. "What is this place?" I asked, craning my neck to look at the pale yellow building with black lattice balconies.

"It's her house," said Cokie. "Willie Woodley's."

"*Her* house? But Willie's a man's name," I said.

"Stop it, Josie. Willie is a woman's name. Now, keep quiet!" said Mother, smacking my thigh. She smoothed her dress and fidgeted with her hair. "I didn't think I'd be so nervous," she muttered.

"Why are you nervous?" I asked.

She grabbed me by the hand and yanked me up the walk. Cokie tipped his hat to me. I smiled and waved back. The sheers in the front window shifted, covering a shadowy figure lit by an amber glow behind the glass. The door opened before we reached it.

"And you must be Louise," a woman said to Mother.

A brunette in a velvet evening dress hung against the door. She had pretty hair, but her fingernails were chewed and frayed. Cheap women had split nails. I'd learned that in Detroit.

"She's waitin' for you in the parlor, Louise," said the brunette.

A long red carpet ran from the front door to a tall staircase, crawling up and over each step. The house was opulent, gaudy, with deep green brocades and lamps with black crystals dangling from dimly lit shades. Paintings of nude women with pink nipples hung from the foyer walls. Cigarette smoke mingled with stale Eau de Rose. We walked through a group of girls who patted my head and called me sugar and doll. I remember thinking their lips looked like someone had smeared blood all over them. We walked into the front parlor.

I saw her hand first, veiny and pale, draped over the arm of an upholstered wingback. Her nails, glossy red like pomegranate seeds, could pop a balloon with a quick flick. Clusters of gold and diamonds adorned nearly every finger. Mother's breathing fluttered.

I approached the hand, staring at it, making my way around the back of the chair toward the window. Black heels poked out from beneath a stiff tailored skirt. I felt the bow in my hair slide down the side of my head.

"Hello, Louise."

The voice was thick and had mileage on it. Her platinum-blond hair was pulled tight in a clasp engraved with the initials W.W. The woman's eyes, lined in charcoal, had wrinkles fringing out from the corners. Her lips were scarlet, but not bloody. She was pretty once.

The woman stared at me, then finally spoke. "I said, 'Hello, Louise.'"

"Hello, Willie," said Mother. She dragged me in front of the chair. "Willie, this is Josie."

I smiled and bent my scabby legs into my best curtsy. The arm with the red nails quickly waved me away to the settee across from her. Her bracelet jangled a discordant tune.

"So . . . you've returned." Willie lifted a cigarette from a mother-of-pearl case and tapped it softly against the lid.

"Well, it's been a long time, Willie. I'm sure you can understand."

Willie said nothing. A clock on the wall swung a ticktock rhythm. "You look good," Willie finally said, still tapping the cigarette against its case.

"I'm keeping myself," said Mother, leaning back against the settee.

"Keeping yourself . . . yes. I heard you had a greenhorn from Tuscaloosa last night."

Mother's back stiffened. "You heard about Tuscaloosa?"

Willie stared, silent.

"Oh, he wasn't a trick, Willie," said Mother, looking into her lap. "He was just a nice fella."

"A nice fella who bought you those pearls, I guess," said Willie, tapping her cigarette harder and harder against the case.

Mother's hand reached up to her neck, fingering the pearls.

"I've got good business," said Willie. "Men think we're headed to war. If that's true, everyone will want their last jollies. We'd work well together, Louise, but . . ." She nodded in my direction.

"Oh, she's a good girl, Willie, and she's crazy smart. Even taught herself to read."

"I don't like kids," she spat, her eyes boring a hole through me.

I shrugged. "I don't like 'em much either."

Mother pinched my arm, hard. I felt the skin snap. I bit my lip and tried not to wince. Mother became angry when I complained.

"Really?" Willie continued to stare. "So what do you do . . . if you don't like kids?"

"Well, I go to school. I read. I cook, clean, and I make martinis for Mother." I smiled at Mother and rubbed my arm.

"You clean and make martinis?" Willie raised a pointy eyebrow. Her sneer suddenly faded. "Your bow is crooked, girl. Have you always been that skinny?"

"I wasn't feeling well for a few years," said Mother quickly. "Josie is very resourceful, and—"

"I see that," said Willie flatly, still tapping her cigarette.

I moved closer to Mother. "I skipped first grade altogether and started in the second grade. Mother lost track I was supposed to be in school—" Mother's toe dug into my ankle. "But it didn't matter much. She told the school we had transferred from another town, and I just started right in second grade."

"You skipped the first grade?" said Willie.

"Yes, ma'am, and I don't figure I missed anything at all."

"Don't ma'am me, girl. You'll call me Willie. Do you understand?" She shifted in her chair. I spied what looked like the butt of a gun stuffed down the side of the seat cushion.

"Yes, Mrs. Willie," I replied.

"Not Mrs. Willie. Just Willie."

I stared at her. "Actually, Willie, I prefer Jo, and honestly, I don't much care for bows." I pulled the ribbon from my thick brown bob and reached for the lighter on the table.

"I didn't ask for a light," said Willie.

"No, but you've tapped your cigarette fifty-three times . . . now fifty-four, so I thought you might like to smoke it."

Willie sighed. "Fine, Jo, light my cigarette and pour me a Scotch."

"Neat or on the rocks?" I asked.

Her mouth opened in surprise, then snapped shut. "Neat." She eyed me as I lit her cigarette.

"Well, Louise," said Willie, a long exhale of smoke curling above her head, "you've managed to mess things up royal, now, haven't you?"

Mother sighed.

"You can't stay here, not with a child. You'll have to get a place," said Willie.

"I don't have any money," said Mother.

"Sell those pearls to my pawn in the morning and you'll have some spending money. There's a small apartment on Dauphine that one of my bookies was renting. The idiot went and got himself shot last week. He's taking a dirt nap and won't need the place. The rent is paid until the thirtieth. I'll make some arrangements, and we'll see where you are at the end of the month."

"All right, Willie," said Mother.

I handed Willie the drink and sat back down, nudging the bow under the settee with my foot.

She took a sip and nodded. "Honestly, Louise, a seven-year-old bartender?"

Mother shrugged.

That was ten years ago. She never did buy me the doll.

TWO

They thought I couldn't hear their whispers, their snickers. I had heard them for ten years. I cut across Conti toward Chartres, clutching my book under my arm. The vibration of my humming blocked out the sound. Courtesan, harlot, hooker, whore. I'd heard them all. In fact, I could look at someone and predict which one they'd use.

"Hello, Josie," they'd say with a half smile, followed by a sigh and sometimes a shake of the head. They acted like they felt sorry for me, but as soon as they were ten steps away, I'd hear one of the words, along with my mother's name. The wealthy women pretended it singed their tongue to say *whore*. They'd whisper it and raise their eyebrows. Then they'd fake an expression of shock, like the word itself had crawled into their pants with a case of the clap. They didn't need to feel sorry for me. I was nothing like Mother. After all, Mother was only half of the equation.

"Josie! Wait up, Yankee girl."

Frankie, one of Willie's information men, was at my side, his tall, slinky frame bending over mine. "What's the rush?" he asked, licking his fingers and smoothing his greased hair.

"I have to get to the bookshop," I said. "I'm late for work."

"Sheesh, what would ol' man Marlowe do without you? You spoonin' him applesauce these days? I hear he's just about dead."

"He's very much alive, Frankie. He's just . . . retired." I shot him a look.

"Ooh, defensive. You got something goin' with Marlowe?"

"Frankie!" What a horrible thought. Charlie Marlowe was not only ancient, he was like family.

"Or maybe you got a thing for his son, is that it? You got eyes on looping with Junior so you can inherit that dusty book nook you love so well?" He elbowed me, laughing.

I stopped walking. "Can I help you with something, Frankie?"

He pulled me onward, his voice low. "Actually, yeah. Can you tell Willie that word on my side is that Cincinnati's comin' down?"

A chill ran beneath the surface of my skin. I tried to keep my step steady. "Cincinnati?"

"Can you let her know, Josie?"

"I won't see Willie till morning, you know that," I said.

"You still not going near the place after dark? Such a smart one, you are. Well, give her word Cincinnati's around. She'll want to know."

"I hope I don't forget," I said, opening my palm.

"Oooh. Beggar woman!"

"Businesswoman," I corrected him. "Remember, Willie doesn't like surprises."

"No, she don't," he said, digging in his pocket. "What do you do with all this bank, Josie? Be a lot easier if you just lifted your skirt."

"The only reason I'd lift my skirt is to pull out my pistol and plug you in the head."

My money was none of Frankie's business. I was getting out of New Orleans. My plan included bus fare and cash reserves to cover a full year of living expenses, enough time to get me on my feet. A business book I read in the shop said that it was always best to have at least twelve months' savings. Once I had the money, I'd decide where to go.

"All right, all right," he said. "You know I'm only joking."

"Why don't you just buy a book from me at the shop, Frankie?"

"You know I don't like to read, Yankee girl. Don't think anyone likes to read as much as you do. What you got under your arm this time?"

"E. M. Forster."

"Never heard of it." He grabbed my hand and dropped some coins in my palm. "There, now don't forget to tell her. I won't get paid if you forget."

"You know when he'll hit town or where he's holing up?" I asked.

"Nah. Not yet. For all I know, he's already here." Frankie twitched and looked over his shoulder. "See ya, kid."

I grabbed my skirt and quickened my pace toward the bookshop. It had been two years since the incident. Cincinnati hadn't been back in the Quarter, and no one missed him. He claimed he worked on the fringes for Carlos Marcello, the godfather of the New Orleans mafia. No one believed him, but no one outright challenged him on it, either. Cincinnati proudly wore expensive suits—suits that didn't quite fit him. It was rumored that his clothes were stolen from corpses, people he had killed for Carlos Marcello. Cokie said it was bad mojo to wear a dead man's suit.

Carlos Marcello ran the syndicate and owned land just outside Orleans Parish. Talk amongst the locals was that Marcello stocked his swamps with alligators and dumped his dead bodies there. A postman once told Cokie that he saw shoes floating on top of the filmy swamp. Willie knew Carlos Marcello. She sent girls out to his Town and Country Motel when the heat was on the house on Conti. That's where Mother met Cincinnati.

Cincinnati had a thing for Mother. He brought her expensive gifts and claimed she looked just like Jane Russell from the Hollywood magazines. I guess that meant I looked like Jane Russell, too, but maybe Jane Russell without makeup, nice clothes, or styled hair. Our brown eyes were set a bit far apart, and we had high foreheads, a mess of dark hair, and lips that always looked pouty.

Mother was crazy about Cincinnati, even once claimed they were in love. Sometimes Mother was embarrassingly stupid. It was bad enough she turned tricks with a criminal like Cincinnati, but in love with him? Pathetic. Willie hated Cincinnati. I despised him.

I cut through the skinny street near the jeweler, dodging a man peeing against the wall. I used E. M. Forster to wave the smell of moldy oak away from my face as I stepped quickly across the wet flagstones. If the Quarter smelled this bad in cool weather, it would reek this spring and be simply rancid by summer. I made my way up Toulouse toward Royal and heard Blind Otis singing the blues, stamping his foot and sliding a dull butter knife across his steel strings.

Bar and restaurant owners stood on ladders, decorating their doors and windows for the night's festivities. At midnight, 1950 would finally arrive. A fizz of excitement perked through the streets. People were anxious to put the decade, and the war, behind them. A pair of lovers cut in front of me to chase a taxi while a small man in ragged clothing stood up against a building saying "hallelujah" over and over again.

Last time Cincinnati was in town, he got drunk and beat Mother. Willie kicked down the door and shot at him, grazing his leg. I drove Mother to the hospital in Cokie's cab. After he sobered up, Cincinnati actually had the guts to come to the hospital. I threw hot coffee on him and told him I'd called the cops. He left town limping, but not without promising to come back.

"Just you wait," he whispered, licking his teeth. "I'm gonna get you, Josie Moraine."

I shook off the shiver.

"Hey, Motor City."

I turned toward the voice. Jesse Thierry sat on his motorcycle, staring at me from across the street. Jesse was quiet and often spoke through only a nod or a smile. Sometimes I thought he was watching me, which was ridiculous, because Jesse Thierry would have no interest in someone like me. He might be quiet, but his looks were not. He was striking and edgy, in a way that made me feel uncomfortable. Others didn't find Jesse's looks unsettling. Tourists turned to look at him. He was constantly trailed by girls.

"You need a ride?" he asked. I shook my head.

"I want a ride, Jesse!" said a blonde next to him.

He ignored her. "You sure, Jo?"

"I'm sure. Thanks, Jesse."

He nodded, fired up the bike, and sped away, leaving the girls on the sidewalk.

The noise faded as I turned onto Royal. The deep blue sign with gold lettering came into view, hanging from a wrought-iron bracket above the door: MARLOWE'S BOOKSHOP. Through the window, I could see Patrick sitting at the counter. The bell tinkled overhead as I entered the store, and the calming smell of paper and dust surrounded me.

"How is he today?" I asked.

"Today's a good day. He knows my name. I think for a second he even remembered I'm his son," said Patrick, leaning back on his usual chair behind the counter.

"Wonderful!" I meant it. Some days Mr. Marlowe didn't recognize Patrick. Sometimes he swore at him, even threw things at him. Those were bad days.

"Your pal Cokie came by," said Patrick. "He said to give you this." He slid a folded piece of paper across the counter.

I opened it.

CINCYNATTY.

It was written in Cokie's shaky handwriting.

"I didn't read it, but I think he means Cincinnati," said Patrick.

"You didn't read it, huh?" Patrick had just turned twenty-one but still teased like a boy who milked girls' pigtails at recess.

He smiled. "He doesn't know how to spell it. Is he going to Cincinnati?"

"Mmm . . . must be. Did you save me a paper?"

He pointed to a copy of the *Times-Picayune*, neatly folded on my chair.

"Thanks. I'll take over in a minute," I told him.

"Really, Jo, the *Picayune* is so boring. They intentionally leave out news from the Quarter and . . ."

Patrick's voice trailed off as I made my way through the tall shelves of books toward the squirrelly staircase at the back of the shop. I had kept my own apartment since I was eleven. It wasn't really an apartment, not at first anyway. It was a tiny office with a bathroom attached. I had been sleeping in the bookshop since I was ten, when Mother started her fits and beat me with an umbrella for no good reason. I quickly learned she was happiest when I wasn't around. So I'd hide in the bookshop just before close and sleep under the large desk in the office.

On my eleventh birthday, I crept up the stairs after the store was locked. The office had been transformed. The windows and walls had been washed. The desk was still there, but all the boxes were cleared out and there was a bed, a small dresser, and even bookshelves in the corner. Flowered curtains hung from a rod over the open window, and music floated up from Bourbon Street. A single key hung on a nail. A lock had been installed on the door and a baseball bat leaned up against the bed. We never spoke of the arrangement. I simply began working for Mr. Marlowe in the store in exchange for the lodging.

I unlocked the door and slipped inside, quickly bolting it again. I got down on my hands and knees and pulled up a floorboard underneath my bed, feeling around until my fingers hit the cigar box. I dropped the coins from Frankie inside and put the floorboard back in place. I crawled out from under the bed and snapped the drapes shut. Then I opened the note from Cokie.

CINCYNATTY.

THREE

"I'll be right back," I told Patrick when I came down into the shop.

"Aw, come on. It's New Year's Eve," he complained.

"It's only one o'clock."

"But I've got things to do," he said.

"I'll just be a minute," I told him, rushing out the door.

I ran across the street to Sal's. Willie was a good customer at Sal's restaurant, and he let me use his telephone when I needed it. Actually, Willie was a good customer at many places, and fortunately, those benefits extended to me.

"Hi, Maria," I said to the hostess, pointing to the telephone at the back. She nodded.

I picked up the phone and dialed HEmlock 4673.

Dora answered after only one ring in her fake breathy voice.

"It's Jo. I need to speak to Willie."

"Hey, sugar, she's resting."

Resting? Willie never took naps. "Wake her up."

Dora put the receiver down. I heard her shoes clack and then fade on the hardwood floor as she went to get Willie. I could tell by the way the backs slapped against her heels that she was wearing the red-feathered mules that she bought mail-order from Frederick's of Fifth Avenue. I twisted the telephone cord, and it slipped between my fingers. My hand was sweating. I wiped the moisture on my skirt.

"Buttons and bows," said Willie, not even bothering to say hello.

"What?"

"The tune you were humming. It's 'Buttons and Bows.' Look, I need a little peace before the walls start shaking. What the hell's so important?"

"Cincinnati."

There was silence on Willie's end of the line. I heard the flip and flick of her sterling cigarette lighter and then a long breath as she inhaled and exhaled the smoke. "Who told you?"

"Frankie," I said. "He found me after I left your house. I was on my way to the bookshop."

"When's he in?" asked Willie.

"Said he didn't know, just that he was on his way and that he could be here already. Where's Mother?" I asked.

"Upstairs. She's been a giggling idiot all morning," said Willie.

"You think she knows?"

"Of course she knows. I knew something was up. Dora said she got a phone call two days ago. She's been a complete imbecile ever since." I heard the long intake of breath, the hold, and then the flutter as Willie expelled the curling smoke from her nostrils.

"Cokie knows. He left me a note," I said.

"Good. Cokie's scheduled for a few drop-offs tonight. He'll keep me posted. Are you at Sal's?"

"Yes. Cokie said the Dukes of Dixieland are playing tonight at the Paddock, so I thought I'd—"

"Absolutely not. I don't want you seen in the Quarter," said Willie.

"But, Willie, it's New Year's Eve," I argued.

"I don't give a rip. You're staying in—locked in. You understand?" she said.

I hesitated, wondering how far I could push it. "I hear Cincinnati's in with Carlos Marcello now."

"Mind your own business," Willie snapped. "Come over in the morning."

"It's just—I worry about Mother," I said.

"Worry about yourself. Your mother's a stupid whore." The line clicked and went dead.

FOUR

"Sorry about that," I said to Patrick as I returned to the bookshop.

"You okay?" he asked.

"Fine, why?"

"You have red splotches on your neck. Here, your beloved society page is chock-full today." He tossed the paper at me as I sat next to him behind the counter. His voice elevated to a prissy, nasal tone. "Miss Blanche Fournet of Birmingham, Alabama, who is spending part of her winter season in New Orleans, was the guest of honor at a luncheon given by her aunt and uncle Dr. and Mrs. George C. Fournet. The table was decorated with pale blue hydrangeas, and all the lovely guests had a perfectly boring time."

I laughed and swatted him across the shoulder with the paper.

"Really, Jo. Your obsession with Uptown and the society page is ridiculous. When are you gonna realize that those women are just a bunch of pretentious old biddies?"

The bell jingled, and a tall, handsome man in a tailored suit entered the shop.

"Afternoon," he said, smiling and nodding to us. "How are y'all today?"

The man's accent was Southern, but not from New Orleans. His skin was deeply tanned, making his teeth and broad smile sparkling white, like Cary Grant.

"Fine, thank you. Visiting New Orleans for the holiday, sir?" I asked.

"Is it that obvious?" said the man, grinning.

"I'm sorry, I just meant—"

"No apologies. You're correct. I'm just down from Memphis for the Sugar Bowl."

"Do you play?" asked Patrick, eyeing the man's height and broad shoulders.

"I did. Wide receiver for Vanderbilt. I used to come here with the team, and we'd duke it out with Tulane. Always loved it. New Orleans was a great place to get in trouble, and I did my fair share, mind you." He gave a knowing wink to Patrick. "Y'all in school at Tulane?" he asked.

"I just finished up at Loyola," said Patrick.

"And you, pretty lady?" The gorgeous man looked at me.

College? Yes! I wanted to scream. I'd love to go to college. Instead I smiled and looked down.

"She's trying to make up her mind," said Patrick, jumping in. "You know the type, so smart, they're all fighting over her."

"Are you looking for anything in particular today?" I asked, changing the subject. I casually put two fingers on the counter, signaling to Patrick. It was one of the games we played, trying to guess what type of book the customer wanted. My two fingers told Patrick I was betting a dime that Mr. Memphis was interested in history. Patrick closed his left fist. That meant he wagered sports related.

"As a matter of fact, I am," he replied, taking off his hat. His black hair glistened in the afternoon sun streaming through the front window. "Keats."

"Poetry?" said Patrick.

"Ah, surprised, are you? Well, let's not judge a book by its cover, now. Even football players like poetry," he said.

"Of course they do," I replied. "The poetry section is right this way."

"I've got to run," said Patrick. "Josie will take it from here. Keats is one of her favorites. Nice to meet you, sir."

"Forrest Hearne," said the gentleman, extending his hand to Patrick. "Nice to meet you, too."

I led Mr. Hearne toward the back of the shop to the tall case of poetry books.

"They say Keats fell in love with his neighbor," I told him over my shoulder.

"Yes, but I've read it was a tumultuous affair," he said, challenging me. "Keats demanded that all of the letters between them be burned upon his death. So I guess we'll never know the truth."

I stopped at the stack with my back to Mr. Hearne and quickly scanned the alphabetized books for the letter *K*.

"Here we are, Keats." I turned around. Mr. Hearne was quite close, staring at me.

"Do I . . . know you somehow?" he asked seriously. "There's something about you that seems awfully familiar."

I felt a trickle of sweat between my shoulder blades. "I don't think so. I've never been to Tennessee."

"But I've been to New Orleans, many times," he said, adjusting the knot in his silk tie.

"I must have one of those familiar faces, I guess," I said, stepping away from him and the bookshelf. "Just holler if you need anything else."

I walked back to the counter, humming, aware of his gaze upon me as I slipped between the stacks. How could I be familiar to a former Vanderbilt football player from Tennessee who looked like a movie star and liked poetry? But his expression had been genuine, not like one of the sweet-talking men with bloodshot eyes that I saw at Willie's when I cleaned in the mornings. Sometimes, if I arrived before six A.M., I'd pass a trick on the way out. Most men didn't stay all night. Willie always said she wasn't holding a slumber party unless they wanted to pay good and big for one. No, most men would leave with a grin after they'd done their business. The men who stayed the whole night had a lot of money, but also a lack of something else, like they had a hole in their soul too big to be patched. More often than not, they'd try to make conversation with me before they left in the morning. The conversation was awkward, guilt soaked, and generally included the standard line that I looked familiar. But the way Mr. Hearne asked felt sincere, like it puzzled him somehow.

He walked back to the counter carrying two books.

"Ah, yes, this is a nice choice," I said, examining the volume of Keats he'd selected.

"For Marion, my wife," he said.

"Oh, and *David Copperfield* too."

"That's for me. I must have ten copies by now."

I smiled. "It's my most favorite of all Dickens. It's so inspiring, thinking that *David Copperfield* was based on Dickens's own life, that someone could overcome that kind of suffering and poverty to finally achieve happiness."

I had said too much. He was giving me the look. I hated the look. It was the "You've had it tough, huh, kid?" look. It made me feel pathetic.

Hearne spoke softly. "I know what you mean. I had kind of a Copperfield childhood myself."

I stared at him, shocked that the sophisticated man in front of me could have ever known poverty or suffering. Had he really recast himself? My surprise registered with him.

He nodded. "Decisions, they shape our destiny." Without opening the book, he began to recite from *David Copperfield*. "'Whether I shall turn out to be the hero of my own life, or whether that station will be held by anybody else . . .'"

I nodded and finished it with him. "'These pages must show.'"

We stood, not knowing each other, but understanding each other completely. A car horn honked from the street, severing our stares.

I quickly finished the receipt total and turned the pad to him. "Shall I wrap them for you?"

"No, that's not necessary." He took out a money clip from his interior suit pocket. The man had what Willie called "a head of lettuce." There were so many bills, they burst and flowered from the silver clip. I noticed his shiny Lord Elgin watch as he handed me a fifty-dollar bill.

"I'm sorry," I breathed. "I'm afraid I don't have change for something that large."

"My fault. I forgot to get change at the hotel. Would you take a check?" he asked.

We didn't accept checks, unless they came from customers with an account. We had had our share of rubber bouncers from stragglers in the Quarter. A sign in front of the register displayed our no-check policy. "Of course," I told him. "A check is fine."

He nodded in appreciation and took out his checkbook along with an elegant fountain pen. Forrest Hearne was in high cotton, to be sure.

"What is it that you do in Memphis?" I asked, trying to sound casual.

"I'm an architect and a developer," he said. He signed his check and handed it to me, smiling. "I build things."

I nodded.

He walked to the door, still staring at me with a quizzical expression. "Well, thank you for your help and the conversation. I sure do appreciate it."

"My pleasure."

"And good luck at college, whichever one you choose." He opened the door to leave and stopped suddenly. "I almost forgot—Happy New Year," he said, putting on his hat. "It's gonna be a great one!"

"Happy New Year." I smiled.

And then he was gone.

FIVE

I sat on my bed staring at the check.

Forrest L. Hearne, Jr.

73 East Parkway Avenue North, Memphis, Tennessee

Memphis Bank and Trust Co.

His words seemed to whisper back at me. *Decisions, they shape our destiny.*

I went to my desk and pulled the yellowed sheet of paper out from its hiding place. I had started the list when I was thirteen with the name Tom Moraine, a journalist who had come to the bookshop. One day, when I was mad at Willie, I told her I had found my father and was going to leave. Willie laughed. She told me that Moraine wasn't my father's last name. It was the name of a gambler Mother had run off with when she was seventeen. The marital bliss lasted all of three months and then Mother came back. She kept the ring and the name.

Willie said fathers were overrated, that my father could be one of thousands, most likely some rotten crotch creep that loved clip-on ties. She said I should forget about it. But I didn't forget about it. I couldn't. So the game continued, and for years I added names to the list, imagining that 50 percent of me was somehow respectable instead of rotten. And creepy was certainly relative. After all, what was creepier, a man who loved clip-on ties or a girl who kept a log of fantasy fathers hidden in her desk drawer?

The red neon sign from Sal's across the street blinked and buzzed, washing my curtains and desktop in a rosy glow. The volume outside increased as midnight drew closer. 1950, and the promised opportunity of the new decade, would soon arrive. I added the name Forrest L. Hearne, Jr., to the list, along with the few details I knew about him. I estimated him in his late thirties or early forties.

Football player. Memphis. Architect. Likes Dickens and Keats, I wrote.

Keats . . . He certainly wasn't an average tourist in the Quarter.

He had asked me about college. I had graduated from high school last June but had packed college in mothballs and shoved it up into the attic of my mind, where I wouldn't have to think about it for a while. High school was hard enough, but not because of the course work. That was easy for me. It was constantly trying to stay invisible that was exhausting. When people noticed me, they talked about me. Like the time Mother came to parent day in the eighth grade. She came only because one of

Willie's girls had said my history teacher, Mr. Devereaux, was handsome and a bit wild.

Mother showed up in diamond earrings and a full-length rabbit coat she said had "fallen off of a truck." She was completely naked underneath.

"Don't be such a prude, Josie. I was runnin' late. No one's going to notice," she told me. "Besides, the linin' feels so silky smooth. Now, which one's your history teacher?" She had been drinking and had a hard time keeping the coat closed. All the fathers stared while their wives gripped and pulled at their arms. The kids stared at me. The next day, several students whispered that their mommas had called mine "that whore." And then I felt naked and dirty too.

She must not have found my history teacher interesting. Mother never came back to school, not even for my high school graduation. "Oh, that was today?" she had said, dotting a fake mole on her cheek in front of the mirror. "Did you wear one of those ugly hats with the tassels?" She threw her head back and laughed the laugh I hated. It started innocent enough but then tightened in her throat, traveled up through her nose, and slithered out a cackle. I could see the ugly just pouring out of her.

Willie came to my graduation. She rolled her black Cadillac into the lot and parked in one of the spots reserved for administration. The crowd parted as she strode into the auditorium and took a seat up front. She arrived in an expensive tailored suit with matching hat and gloves, along with her traditional dark sunglasses—which she wore through the entire ceremony. Cokie came too and stood in the back with a large bouquet of flowers, smiling from ear to ear. People whispered about his toffee-colored skin, but I didn't listen. Cokie was the only man I felt truly safe with.

Willie gave me a gorgeous sterling locket from Tiffany & Co. for graduation, engraved with my initials. "Engrave your pieces, Jo, and they'll always find their way back to you," said Willie. It was the most expensive thing I owned, and I wore it every day, tucked within my blouse. I knew if I took it off, Mother might steal it or sell it.

I wrote, *Asked about college*, in the margin near Mr. Hearne's name and tucked the paper back in the drawer.

I heard commotion in the street below, along with voices in unison,

"Five . . . four . . . three . . . two . . . one . . . HAPPY NEW YEAR!!"

Horns honked, and people yelled. I heard glass breaking and rounds of laughter.

I took out my mirror and set to work on my pin curls. I wound my thick hair around my finger, pressed it tight to my scalp, and slid a bobby pin across each curl. New Year's Eve was a mess. I wasn't missing a thing, I told myself. Last year, a salesman from Atlanta decided to show off his riches for the girls at Willie's by burning dollar bills in the parlor. They cooed and ahhed until one of Willie's oriental chairs caught fire. The next day I had to drag the burned-out shell to the alley and got covered in soot. Mother laughed at me. Her bitterness increased with each year. Mother had a hard time getting older, especially among all the young girls in Willie's house. She still looked to be in her twenties and lied about her age, but she wasn't exactly a favorite anymore.

I finished my curls and decided to read a bit until the merriment died down outside. Besides humming, reading was the only thing that blocked out Mother, the Quarter, and allowed me to experience life outside New Orleans. I leapt eagerly into books. The characters' lives were so much more interesting than the lonely heartbeat of my own.

My book was downstairs in the shop. I unlocked my door and stole down the tiny staircase in my nightgown and bare feet, staying within the dark shadows between the stacks so as not to be visible through the front window. I was on the other side of the store when I heard a noise. My shoulders jumped. There was a push at the door. Suddenly, it clicked and the bell jingled. Someone was in the shop.

I looked across the room to the staircase, debating whether I should make a run for my room and my gun. I moved to the side and stopped. Footsteps. They got closer. I ducked behind the stack and heard the deep chuckle of a man's voice. I searched for something to defend myself with. I slid a large book off the shelf in front of me.

"We seeeeee you," taunted the deep voice.

My heart lurched. We? Cincinnati had brought someone with him. A shadowy figure emerged in front of me. I hurled the book at his face with all my might and made a run for the stairs.

"Ow! Josie, what the hell?"

It was Patrick's voice. "Patrick?" I stopped and peeked around the bookshelf.

"Who else would be in the store?" said Patrick as he rubbed

the side of his face. "Sheesh, you really got me." A second figure stepped out beside him.

"What are you doing here?" I asked, moving forward. I smelled stale bourbon.

"We came to get a book," said Patrick.

"Jean Cocteau," said the man with the deep voice, laughing and holding up a book. *"Le Livre—"*

"Shhh," Patrick told him. His friend answered with what sounded like a giggle.

"Who are you?" I asked the man.

"Josie, this is James. He works at Doubleday."

"Doubleday Bookshop? Don't you have enough books of your own over there?" I asked.

"Not this one." He looked me over. "Nice nightgown."

"It's late, and I have to work early in the morning," I said, gesturing them toward the door.

"You're working on New Year's Day? Everything's closed. What do you do?" asked James.

"Family business," said Patrick. "Come on, let's go."

"Make sure you lock the door," I called after him.

Patrick turned and walked back to me. "You think I'd leave my dad's shop unlocked? Jo, what's wrong with you?" he whispered.

"Nothing. You surprised me, that's all. Happy New Year."

"Happy New Year," said Patrick, reaching across to punch me on the arm. He tilted his head and looked at me, then nudged me into the pool of light that spilled in from the front window.

"What are you doing?" I asked him, clutching my book to the front of my nightgown.

"Jo, you really ought to part your hair on the side, instead of down the middle."

"What?" I asked.

His friend laughed.

"Nothing," said Patrick.

SIX

As expected, the house was a mess. I tightened my apron and pulled on the thick rubber gloves Willie insisted I wear. Ashtrays overflowed with cigar butts in the parlor, and empty liquor bottles crowded the tabletops. I spied a silver high-heeled shoe dangling from a planter as I stepped over a rhinestone earring in a sticky puddle of champagne. Something smelled like sour apples. The floors would have to be scrubbed and the rugs beaten. I cringed, imagining the condition of the bathrooms. Happy New Year. I opened the windows and set to work.

I started up in Sweety's room. She lived with her grandmother and rarely spent the night. Sweety was a beautiful quadroon girl, a quarter Negro like Cokie. She had a long, thin neck, jet-black hair, and eyes so sincere you knew she really *saw* you. The men loved Sweety. She was a big earner and worked loyal to Willie. But she kept to herself and didn't socialize with the other women outside the house. I always wondered what she did with her money. Sweety was the only one who left me tips. Sometimes she took her sheets home at night and washed them herself.

Dora was a buxom redhead with wide hips who wore nothing but green. She had every shade imaginable—jade, mint, forest, apple, but absolutely everything was green. Dora was rough-and-tumble. I'd often find her snoring in a collapsed bed with a melted ice pack between her legs. She loved to sleep and could slumber through anything. Dr. Sully came every Wednesday morning to examine the girls, and sometimes Dora slept right through it, naked, with nothing but a green feather boa around her neck.

Evangeline stood only four foot eight and looked like a schoolgirl. She played up the part but was mean as a snake. Evangeline was a reformed kleptomaniac. She didn't trust anyone and slept with her purse over her shoulder—even wore her shoes to bed. But she didn't steal from the dates. Willie had rules. No stealing, no drugs, no freebies, and no kissing up in the rooms. If a man came downstairs with traces of lipstick on his mouth, Willie would throw the girl out. "You think you're sitting under the apple tree? I'm selling sex here!" she'd yell. Evangeline's room was always filthy. Today there were dirty tissues stuck all over the hardwood floor. I had to peel them up one by one.

"Shut up and quit your hummin'. I'm trying to sleep, you little wench!" screeched Evangeline.

I dodged the shoe she threw at me from under her covers. Evangeline had no family. She certainly didn't have a father like Forrest Hearne. I sighed, thinking about Mr. Hearne. He assumed I was attending college. And why not? No one said a girl like me couldn't go to college. Then I laughed. How many college girls cleaned cathouses?

"I said SHUT UP!" screamed Evangeline.

I walked down the hall to Mother's room and turned the knob gently, careful not to make a sound. Cokie had oiled the door for me. Mother hated when it squeaked. I slid quietly into the room and closed the door, smiling. Mother's room smelled of her Silk 'n' Satin powder she bought at Maison Blanche. As usual, her stockings hung over the chair, but her black garter belt wasn't there. I peeked into her high, red-canopied bed. Mother wasn't in it.

The bell tinkled downstairs. Willie was awake. I picked up my pail, left Mother's room, and headed down to the kitchen.

Sadie, the cook and laundress, was scurrying around the sink.

"Happy New Year, Sadie," I said.

She nodded, smiling with her mouth closed. Sadie was mute and never spoke a word. We didn't even know her real name. Willie named her Sadie because she once knew a sweet crippled horse named Sadie. The horse ended up getting shot. Willie said she wished we were all mute like Sadie.

I set to making Willie's chicory coffee. Like many in New Orleans, Willie was particular about her coffee. I perfected her brew when I was twelve, and she'd insisted I make her coffee ever since. There wasn't really a secret. I bought the coffee from Morning Call and added a little honey and cinnamon. With the pail in one hand and the coffee tray in the other, I walked through the parlor and back to Willie's door. I tapped my foot gently against the bottom.

"Open," said the hoarse voice.

I pushed the door with my hip, catching it again and closing it with my foot. Willie's apartment was nothing like the rest of the house. Potted palms throughout her sitting room and bedroom gave it a tropical feel. Willie's rolltop desk sat on an antique Aubusson rug next to a buttercream marble fireplace. An ornate birdcage hung empty from the ceiling in the corner. As usual, Willie sat in the center of her high bed, propped against the pillows in her black silk kimono, platinum hair combed, red lipstick freshly applied.

"Happy New Year, Willie."

She scraped a file across her long fingernail. "Hmm . . . is it?" she said.

I put the pail down and set the tray of coffee on her bed.

She took a sip and then nodded in approval. "Paper?"

I pulled the paper out from the back of my apron and handed it to her.

"How bad is it?" she asked, propped against her thick pillows.

"I've seen worse," I told her. It was true. I had seen much worse, like when the insurance salesman from Florida got so drunk he fell down and hit his head. There was blood everywhere. It looked like someone had slaughtered a hog on the floor. I scrubbed for days and still couldn't get the stain up. Willie eventually bought a large oriental rug to put over the spot. She even rearranged the furniture. But the stain was still there. Some things just won't go away, no matter how hard you scrub.

"So, what do you have?" she asked.

I picked up the pail. "Well, first, this huge thing." I pulled an enormous red shoe out of the bucket.

Willie nodded. "From Kansas City. He paid two bills to dress up in stockings and dance with the girls."

"And he left a shoe?" I asked.

"No, the other one's under the settee in the parlor. I keep them up in the attic for guys like him. Wipe them off and put them back up there. What else?"

I pulled a twenty-dollar bill out of the pail. "In Dora's toilet tank."

Willie rolled her eyes.

I produced a silver cigarette lighter from the bucket. "On Sweety's bedside table."

"Well done. It belongs to an Uptown attorney. What a horse's ass. Thinks he's so smart. He doesn't know the difference between piss and perfume. I'll have fun returning that to him. Maybe I'll drop by his house at dinnertime."

"And this," I said. "I found it in the upstairs hallway." I held up a bullet.

Willie put out her hand.

"Did you have one of the bankers here last night?" I asked.

"This isn't from a banker's gun," said Willie. "It's for a .38."

"How do you know?"

Willie reached under her pillow and pulled out a gun. With a flick of her wrist she opened the cylinder, slid the bullet in the chamber, and snapped the cylinder back into place. "That's how I know. Get your mother."

"She isn't here," I said. "Her bed is empty, and her garter belt isn't on the chair."

"Such a liar. Said she didn't feel well. She had that sack of trash in my house. I haven't gotten a report from Frankie. Did anyone see Cincinnati last night?" asked Willie.

"I don't know. For a minute I thought he was in the store, but it was only Patrick. He scared the bejesus out of me."

"Patrick, hmph. He's nothing like his father, that's for sure. How's Charlie doing?"

"Talking crazy. I feel so bad for Patrick. I'm going to stop by today," I told her.

"Charlie's not crazy. His brain is a touch soft somewhere—that happens to some people. Happened to Charlie's dad." Willie sighed. "But don't go saying he's crazy, or he'll be hauled off to the mental ward at Charity. I won't let that happen. Not to a good man like Charlie. He took you in when none of us could be bothered. Here," said Willie, throwing the twenty from Dora's toilet at me. "Buy him groceries or whatever he needs. Let me know if he wants a girl sent over."

I nodded. Charlie had been good to me. One day when I was fourteen, I told Charlie that I hated Mother. "Don't hate her, Jo," he told me. "Feel sorry for her. She's not near as smart as you. She wasn't born with your compass, so she wanders around, bumping into all sorts of walls. That's sad." I understood what he meant, and it made me see Mother differently. But wasn't there some sort of rule that said parents had to be smarter than their kids? It didn't seem fair.

"So what else don't I know?" said Willie.

"Evangeline's flying the red flag, and Dora ripped her velvet gown across the bosom again. I still have rooms to clean, so that's all I know right now."

"Ripped her dress, again? Like watermelons, those things. Okay, Evangeline is off for five days. Tell her to move upstairs to the attic. Have Sadie mend the gown. Now get out. I want to read the paper."

I nodded and picked up the pail to leave. "Say, Willie, there was a man from Memphis that came by the shop yesterday. Tall, said he was an architect and played ball for Vanderbilt."

"Good-looking guy with an expensive suit and watch?" asked Willie, not looking at me. She sipped her coffee and opened the paper.

My heart sank. "Yes, that's him. He came here?" I asked.

"No, he wasn't here."

Thank goodness. Forrest Hearne didn't seem like the type. "But you've heard of him?" I asked.

"Yeah, I heard of him," said Willie. "He's dead."

SEVEN

"No one's talkin'," said Cokie, "not even Frankie. So you know somethin' ain't right."

"Willie said she didn't know details, just that he was dead," I told Cokie on the sidewalk. "She didn't want to talk about it. Said it wasn't any of her business." I stared at the pavement. I couldn't believe that Forrest Hearne, the lovely man from Tennessee, was dead. "Who told you?" I asked Cokie.

"Saw Eddie Bones last night. He looked like he seen a ghost. I asked him what happened, and he said a well-to-do businessman done died, right there at the table in the club 'bout four A.M."

Eddie Bones was the bandleader at the Sans Souci, a club on Bourbon Street.

"So someone shot him in the club?" I asked.

"Bones didn't say nothin' 'bout a gun," said Cokie.

"Well, he couldn't have just keeled over. You didn't see this guy, Coke. He was a real gentleman, healthy and strong. He didn't look like a boozer or a doper. He was in town for the Bowl. But he had cash, lots of it, and all of a sudden he's dead? Where's Eddie Bones now?"

"Headin' to Baton Rouge," said Cokie. "Said he had a gig up there."

"He's leaving town? Well, how are we going to find out what happened?"

"Why you so curious?" asked Cokie. "Ain't the first time someone's died in the Quarter."

"I . . . just need to know. Where do you think Mr. Hearne is now?"

"I guess he'd be at the coroner's."

A loud rumble fired across the street. I looked up and saw Jesse Thierry on his motorcycle. He nodded to me. I nodded back.

Cokie waved to him. "Come on, now. This ain't no way to spend New Year's. Get in the cab before your momma comes walkin' up with that no-good Cincinnati and all hell breaks loose."

"Cokie, I need you to go to the coroner. Find out what happened," I told him.

"Now, why you think he goin' tell me about some rich dead man?"

"You could tell him Willie wants to know," I said.

"Josie girl, you crazy. You goin' get yourself in heaps o' trouble. Get in the cab. I'll take you over to Marlowe's. That poor ol' man needs some black-eyed peas to bring in the New Year."

I stared out the window as Cokie drove me over to Patrick's.

The Sans Souci wasn't exactly a fine establishment. The owner was a hustler and had B-girls in his club. Bar girls, like Dora's sister, acted like normal patrons but they actually received a commission from the club. They chatted up the customers, encouraging them to buy expensive drinks or bottles of champagne. The more drinks the customer bought, the more money the girls made.

A line from Keats echoed in my head. "A thing of beauty is a joy forever . . . it will never pass into nothingness." No. Something wasn't right.

Cokie dropped me off in front of the Marlowes' pale green town home, surrounded by its black fleur-de-lis fence. I thought it was lovely. Patrick couldn't stand it. He said it was so passé it was embarrassing. Lately, it did smell a bit like old people inside, but I never mentioned that to Patrick.

I heard the piano as I approached the door. I stopped and leaned against the railing to listen. Patrick played so expressively that I often learned more about him from how he played than the things he told me. Despite our friendship, there had always been a low fence between us. I couldn't figure out if I was the one who put it there, or Patrick. This morning he was playing Rachmaninoff, *Rhapsody on a Theme of Paganini*. He was happy, peaceful. It amazed me how some people could touch an instrument and create something so beautiful, and when others tried, like me, it just sounded like mangled noise. I knocked on the door and the piano stopped abruptly.

"Happy New Year!" I said, holding up a bag I had packed in Willie's kitchen.

Patrick's glossy blond hair was disheveled and he still had imprints of waxy lipstick on the side of his face.

"Ah, now I see why you're playing romantic Rachmaninoff. Got lots of smooches at midnight, did you?" I said, pushing past him into the house. Something about the lipstick bothered me.

"No, it was after midnight. I think people felt sorry for me because of this." Patrick turned the left side of his face to me. A large bruise, the color of a plum, swelled across his temple into his hairline.

"Patrick! What happened?"

"What happened? You clocked me with a book. Don't you remember?"

I sucked in a breath. "Oh, Patrick, I'm so sorry."

"That's okay. I told everyone I beat up a thief who was trying to rob an old woman on Bourbon," said Patrick. "I'm a hero."

Patrick was a hero, to me anyway. When he was six, his mother left Charlie and ran off to the West Indies to marry a sugar baron. Charlie was devastated but did right by Patrick and raised him well. Unlike me, Patrick held no grudge against his mother, just shrugged and said he understood. He looked forward to his trips to the West Indies to see her. Charlie treated Patrick more like a colleague than a son. They built the business together and, until recently, worked side by side every day.

Mr. Marlowe sat in the living room on a chair near the window, clutching a tattered heart-shaped box that once held Valentine chocolates. "That's new," I whispered to Patrick.

"I don't know where it came from. He won't let go of it," said Patrick. "Even sleeps with it. But I don't care. At least he's staying put."

A few months before, Patrick's father went through a period where he would get up in the middle of the night and try to leave the apartment in his pajamas. Patrick installed locks on the door that could only be opened with a key, but then Mr. Marlowe tried to climb out of a window. Willie got some medicine from Dr. Sully that helped, but now Mr. Marlowe rarely spoke.

"Happy New Year, Charlie!" I said, bending down and putting my hand on his knee.

His milky blue eyes slowly wandered over to my face. He stared at me with such a blank expression that I wondered if he even saw me. He squeezed the pink satin box against his chest and turned his head away.

"Do you know what's inside the box?" I asked Patrick.

"I have no idea. Like I said, he won't let me near it. I couldn't even comb his hair today. Look at him. He looks like Albert Einstein."

"Don't worry. I'll comb his hair."

I crossed from the living room under the wide arch into the kitchen. I waved the twenty-dollar bill at Patrick and put it under the cookie tin on the shelf above the sink. "From Willie, via Dora's toilet tank."

"How bad was it this morning?"

"It wasn't horrible," I said, pouring myself a cup of coffee and unpacking the bag. "Sticky floors. Evangeline was cranky and threw a shoe at me. She'll be in the attic for five days."

"By the look on your face, I thought it was something really bad," said Patrick, teetering back on the kitchen chair.

"There is something bad," I said quietly over my shoulder from the stove. "Really bad."

"What?"

"Remember that nice man from Memphis who came into the shop yesterday?"

"Of course. The rich football-playing poet," said Patrick.

"Yeah, him." I turned around from the sink. "He's dead."

Patrick's chair thumped down against the floor. "What?"

I brought my coffee to the table and sat down. "He died in the Sans Souci last night."

"Where'd you hear about it? I didn't hear a thing."

"Willie told me, but said she didn't know any details. I just can't believe it. Cokie talked to the bandleader, and he said that Mr. Hearne just slumped over and died at the table."

Patrick crossed his arms and raised an eyebrow.

"Exactly. Did that man not look fit as a fiddle?"

"I'll say he did," said Patrick. "I would have taken him for a Vandy football player now. Did he end up buying anything yesterday?"

"Keats and Dickens. And the man had a bankroll something huge, along with a Lord Elgin watch and an expensive fountain pen."

"Keats and Dickens, huh?" said Patrick. "That doesn't sound like a mess of a man." Patrick turned away from me. "It's a shame. He seemed like such a nice man."

I nodded. "Thanks for covering for me about the college stuff. I would have been embarrassed after he assumed I was at Newcomb."

"But it's true, Jo. You could have your pick. Even Newcomb at Tulane."

I looked down at my fingers laced around the warm coffee cup. Patrick had told me I could get scholarship money from any of the local colleges. But I hated the idea of seeing people from high school, being the girl whose mother was a whore and walked around naked in a fur coat. I'd never have a chance to be normal.

Willie said normal was boring and that I should be grateful that I had a touch of spice. She said no one cared about boring people, and when they died, they were forgotten, like something that slips behind the dresser. Sometimes I wanted to slip behind the dresser. Being normal sounded perfectly wonderful.

"Mr. Vitrone died," said Patrick, pointing to the obituaries spread out on the kitchen table. Patrick combed the death notices daily, looking for leads on books or rare volumes that might be for sale. "He had a nice collection of Proust. I think I'll pay my respects to his wife and see if I can buy them off her."

I nodded. "So what were you doing with someone from Doubleday?" I asked.

"Ran into him at the Faberts' party. We started heckling each other about who had a more diverse inventory," said Patrick.

"Arguing about inventory? Doubleday has a lot more books," I said.

"I know." Patrick laughed. "Liquid confidence, I guess."

"Yeah, you smelled like a distillery. And I didn't appreciate you embarrassing me in front of him."

"Well, what are you doing skulking around the store in your nightgown?" said Patrick. "And then you acted so weird, almost scared of us."

"I had forgotten my book in the shop and came down to get it. You're lucky I didn't have my gun, especially after that comment about my hair."

"For a girl who reads the society page as much as you do, I'm surprised you haven't noticed that all the Uptown brats part their hair on the side now. It would look nice on you, flattering to the shape of your face. C'mon, it's a new year. Time to reinvent yourself," said Patrick. "Hey, I saw your mom at six this morning walking arm in arm toward the Roosevelt Hotel with some tall guy. Black suit. Didn't fit him properly."

"Did she see you?" I asked.

"No," said Patrick. "The guy looked rough, but kinda familiar. You know who it was?"

"I have no idea," I said, staring into my coffee cup.

EIGHT

January 2nd was always slow in the bookstore. People were too tired to go out or had spent too much money on holiday shopping to think about buying books. Patrick and I amused ourselves with one of our games. We'd give each other a choice of two literary characters, and we had to choose which one we'd marry. We played the game for hours, often howling with laughter when the choices were less than pleasing.

"Darcy or Gatsby," said Patrick.

"Oh, come on. Can't you do any better than that?" I scoffed. "That's obvious. Darcy."

"I just don't see why women love him so much. He's so uptight. Gatsby's got style."

"He's not uptight. He's shy!" I insisted.

"Look, here's one," Patrick said, motioning with his eyes to the window.

Droplets of rain began to fall on the sidewalk. An attractive girl with neatly styled auburn hair and a monogrammed sweater stood outside the shop, looking at the books in the window display.

"Romance," said Patrick.

I shook my head. "Thrillers."

The bell jingled, and the girl entered the shop.

"Happy New Year," said Patrick.

"Why, thank you. Happy New Year," she said. She spoke sprightly with an articulate cadence.

"Can we help you find something?" I asked.

"Yes, a book for my father." She opened her purse and rummaged through. "I'm sure I put the slip of paper just here." She began emptying the contents of her purse onto the counter. "Oh, how embarrassing."

"Well, I'm sure we can find something you'd like," said Patrick, setting the bait. "Perhaps a romance, like *Gone with the Wind*?"

She made a face. "No, thank you. Not really my cup of tea. I have nothing against *Gone with the Wind*, mind you. In fact, the author attended my college, and it would be quite sacrilege if I didn't just love her."

"Margaret Mitchell?" I said. "Where do you go to college?"

"I'm in my first year at Smith. Oh! Here it is." She opened a small scrap of paper. *"Fabulous New Orleans."*

"By Lyle Saxon." Patrick nodded. "Let me get it for you. The Louisiana shelf is right in front here."

Smith. Northampton, Massachusetts. I had read about it in the library. It was one of the Seven Sisters colleges and, along with Vassar and Radcliffe, was considered one of the most prestigious for women in the country. And, unlike Louisiana, Massachusetts had no segregation.

The girl looked around the bookshop and took a deep breath. "That smell, I just love it, don't you?"

"Yes," I agreed.

"And how lucky you are to work here. I could live in a place like this."

"Actually, I do," I said.

"You do? Where?" she asked.

"In an apartment above."

"You have your own apartment?" The girl looked at me with a mixture of astonishment and intrigue. "Forgive me. I've been incredibly rude." She thrust her hand out to Patrick. "Charlotte Gates."

Patrick grinned at her stiff, official introduction. "Patrick Marlowe."

"Marlowe. Yes, of course. The shop is yours."

The girl wore cultured pearls underneath her round white collar. She was sophisticated, yet had a dash of boldness generally absent among the debutantes of New Orleans.

"Charlotte Gates," she said, extending her hand to me.

I paused. "Josephine Moraine," I replied.

Patrick coughed. I shot him a look.

"Josephine, what a lovely name. I've always loved the name Josephine, ever since I read *Little Women*, I absolutely adored Josephine March. Oh, but don't cut off your beautiful brown hair like Jo March did. Yours is so lovely. I wish my hair looked attractive parted on the side like that. It's all the rage, you know."

"Jo, I mean Josephine, has always worn her hair parted on the side," said Patrick, suppressing a smile.

Charlotte nodded at Patrick. "Some people are just born with style. Josephine is obviously one of them."

This woman with an Uptown pedigree from an elite college had just paid me a genuine compliment. I opened my mouth, then closed it. I didn't know what to say or how to react. Fortunately, Charlotte Gates continued to ramble.

"I'm majoring in English, and I still can't get enough of reading. To work in a shop like this would be heaven."

"Oh, sure, it's heaven," said Patrick.

Charlotte grinned. "Josephine, men just don't understand, do they?"

"Not at all," I agreed. "For example, Patrick asked if I would rather marry Gatsby or Mr. Darcy."

"No, he didn't! Who in the world would choose Gatsby over Darcy?" Charlotte caught on and turned to me. "Josephine—Ethan Frome or Gilbert Blythe from *Anne of Green Gables*?"

"Oh, Ethan Frome," I said quickly.

"Out of pity," said Charlotte, with an understanding nod.

"A bit," I agreed. "But Ethan Frome had a hidden depth, something waiting to be discovered. And that cold, dark winter setting in New England. I thought it was beautiful," I said.

Charlotte perked up. "It was set in Massachusetts, you know. And it's quite cold and snowy like that right now."

"It sounds lovely," I said. I meant it.

Patrick rolled his eyes. "Perhaps Josephine should consider Smith, then," he said with a snicker. "She doesn't seem interested in schools in Louisiana."

"Stop it," I muttered.

"Are you applying to colleges?" Charlotte leaned over the counter. "Oh, Josephine, do consider Smith. It has a wonderful literary legacy. In addition to Margaret Mitchell, there's a promising talent named Madeleine L'Engle who graduated from Smith."

"Smith? Oh, I don't know," I said.

"Why not? You're obviously an accomplished woman, practically running a publishing business and living on your own in a unique and decadent city like New Orleans. So many eccentric characters, I can't imagine what you've experienced here," she said with a wink.

"We have some interesting people at Smith too. I'm part of a new group on campus," continued Charlotte. "The Student Progressives. We promote opportunities for minorities and women. Perhaps you heard about the Amherst fraternity that lost their charter because they pledged a Negro man? We wrote to our congressmen and picketed."

I had heard about it. Cokie showed me the article in the paper. Several colleges out East supported the Phi Psi chapter in their decision to invite a Negro man into the fraternity. Smith was one of them. I was elated, but couldn't talk about those things with most women in the South.

Charlotte leaned toward me over the counter and lowered her voice to a whisper. "Let me just tell you, I have no interest in knitting argyles. And all of those little books about domestic servitude? Straight into the trash."

Patrick erupted with laughter and pointed at me. "She tried to convince my father not to carry those booklets in the store."

"Of course she did," said Charlotte. "She's a modern woman. Josephine, you really should consider Smith. Let me send you some information."

Charlotte took down the address of the shop and talked nonstop about Smith, the campus, the professors, and how she knew we'd be joined at the hip if I were in Northampton. Charlotte was a member of both the fencing and flying clubs at Smith and even had her pilot's license. We chatted for an hour until she had to meet her parents at their hotel.

"I know this is last minute," said Charlotte, "but my aunt and uncle are having a get-together tonight for my parents. They live Uptown. I'd just love if you'd both come."

"Uptown?" I blurted.

"Oh, yes, I know, they're ridiculously stiff. But come, and we'll have a good laugh at everyone. Do come!"

Me? At an Uptown party? My mouth hung agape.

"Sure, we'd love to," said Patrick, handing Charlotte the book she had purchased for her father. "Just give us the address." While Charlotte scribbled down the address, Patrick motioned for me to close my mouth.

"See you tonight!" Charlotte hurried out of the store, smiling and waving from the wet street.

"Are you crazy? An Uptown party?" I said.

"Why not? I think you're the one that's crazy, *Jooosephine,*" mocked Patrick. "Since when?"

"Well, Josie is nearly short for Josephine and Josephine is so much more . . . I don't know."

Josie sounded like a cheap nickname. Why couldn't Mother have named me Josephine?

"Seems like you've made a new friend," said Patrick. "I like her. She's smart."

Charlotte *was* smart. She even knew how to fly a plane. She was also witty and fun. And she seemed to truly like me. Actually, she seemed impressed with me. A twinge of happiness bounced around in my chest. Charlotte lived across the country. She didn't know about Mother, Willie's, who I was, or what I came from.

"She sure was giving you the hard sell on Smith."

"Yes. It sounds wonderful, doesn't it? Who knows, maybe I would like to go to Smith," I told Patrick.

"Yeah, well, I'd like to go to the Juilliard School, but I don't see that happening either. But in the meantime, what a great idea you had to part your hair on the side."

I wadded up some paper and threw it at him.

NINE

Patrick left to pay his respects to the widow Vitrone and make a deal on Proust in the process. I pushed the book cart among the aisles, shelving the new titles we had taken in last week. Patrick did the buying and pricing. I did the organizing. It had been our system for years. I slid the new romance by Candace Kinkaid into place. *Rogue Desire.* How did she come up with such bad titles? Creating bad titles could be a fun game for Patrick and me . . . or maybe even me and Charlotte.

Why couldn't I go to Smith? I had made nearly all A's in high school and took the College Board Tests because they seemed fun. True, my extracurricular was limited to cleaning a brothel and spending time with Cokie, not exactly something you'd put on a college application. But I had a lot of experience from working in the bookshop and, on average, read at least 150 books per year. I was fairly well versed in all subjects.

What would the girls from high school—the ones with two parents and a trust fund—say when I ran into them at Holmes department store? "Oh I'm sorry, I'm in such a rush," I'd tell them. "You see, I'm off to Smith in the fall and I'm just here picking up my monogrammed sweaters. Why, yes, Smith *is* out East. I just didn't find the curricula of the Southern schools compelling whatsoever."

I couldn't wait to receive the information from Charlotte. I planned to start a list with all my questions and would go back to the library to read up on Smith.

The bell jingled as I was reaching up to the top shelf. "I'll be right with you," I called out. I dusted off my palms, straightened the dip in the front of my hair, and stepped out to help the customer.

"My apologies, I was—"

I jerked to a halt. Cincinnati leaned up against the shelf in front of me, cigarette dangling from his mouth. The black suit jacket hung large on his slender shoulders. His handsome had gone rotten, like bad fruit. His gray eyes were still thin slits and now matched a silvery scar across the bridge of his nose. He stood staring for a moment, then stepped closer.

"Well, lookie this. I almost didn't recognize you. You've grown up something, now, haven't you?" He eyed my blouse, rolling the cigarette between his lips. "You spreadin' your legs for Willie?"

"No," I said quickly.

"That's a shame." He smashed his cigarette against the side of the bookshelf and moved closer. "I might actually take a turn with you myself," he said, leaning in toward my face, "seein' as we have a score to settle."

"I don't know what you're talking about." I could feel my

pistol, strapped against my right leg under my skirt. I just needed the opportunity to reach for it. But lifting my skirt did not seem wise, considering the circumstances.

"Don't know what I'm talking about?" sneered Cincinnati. He held up his left hand, displaying a shiny red patch. "Some little witch burned me, burned me bad. And some old hag shot me in the leg. You know what it feels like to be burned, little girl?" He took a step toward me. "You wanna feel it? I bet you do. I bet you're like your momma."

"I'm nothing like my mother," I told him, edging away from the stacks into the center of the store in order to be visible from the front window.

"Where you sliding to? You scared of me, Josie Moraine? You scared I'm gonna cut you up in little pieces and dump you in Marcello's swamps?" He laughed, revealing brown tobacco stains on his bottom teeth. He grabbed me by the wrist, pulling me to him. "You'd be such sweet eatin' for those gators."

The door to the shop flew open. "Get your hands off her!" Cokie ordered. He was carrying a tire iron.

Cincinnati barely looked at Cokie. "Mind your own business, old man."

"I'll mind some business with this iron through your head." Cokie raised the tire iron. "I said get your hands off her."

Cincinnati let go of my wrist. "Oh, I see how it is. She's your property. You keep her locked in this bookshop and stop by for a poke whenever you feel like it."

"That ain't how it is," said Cokie.

"No? Well, how is it?" said Cincinnati, moving toward Cokie, taunting him. "Look at you. I can't tell if you're more cream or more coffee. Oh, wait, let me guess. Your granny was a real pretty maidservant, and she got bent over by the boss man, huh?"

Click, click.

Cincinnati spun around toward me. "All right," he said, casually raising his hands. "Let's not get crazy, Josie."

"Crazy Josie—I kinda like the way that sounds." I clutched my gun with both hands the way Willie had taught me. "Why don't you get out of here before I do something crazy."

Cincinnati laughed. "Take it easy, baby. I just came to give you a message from your momma."

"Is that what you were doing? Giving me a message?" I said, keeping my gun drawn and steering him toward the door.

"Yeah, your momma said to meet her at the Meal-a-Minit at three o'clock. She's got something to tell you." Cincinnati took out a cigarette and lit it slowly, just to show me that my gun didn't bother him a bit.

Cokie's eyes were the size of half-dollars. The tire iron trembled slightly in his hand. He was terrified of guns.

"Lookin' good, Josie," said Cincinnati. He pointed his cigarette at me. "I'll be waitin' to see you again." He pushed past Cokie and left the store.

"Sweet Jesus, put that thing down before someone in the street sees you," said Cokie.

I lowered my arms, unable to release my grip on the gun.

"You okay?" asked Cokie. "He didn't hurt you none, did he?"

I shook my head, finally taking a breath. "Thanks, Coke. Were you following him?"

"I got some eyes around. Frankie said he saw him walkin' this way from the Roosevelt Hotel. I don't know why your momma mess with that man. He's evil. I can see it in his eyes."

He was right. There was something ice-cold, dead in Cincinnati. I exhaled and began to release my cramped fingers.

"Cokie, were you able to go by the coroner?" I asked.

"Jo, what's wrong with you, girl? Thirty seconds ago, you had guns on a criminal, and now you're asking about that dead man from Memphis? What's the story?"

What *was* the story? Forrest Hearne was a mystery, like looking down a dark well. But I knew in the deepest pit of my stomach. Something wasn't right.

"There's no story. He came into the shop on New Year's Eve, and I met him, that's all. He was a really nice man, and now he's dead. So, did you talk to the coroner?"

"I did. I went to see Dr. Moore myself," said Cokie. "And I had to wait around outside until he left for lunch. I wasn't goin' in that morgue with all them dead bodies. He wasn't too happy to see me. He said he was a busy man—"

"And?"

"Dr. Moore said the rich man from Memphis died of a heart attack."

I shook my head. "No."

"Well, now, Josie, that's what the man said. He the coroner."

The door burst open with a yell. I drew my gun, and Cokie whipped around, raising the tire iron.

Patrick jumped back, looking from the tire iron to my gun. "What's wrong? It's just Proust!" he said, holding a large box of books.

TEN

I sat in the vinyl booth at the Meal-a-Minit, facing the door. The diner was air-cooled in the summer, but now the air was thick and the sweat behind my knee ran down my calf, making it stick to the booth. I picked at a cigarette burn in the red vinyl and watched the ceiling fan spin, letting my eyes blur on the rotating blades. Willie had sent a thug named Sonny to sit in the booth in front of me. He was reading a paper. I didn't think Cincinnati would come with Mother, but I couldn't be sure. I arrived ten minutes early. Mother was twenty minutes late. Typical.

Jesse Thierry was sitting in the booth across from me. He dropped some coins on the table.

"Thanks, darlin'," said the waitress. "Say hi to your granny for me." Jesse nodded. I watched out of the corner of my eye as he pulled on his leather jacket to leave. He caught me looking and smiled.

"Happy New Year, Motor City," said Jesse. He left the diner.

A fat man with a pink face walked by and stopped at the booth. "Well, hello there, Josie. Remember me?"

Walter Sutherland. He was an accountant at a matchbook factory and one of the men who sometimes spent the night at Willie's. I had run into him once or twice in the mornings. He had a way of looking at me that made me wish I was wearing a winter coat.

"Hello," I said, avoiding direct eye contact.

"Are you alone?" he asked.

"I'm meeting my mother," I told him.

"Oh. Are you"—he lowered his voice—"working yet?"

I turned to face him. "No."

He looked at me, adjusting his waistband as he bit his bottom lip. "You'll tell me if you start, won't you? I want to be the first," he whispered.

"I won't work at Willie's."

"Well, it doesn't have to be at Willie's. I know it must be hard for you, Josie. If you ever need money, you let me know. We could work out a nice arrangement. I'd pay handsome to be the first." He mopped his sweaty forehead. "And I wouldn't tell a soul. It could be our secret, Josie."

"Get lost, butterball," said Sonny from the booth in back of me.

Walter scurried out like a frightened squirrel, passing Mother as she walked in.

Mother wore a new red dress with jewelry I had never seen. She slid into the booth, laughing.

"Walter Sutherland. What a pathetic old pig. He's slow as molasses and then wants you to hug him all night while he cries.

I'm so glad he's never picked me. He's loaded, though. He generally goes with Sweety. She's made a mint off him."

I nodded.

Mother looked at her wrist, admiring her diamond bracelet. "You changed your hair, baby. Looks real pretty."

"Thanks. You look good too. New dress?"

"Yeah. Cinci's taking me to Antoine's tonight for dinner. You know how I love Antoine's. It's been years since I've been able to go."

The saliva in my mouth soured. The thought of Mother having a fancy dinner with Cincinnati at Antoine's was revolting. And what if one of the patrons recognized her stolen jewelry on Mother?

"New Year's Eve was a real ball this year. You have a good time?"

Mother had told Willie that she didn't feel well on New Year's Eve. Now she was saying she'd had a ball. "Yes," I said. "I stayed in and finished a book."

Mother rolled her eyes. "You better get your nose out of those books and get busy livin', Jo. In a couple years, you'll be past your prime. You'd be something to look at if you wore a little more makeup and a better bra. I was a real knockout at your age . . . until I had you."

The waitress arrived at our table. Mother ordered a sweet tea. I saw Sonny over Mother's shoulder, still buried in the newspaper. His ashtray was already overflowing with butts.

"Mother, I've been wondering . . . why did you name me Josie instead of Josephine?"

"What are you talking about? Her name wasn't Josephine."

"Whose name?" I asked.

Mother took a compact out of her purse to inspect her lipstick. "Besides, aren't you happy I didn't name you Josephine? That sounds like a fat old washwoman. Josie's much sexier."

Sexier. I looked across the restaurant and saw a mother sitting next to her daughter in a booth, helping her read the menu. She smoothed the little girl's hair and put her napkin on her lap.

"Whose name was Josie?" I asked.

"Josie Arlington. She was the classiest madam in Storyville years ago. Had a house on Basin. Willie used to talk about her all the time, said she died on Valentine's Day. So when you were born on Valentine's Day, I thought of Josie Arlington and named you Josie in her honor."

"You named me after a madam?"

"Not just any madam, the most high-class madam that ever existed. She was a smart woman. With your brains, Jo, you'd make a fine madam yourself."

"I have no interest, Mother." Humiliation bubbled inside of me. I thought about explaining to Charlotte Gates that I wasn't named after a virtuous character in *Little Women*. I was named after a woman who sold five-dollar hookers on Basin Street. And my mother thought I should be proud of that.

"Don't get on your high horse, Jo. What, you think you're gonna be Cinderella?" She tipped her head back and laughed. Ugly. "You think your life is going to be some fairy tale, hon, like in one of your books?"

The waitress brought Mother her iced tea. I knew what to do. I should have ended the conversation there. I should have left. Instead, I sat in the booth staring at her, wishing that she could be like other mothers, wishing that she were different. Mother would never square up. I knew that.

"So, what did you want to tell me?" I asked.

"We're leaving," said Mother.

"What do you mean?"

"Me and Cincinnati." Mother leaned in toward the table. "We're going to California. I need you to tell Willie for me, but wait until tomorrow, after we're gone."

"You're going to California." For some reason, I wasn't surprised.

She tousled her hair. "It's time to get outta Dodge. This could finally be my break, going to Hollywood."

My mother was ridiculous. "Mother, I don't think it's wise for you to go anywhere with Cincinnati. He's dangerous. He beat you. I don't want that to happen again."

"Oh, he's changed, baby. Look at the gorgeous bracelet he bought me." She extended her arm.

"Who cares, Mother? It's probably stolen."

"You don't know what you're talking about."

"Maybe not, but I know you're too old for Hollywood."

That did it. I had taken my foot off the brake, and we were barreling toward blackness. Soon we'd be a hideous, mangled mess. Mother lurched over the table and grabbed my wrist.

"I am *not* too old," she said through her teeth. "You're just jealous, and you know it. You're lucky I didn't throw you in a trash barrel, you little ingrate. I sacrificed everything for you, so don't tell me what I am."

I took a breath and tried to speak quietly. "You don't mean that, Mother. Stop it. You're making a scene." I tried to pull my arm from her grasp. "And you're hurting me."

"I'm hurting *you*? Oh, that's ripe. You ruined my body and tied me down during the best years of my life. I could have been famous. And you say I'm hurting you?" Mother released my arm, pushing it away from her. She leaned back against the booth and began digging in her purse. She pulled out a small flask and took a swig. "This is finally my chance, Jo, and I'm takin' it."

"Fine, take it."

"I don't think you understand. Don't expect me to come back."

"I understand. I just wish you'd find someone other than Cincinnati. He's a no-good criminal, Mother. You don't want to get messed up in that."

"You don't know anything about him." She pulled a huge wad of bills from her purse and threw one on the table. "There. This one's on me."

Generous. I hadn't ordered anything.

Mother stood up and smoothed her dress. "Don't forget to tell Willie. I'll try to write, but I'll probably be too busy." She put a hand under her curls and bounced them a bit. "Maybe you'll read about me in the papers!" She kissed the air in my direction and then walked out.

I closed my eyes and clenched my teeth, hoping to stop any tears that might be forming. I hummed Patrick's Rachmaninoff piece and felt my shoulders relax. I saw his torso swaying over the ivory keys, his father healthy again, standing and listening in the doorway. I saw Charlotte smiling and waving to me from the street and then suddenly, the image of Forrest Hearne, frantic, mouthing my name and waving the copy of Keats he had bought. I gasped at the image of Hearne and opened my eyes. Sonny was staring at me. The fluorescent lights buzzed and the ceiling fan creaked overhead.

ELEVEN

I snuck through the back door at Willie's, dressed for Charlotte's party. Dora's boisterous laughter echoed from the kitchen as I hurried down the rear hallway. It would only take five minutes to iron my cream linen blouse. I couldn't wear it to the party limp and full of folds. Since I didn't own an iron, I generally ironed my clothes in the morning at Willie's. I told myself I'd be in and out before anyone saw me.

I pushed through the laundry room door, startling Sweety, who was wearing a peach chiffon cocktail dress and talking to Sadie. Sweety stopped midsentence. They both turned to me, eyes wide.

"Jo, what are you doing here?" asked Sweety, her voice thick with concern. Sadie stared at me with her mouth hanging open.

"I—I'm going to a party, and I need to iron my blouse," I stammered.

"What kind of party, honey?" said Sweety, still looking at me intently.

"Uptown," I said. "A girl I met in the bookshop. I need to hurry."

Sadie's shoulders relaxed.

"Uptown? Well, how fun, Jo. Hurry and take your blouse off. The iron's hot. Sadie, girl, put my sash aside. Let's iron Jo's blouse so she can be on her way," said Sweety, gesturing with her slender arms. Even the way Sweety moved was gentle and lovely, like a ballerina. The sheer peach fabric swayed about her as she shifted out of the way. I couldn't imagine her with fat, sweaty Walter Sutherland. I pushed the thought aside.

I unbuttoned my blouse and moved toward the ironing board. Sadie held up her hand and took the blouse from me. "Thanks, Sadie."

"So, who are you going to the party with?" asked Sweety.

"A party?" boomed Dora, erupting through the door in a green satin robe with feathered slippers to match. She held a cup of coffee in one hand while dangling a cigarette in the other. Her makeup was freshly applied, and her red hair was piled high in rollers. "Now, who's goin' to a part—Jo, what are you doin' here?" Dora's eyes scanned my body, taking in my camisole, styled hair, and lipstick. "Why, baby girl, look at you. You're puttin' on the dog. Look at that new hairdo. Are you joining up—"

"Jo's going to a party," interrupted Sweety. "She's in a hurry." Sadie nodded.

"Oh, good," said Dora. "Well, who you goin' with, doll?"

"Patrick Marlowe," I replied.

"Mmm, mmm, now there's a sweet thing," said Dora. "Why

doesn't he ever come by the house so I can throw him around a bit?" Dora jostled her large chest and hooted. I just shook my head.

"He is a sweet boy. That's why he doesn't come here," said Sweety. "You'd scare him right to death, Dora."

"Well, Jo, you tell that gorgeous book boy that he needs to take lil' ol' Dora to a party sometime. I'd like to run my fingers through that shiny blond hair of his. He can read me some poetry from his bookstore." She cleared her throat. "Roses are red, and Dora is green. Give her your dollars, and she'll make you scream."

We burst out laughing. I buttoned my warm blouse and thanked Sadie.

"*Green* and *scream* don't exactly rhyme," said Sweety.

"Of course they do! Now don't you go criticizin'. I just might become a poet myself," bellowed Dora, holding her coffee and cigarette in her best literary pose until we all started laughing again.

Willie walked through the door and folded her arms across her chest. Her platinum hair was pulled back tight, her pale face severe against the red lipstick and black dress she wore.

The laughter quickly died.

"Contrary to what you might think, Dora, I'm not running a rodeo. Get dressed, now!" barked Willie. She turned to me. "What the hell are you doing here?"

"I had to iron my blouse."

"You're supposed to do that in the morning. I've got dates coming." Willie eyed my freshly pressed blouse. "Where are you going?"

"To a party." I smoothed my skirt.

"And am I supposed to be a mind reader? What party? Where? With who?"

Dora made a face and ducked out of the room.

"Uptown. Prytania Street. With Patrick." I rattled off some vague details about Charlotte Gates and her invitation.

"I don't know of a Gates family Uptown," said Willie, staring at me.

"No, Charlotte's from Massachusetts. The party is at her aunt and uncle's."

"And do her aunt and uncle have a name?" pressed Willie.

"I didn't ask. Charlotte gave Patrick the information. We won't be there long."

Willie nodded. "You'll take Mariah."

"No, thank you, Willie. We're gonna take the streetcar."

I hated Mariah, Willie's big black Cadillac. It had red interior, whitewall tires, and stuck out like a sore thumb. Everyone in the Quarter knew Mariah was Willie's car. I didn't want to be seen in it. Cokie loved Mariah.

"Did you see your mother?" asked Willie. I nodded. "Well, what did she want?"

I hesitated, wondering how much of the conversation Sonny had heard and reported to Willie. Mother had told me not to tell Willie she was leaving until tomorrow, when she was gone.

"She wanted money," I lied. I felt a twitching near my eye. "To have dinner at Antoine's with Cincinnati. She wanted me to ask you for an advance. You know how she's always talking about Antoine's."

"Like I'd give her a dime to do anything with that no-good hop, after what he pulled the other night."

"Was Cincinnati responsible?" said Sweety.

"Responsible for what?" I asked.

"Get out of here," said Willie, flipping her jewel-adorned fingers at me. "I have a business to run." She left the room in a huff.

Sweety looked at me. "Your momma's always loved Antoine's."

I nodded and pretended to fiddle with my purse. "What was Cincinnati responsible for this time?" I asked.

Sweety pulled the chiffon of her dress through her long fingers. "Say, you know what you need for your party, Jo? You need this string of pearls." She removed her necklace. "Put that locket in your purse and wear these tonight. All the gals Uptown love pearls."

"Oh, I don't want to take your pearls, Sweety. They look so pretty with your dress," I told her.

Sweety gave me a quiet smile. "Jo, honey. You and I both know that the fellas comin' here don't care nothin' 'bout pearls."

Sweety stood on her tiptoes, face-to-face with me while she fastened the clasp behind my neck. Her skin smelled like fresh honeysuckle. She was so kind and generous, it made me think of the line from *David Copperfield,* that a loving heart was better and stronger than wisdom. I stood staring at Sweety, wondering how she had ended up at Willie's, wishing that she could have changed her course for something better, like Forrest Hearne.

"Those look perfect on you," said Sweety. "Now, you go and have yourself a real good time."

I met Patrick on St. Charles Avenue, just in time to catch the streetcar.

"You look nice," he said. "Where'd you get the pearls?"

"Sweety," I told him. Patrick looked nice too. The bruise was less noticeable. He wore crisp khakis with a blazer and tie. The streetcar chugged along St. Charles. The closer we got, the more knotted my stomach became. I wouldn't know a soul at the party, or worse, what if I did know someone? Either scenario was disastrous. The air suddenly felt thick, difficult to breathe.

"What if this is a horrible mistake?" I croaked.

"Oh, it'll be horrible fine, just a bunch of pretentious rich people with shelves of expensive books they've never read."

"Maybe we should go back."

"C'mon, Jo, this is the stuff you pore over in the society page. You'll finally be able to read about a party that you attended."

"I don't even know their name," I whispered. "What am I doing?" I stared out the window, watching the streets become cleaner and less crowded as we rode Uptown.

"John and Lillian Lockwell," read Patrick from the piece of paper Charlotte had given him. "This is our stop. Ready?"

TWELVE

We got off on St. Charles and walked one block down to Prytania. The first thing I noticed was how peaceful it was. The road felt so wide. No one was pushing, yelling, or selling things in the street. I wanted to throw open my arms and run across the pavement. Birds chirped, and the perfume of winter jasmine floated out onto the sidewalk, hanging around the shrubbery. Large oaks lined the street where wealthy shipbuilders, oil operators, and professional men lived. I stared at the enormous homes, the landscaping and flower beds immaculate. It was as if dollar bills, instead of leaves, hung from the trees. Carnival season was soon to begin and I imagined these homes flying flags of purple, gold, and green to symbolize prior queens or Carnival royalty. We passed a couple, who nodded and greeted us. I noted the woman's posture and tried to straighten my back.

I had never been amongst such wealth. Just last week, I had stopped by the funeral of one of Cokie's friends, a Negro trumpet player named Bix who lived in the Quarter. His family was so poor they'd put a plate on the chest of the corpse, and people dropped coins in to pay for the undertaker and the brass band procession. Uptown, families rented half a dozen butlers just to serve drinks at their funerals. Tragedy was a big social event, and everyone wanted in on it. Sure, I saw wealthy people and tourists in the Quarter, but I had never been to their homes. I wondered if Forrest Hearne had lived in a neighborhood like this.

Patrick stopped in front of a sprawling Greek Revival mansion with double galleries and a long walkway lined with perfectly manicured hedges. The lights were ablaze, the house alive with guests and merriment.

"This is it," said Patrick. He didn't even pause, just marched toward the front steps, leaving me to scurry along behind him like a duckling chasing its mother.

The scent of Havana tobacco draped thick from the magnolia trees in the front yard. Ice cubes mingled and clinked against the sides of crystal tumblers. Patrick said hello to a group of men sitting on the veranda. I heard the pop of a champagne cork and laughter from inside.

We walked through the open door into an enormous entry hall that buzzed with activity. I clutched Patrick's elbow, wishing I owned something better than my faded linen blouse. The tinkling of a piano drifted from a nearby alcove, and Patrick moved toward it as if pulled by a magnet.

We entered a beautiful drawing room with flocked wallpaper and plush sofas and chairs. People gathered in clusters around the room while a man in a black suit played "It's Only a Paper

Moon" on the piano. The furnishings were expensive, but different from Willie's. Willie's furniture had an exotic feel, with sensual colors and curves. This was elegant, refined, and so clean I could practically see my reflection in everything.

"Not a single smoke or bloodstain," I whispered to Patrick.

"Not that you can see," said Patrick out of the corner of his mouth.

A circular mahogany table was covered with sterling frames of all shapes and sizes, boasting the legacy that was the Lockwell family. There were photos of babies, teenagers, grandparents, a golden retriever, the family at the shore, at the Eiffel Tower, all with smiling faces advertising how happy and valuable their lives were. There was even a photo of Charlotte in a small oval frame.

I stared at the pictures. If someone meant something to you, you put their photo in a silver frame and displayed it, like these. I had never seen anything like it. Willie didn't have any framed photos. Neither did Mother.

"Josephine!" Charlotte was suddenly at my arm, looking radiant in a mint green cashmere sweater, her auburn hair held neatly in place by a black velvet headband. "I'm so glad you're here!"

"Thank you for inviting us."

"Well, don't worry. I won't leave your side. I know it's horribly uncomfortable to be at a function where you don't know anyone."

I nodded. Charlotte understood. It was as if she'd heard my thoughts on the way over. Or perhaps my face was splotched again.

"Hello, Patrick. Did you have any trouble finding the house?" asked Charlotte.

"Not at all. But then a place like this is hard to miss, isn't it?" said Patrick.

"Yes, a quality that my aunt is all too proud of," whispered Charlotte. "They're not exactly the understated type, if you know what I mean."

"That's a lovely photo of you," I said, pointing to the frame.

"Oh, that's a couple years old now. I just had a new photograph taken at Smith. Here, let me introduce you."

Charlotte pulled both Patrick and me over to an attractive middle-aged couple across the room. "Aunt Lilly, Uncle John, these are my friends Josephine Moraine and Patrick Marlowe."

"How do you do?" said Mrs. Lockwell. "Marlowe, I know that name. John," she said, swatting her husband's arm, "why do we know the name Marlowe? Is your mother in the Junior League, dear?"

"No, ma'am," said Patrick. "My mother lives in the West Indies."

"Is your father an attorney?" asked Mr. Lockwell.

"No, sir, my father is an author and a bookseller. We own a bookshop in the Quarter."

"Well, now isn't that quaint. We just love books, don't we, John?"

Mr. Lockwell paid little attention to his wife and instead looked about the room, eyeing all the other women. "And where are you in school, Patrick?" asked Mrs. Lockwell.

"I just finished up at Loyola," said Patrick, gratefully accepting a beverage from one of the waiters that was circulating.

"And you, Josephine? Have I seen you at Sacred Heart with our Elizabeth?" asked Mrs. Lockwell.

"Josephine lives in the French Quarter, Aunt Lilly. Isn't that exciting?" said Charlotte.

"The Quarter. Oh, my," said Lilly Lockwell, putting an affected hand to her chest. "Yes it is. What did you say your last name was, dear?"

"Moraine."

"John." She swatted her husband's arm. "Do we know the Moraines in the Quarter?"

"I don't believe we do. What line of business is your family in, Josephine?"

Mr. Lockwell looked at me. Mrs. Lockwell looked at me. Charlotte looked at me. Their faces felt an inch from mine.

"Sales," I said quietly.

"What a lovely piano," said Patrick, quickly changing the subject. "A Steinway baby grand, isn't it?"

"Why, yes. Do you play?" said Lilly, speaking to Patrick, but with her eyes still fixed on me.

Patrick nodded.

"Well, then you certainly appreciate a nice piano." Mrs. Lockwell smiled, raising her glass in a private toast to her Steinway.

"Yes, I have a Bösendorfer grand," said Patrick.

Aunt Lilly's eyes snapped off of me and locked onto Patrick.

"A Bösendorfer? Well, well, now, that's a piano!" roared Mr. Lockwell.

"Indeed. You must play for us tonight, Patrick. Don't be shy, now," said Lilly.

"Oh, Aunt Lilly, don't steal my friends. I was just going to give them a tour of your magnificent house," said Charlotte, pulling us away from her aunt and uncle, who stood, heads cocked, staring at Patrick and me.

Charlotte didn't give us a tour of the house. She grabbed a plate of canapés from a server, pulled us into a library on the main floor, shut the doors, and flopped down on a sofa.

"It's exhausting, I tell you. And embarrassing. *'And what did you say your last name was?'*" said Charlotte, mimicking her aunt. "My apologies to you both. They drink like fish and ask the most probing questions!"

"Welcome to the South." Patrick laughed.

We talked with Charlotte for over an hour in the library. I tried to keep my posture straight in the thick leather chair and from time to time put my hand to my neck to make sure I hadn't lost Sweety's pearls. Charlotte settled right in and kicked her shoes off, folding her bobby socks under her skirt on the sofa. Patrick focused on inspecting the books in the Lockwells' collection, pausing only to comment on a certain title or volume. We hooted and howled when Patrick discovered Candace Kinkaid's *Rogue Desire* tucked away on a high shelf.

A man poked his head into the library. "Can I hide out with you? Sounds like it's more fun in here."

"Dad! Come meet Josephine and Patrick," said Charlotte.

An elegant man in a blue suit entered the library. "Well, now, you must be Patrick with the Bösendorfer grand."

"Ugh—are they still talking about that?" said Charlotte.

"Yep. And, Patrick, I'm afraid that you're going to have to play. My sister won't stop until she hears what Bösendorfer fingers sound like on a Steinway. George Gates," he said, extending his hand to Patrick. "And you must be Josephine," he said, turning to me. "Charlotte hasn't stopped talking about you."

"Most people call Josephine Jo." Patrick smiled. I shot him a look.

Mr. Gates discussed books with Patrick, inquiring about some rare volumes he wasn't able to locate out East. He then convinced Patrick to get the piano recital over with, and they left the library.

"Your father's so nice. Funny, too," I told Charlotte.

"Yes. Is your dad funny?" she asked.

I looked at her, wondering if my expression gave me away. "My father . . . my parents aren't together," I told her.

Charlotte sat up at once and put her hand on my knee. "Don't worry, Jo. Half of the married couples here tonight aren't together. Not really, anyway. But they'd never be honest about it like you. Right before you arrived, Mrs. Lefevre told us that she held a gun to her husband's head in the bedroom last night because he smelled like Tabu." Charlotte shook her head, whispering. "Mrs. Lefevre does not wear Tabu. But a gun? Can you imagine the insanity of that?"

I shook my head, feeling the cold steel of my pistol against my leg under my skirt. Unfortunately, I knew that insanity all too well.

"No one's life is perfect. I find it much more interesting when people are just honest about it," said Charlotte.

Honest. But what would Charlotte think if I told her the truth? That my mother was a prostitute, that I didn't know who my father was, that most men scared me, so I created make-believe dads like Forrest Hearne.

"Charlotte!" A tall, spindly girl with an overbite ran into the library. "Mother says you're friends with that boy Patrick Marlowe. You must introduce me!"

"Elizabeth, Patrick's too old for you. You're still in high school. I don't think Aunt Lilly would approve."

"I don't care what Mother thinks," said Elizabeth. "He's really handsome. And have you heard him play the piano?"

"Jo, this is my cousin Elizabeth Lockwell."

Elizabeth didn't even glance my way. She twisted her hair around her finger and slung her hip to the side. "Mother said Patrick came with some sad-looking waif from the Quarter. Is she his girlfriend?"

I made a quick exit from the room.

THIRTEEN

I found Patrick by the piano, surrounded by women in expensive dresses. Patrick caught sight of me and cut through the crowd.

"Ready, Jo?" said Patrick, putting his arm around me. "Save me," he whispered.

"Yes, unfortunately, I have to get back," I said loudly.

Elizabeth appeared, still twirling her hair around her finger. "Hello, Patrick. I'm Elizabeth Lockwell. Call me Betty. This is my house, and that's my piano."

"Well, now, sweetheart, you haven't learned to play yet." Mr. Lockwell laughed.

Mrs. Lockwell continued to stare at us. "Such a shame you have to leave already, Patrick. John and I will have to stop by your shop in the Quarter. We love books and have quite a large library."

"Yes, I saw. Candace Kinkaid is a big seller in our shop too," said Patrick with all sincerity.

"Thank you for having us," I said.

"Our pleasure, Joanne," said Mrs. Lockwell.

Patrick pulled me toward the door, with Elizabeth trailing close behind like a bucktoothed puppy.

Charlotte grabbed my arm as we reached the foyer. "Jo, I'm so sorry," she whispered. Her face crumpled. "My relatives are so obnoxious."

"No, there's nothing to be sorry for. Really." I saw Elizabeth bouncing on her toes, talking to Patrick.

"But you haven't even met my mother yet," said Charlotte. "She's in the backyard."

A woman near the door burst into sobs. "They're all just pigs in nice suits! Here he is, pretending he's a good husband when just last night I found dime-store lipstick on his chest. Now I know where my jewelry went." The woman continued to cry, spilling her drink down the front of her dress.

I turned to Charlotte and she shook her head. "Obviously one too many juleps."

"This town is filthy!" wailed the drunk woman. "Poor Forrest Hearne. They told his sweet wife it was a heart attack. It's criminal! They ought to burn the Quarter to the ground."

I turned back and stared at the woman.

"Jo!" called Patrick from across the foyer.

"I'll write to you as soon as I get back," said Charlotte. "I'll send you the information on Smith."

I nodded. Patrick grabbed my arm and herded us through the door and down the front walk, trying to escape Elizabeth Lockwell, who trailed alongside us, close enough to be Patrick's shadow. People stood in groups, smoking and drinking under mossy oaks in the front yard. A husky boy about Patrick's age stood alone at the end of the hedgerow.

"Patrick, this is my brother, Richard," said Elizabeth.

Richard stared at Patrick. His eyes narrowed. "I saw you on New Year's Eve with your friend."

"Fun night, wasn't it?" said Patrick, not stopping to shake his hand.

"Is that what you consider fun?" said Richard, turning to watch Patrick exit. He grabbed his sister's arm. "Stay away from him, Betty."

We walked a few steps, silent. Richard Lockwell certainly seemed the brutish type. The chaos of the party dissipated and was replaced by the thrum of cicadas. And how did the woman at the party know Forrest Hearne?

"You okay, Joanne?" asked Patrick.

I burst into laughter.

"Seriously, Jo. That's Uptown. What do you want with idiots like that?"

"Charlotte's not an idiot," I said.

"Agreed. She's great, and her dad's swell, too. Come on, let's get out of here," said Patrick.

We took a step into the street to cross. Headlights snapped on and approached, blinding us.

"Who is that?" I said, grabbing Patrick's arm.

"I can't see. Move, Jo!" Patrick pulled me back onto the sidewalk as the black sedan approached. I recognized the car. Mariah.

Cokie's head appeared in the driver's window. "Come on, get in," he said.

I looked around and quickly jumped into the backseat. "Cokie, what are you doing here?"

"Willie sent me, said she didn't want you walkin' or takin' the streetcar."

I ducked down in the backseat as the car rolled by the Lockwells' house, praying Richard and Elizabeth Lockwell were not standing on the sidewalk.

"Now, Josie girl, how can you be embarrassed of this here fine automobile?" Cokie beamed. "Ooooee, no one can catch me in my black Cadillac."

"Yeah, it's those people who should be embarrassed, Jo."

"Was there a lot of carryin' on in there?" asked Cokie.

"I don't know," I said.

"You don't know?" said Patrick, turning around from the front seat. "Jo, they have a baby grand piano, but no one in the family plays. They have shelves of books they've never read, and the tension between the couples was so thick it nearly choked us."

"Let me tell you something 'bout those rich Uptown folk," said Cokie. "They got everything that money can buy, their bank accounts are fat, but they ain't happy. They ain't ever gone be happy. You know why? They soul broke. And money can't fix that, no sir. My friend Bix was poor. Lord, he had to blow that trumpet ten hours a day just to put a little taste in the pot. Died poor, too. You saw him, Jo, with that plate on his chest. But that man wasn't soul broke."

"Soul broke. That's it." Patrick nodded.

"They had family photographs in nice frames," I said as I shrugged further into the musky leather interior. I wished Willie hadn't sent Mariah. Was she trying to spy on me?

"And you be careful of that Richard Lockwell," said Cokie. "He's a kitten killer."

"He's a ladies' man?" Patrick laughed.

"Aw, no, that ain't what I mean. When he was young, he hung four kittens in the Quarter. Lord, you should have seen people chase him. He's not right in the head."

I looked out the window, humming "It's Only a Paper Moon" as the Cadillac rolled down St. Charles toward Canal. The Uptown women were wary of the Quarter and everything associated with it. They thought the Quarter was responsible for all corruption. They wanted to believe their husbands were virtuous men of society—good men, like Forrest Hearne—and that the Quarter sucked them in against their will, grabbing them by the ankles and pulling them under.

Mother was probably enjoying oysters Rockefeller at Antoine's now, washing it all down with whiskey and smoke. I could see her. She'd drape her arm across her chest for everyone to admire her stolen jewelry and then slide her foot into Cincinnati's crotch under the table. Mother was prettier than all the women at the Lockwells' party, but she didn't carry herself with the same poise or confidence as the other ladies. I didn't agree with Cokie. It wasn't just rich folks.

Mother was soul broke, too.

FOURTEEN

I hurried through the noisy morning streets to get to Willie's on time. I had written several notes to Sweety and finally just settled on *Thank you for the pearls—Jo.*

I spotted Jesse on the corner of Conti and Bourbon, his grandad's flower cart bursting with snaps of color. I stopped to buy two pink lilies.

"Hey, Motor City. You look nice this morning."

"Aw, come on, Jesse." I motioned to my cleaning clothes and laughed.

He smiled. "Better than me in this flower apron."

Jesse and I had gone through parts of grade school and high school together. He lived with his grandparents on Dauphine but spent some years with family in Alabama. When he was in New Orleans, he helped his grandfather, who sold flowers in the Quarter. Once, when I was eleven, Mother was cranky and slapped me across the face in the street. Jesse marched up to her, threw a pail of water on her, and walked away. I wondered if he remembered that.

Occasionally he stopped by the shop to look at engineering books, but he rarely bought anything. He spent most of his time working on cars.

"How are Willie's nieces doing?" he asked, pulling up the two flowers I had chosen. "Nieces" was the term Willie used for the girls in her house.

"Everyone's fine." I smiled. "You?"

"Just started my first semester at Delgado. It's not Tulane, but I'm excited about it."

Jesse Thierry was going to college? "Oh, Jesse, that's wonderful."

He nodded. "Thanks. And what about you? Don't pretend you're not the smartest girl in New Orleans." A stray piece of hair, the color of dark cinnamon, fell over his ear. His voice dropped, and he looked at me with sincerity. "And now that your mom has relocated, maybe you'll have more time on your hands."

I looked up from my coin purse. How did he know about Mother? I paid for the flowers, trying to avoid eye contact, and thanked Jesse as I walked away.

Mother and Cincinnati had planned to hit the road after their dinner at Antoine's. I had looked at an atlas in the bookshop before I went to bed, wondering how long the drive west to California would take. If they didn't stop to see any sights, I estimated they'd make it in four days. It would take less than four days, however, for Cincinnati to hit her.

• • •

I walked into the kitchen at Willie's. Sadie had Willie's tray already prepped with the coffee and newspaper. She pointed to the tray urgently as soon as I walked in.

"Willie's awake already?"

Sadie nodded. I handed her one of the lilies.

"Thank you for ironing my blouse, Sadie. And for getting Willie's tray ready."

Sadie looked from the flower to me, smiling, almost embarrassed. Her smile broke, and she pointed emphatically toward Willie's room.

I grabbed my apron and the tray and walked through the parlor, swaying around a man's necktie hanging from the chandelier. As I approached Willie's door, I looked down at the paper.

MEMPHIS TOURIST'S DEATH DECLARED A HEART ATTACK

I stopped just short of Willie's door to read the article but didn't have the chance.

"Are you going to stand out there, or are you going to bring me my coffee?" growled Willie's voice from behind the door.

"Good morning, Willie." I made my way into the room.

Willie's hair and makeup were perfect. She wore a smart beige suit and was sitting at her desk writing. "I want my coffee."

"You're up early. Is everything all right?"

"Can't I get up early?" she snapped.

"Of course, it's just . . . you're not usually awake, not to mention dressed, at this hour. Where are you going?"

"Not that it's any of your business, but I have a meeting with my attorney."

"An attorney, this early? Is everything all right?"

"Why do you keep asking that?" Willie continued writing, her head down. "Instead of asking me stupid questions, why don't you tell me when your mother left for California?"

I set the tray on Willie's bed. "Did you see her?"

"No, I didn't see her. But dozens of people told me they heard her bragging on about going to Hollywood with that sad sack. In fact, everyone told me." Willie turned and stared at me. "Except you."

I fiddled with my apron. "She asked me to wait until morning to tell you . . . so it wouldn't disturb last night's business."

Willie threw down her pen. "You know what? Your mother's a stupid, stupid whore!" yelled Willie. "But don't you dare follow in her lyin' footsteps, and don't you *ever* think I'm too stupid to know when you're lying to me. I know your momma a lot better than you think, and there's no way she's takin' me down." Willie was screaming full throttle. Her chin jutted out and her face fired a full crimson.

"Willie, what happened? Did Mother steal from you?"

"What? Your mother's a piece of tail to me, that's all! The only one she's ever stolen from is you! And God willing, now she's gone for good. She can join all the other lying, washed-up losers in Hollywood. And you've got to let her go, Jo. Don't you dare look for her or let her back in. You're not a child anymore. She's on her own. Let Cincinnati shoot her full of holes."

"Willie, stop."

"Look at this room. You're late and everything's a mess! I've asked you for three days to clean my guns, and have you? No! You're off flouncing around, letting people make fun of you at Uptown parties."

Willie grabbed her purse from the bed, knocking the coffee cup off the tray and onto the floor. It broke with a loud crash. She slammed through the bedroom door so hard I thought she might break it. Sweety and Evangeline were standing outside the door in their robes, bleary-eyed and eavesdropping.

"What are you looking at?" yelled Willie. "Get to bed!" Evangeline stepped aside, letting Willie pass.

"Worst whores ever!" Willie screamed from the rear hallway. She banged through the back door, and within seconds, we heard Mariah's engine fire up.

I bent down to pick up the pieces of the broken cup.

"Hey, little wench," said Evangeline, leaning in the door. "Move my stuff into your momma's room. Make sure everything is washed. I don't want her stink all over me."

"Stop it," said Sweety, pulling Evangeline back and closing the door.

I sat on Willie's bed, holding the china pieces, still wet from her coffee. Willie said people were making fun of me. Were they?

I had to get out of New Orleans. I had to get into Smith.

FIFTEEN

Sunlight filtered in from the window, creating a square patch of brightness on the end of the bed. Evangeline was right. The room definitely smelled of Mother. I opened the window and sat on the sill for a moment, looking at her high, canopied bed. I had seen Mother spin her guiles on men in public, but I had never seen her "work" in her room. The deep green wallpaper peeled at the corners, revealing the bare plaster beneath. In the quiet light, the cranberry bed linens showed their age, and the drapery sagging from the canopy split and frayed at the edges. I stared at the bullet hole in the headboard. I still didn't know the story behind that one.

Mother's room was nearly empty. I opened a drawer in her bureau. A bottle of red nail polish rolled over copies of *Hollywood Digest*. I picked them up for the trash, and a piece of paper fluttered out. It was the police report from when Cincinnati beat Mother. After she was discharged from the hospital, Willie insisted she file a report. We took Mother to the station, and after a few minutes of filling out the form, she said she didn't feel well and would finish the report at home. I stared at the form. She hadn't included her last name and even lied about her age.

Name: Louise

Address: 1026 Conti, New Orleans

Age: 28

Marital Status: Single

Children: None

None.

I stared at the word.

"Hey, doll."

I looked up and found Dora leaning against the door frame. She wore a man's dress shirt, green of course, along with skimpy green underwear.

"Heard you had a knock-down-drag-out with Willie this morning. I musta slept through it. You okay?"

"I'm fine." That was my stock answer.

"Don't pay Willie no mind. She's been so cranky lately. Whatcha got there?"

I held up the paper. "An old police report, from when Cincinnati beat Mother."

"Did Louise file a report?" asked Dora.

I laughed. "No, of course not."

"I wouldn't think so. She loves her that Cincinnati."

"I don't understand it. He's a criminal, Dora. He's a really bad man."

"Honey, some gals love bad men. Women love Cincinnati.

He makes 'em feel sexy. And he comes into money from time to time. Now, you may not understand that gals find Cinci attractive, but you do understand that your momma loves money, don't you?"

I nodded and lifted an empty pink coin purse from Mother's drawer. "This was mine. I used to keep my savings in it, hidden under my bed. She took it."

"Oh, sugar." Dora shook her head. She walked over to me and glanced through the police report. She put her hands on my shoulders. "Jo, you listen, you ain't one of us. You're different. Willie knows that."

I stared at my hands. "I want to go to college, Dora."

"College? Well, it's okay to dream, Jo, but I don't know about college. That's a different kettle of crawfish. But I'm sure you could work at one of the nice department stores or maybe even be a hatcheck girl. Honey, I know you love Louise, but you gotta ask yourself—what kind of woman steals money from a child? Evangeline, she's got a condition. But even with her kleptomanny, she wouldn't steal from a baby. Do you understand what I'm sayin'? I'm not trying to be ugly, sugar, but I do suggest that you go about your way." Dora lifted the police report. "And if Louise is sayin' she's not your momma, that might just suit fine."

I stood there, thinking about Dora's question. What sort of a woman steals from her child?

Dora put her hands on her hips. "Now look, help me out with somethin'. Instead of throwing things out, put everything you find in a box and tell Evangeline not to touch it, that you're coming back for it. Let her steal a few things. Maybe then she'll quit sneakin' in my room for a few days."

After Dora left, I stripped the bed and swept the floor of Mother's room. I pulled the broom back from under the bed skirt and heard a sound. A man's sock was caught in the bristles of the broom. I reached down to snatch it up and found it heavy. Something was inside. I shook the sock over the bed, and a gold watch fell onto the mattress. My stomach plunged as my fingers reached for the familiar watch. I turned it over and saw the engraving.

F. L. Hearne.

SIXTEEN

Tick, tick, tick, tick, tick. I heard it all day, pulsing through my head, pumping through the threads of my nerves. I had a dead man's watch. It was the first time I hadn't reported something I'd found to Willie. She was still at the meeting with her attorney when I had finished cleaning, so I left with it, the stolen time bomb ticking in my pocket. When I returned to the bookshop, I inspected the watch. I stared at the second hand as it orbited around the expensive gold face, floating over the words *Lord Elgin* again and again. Was Forrest Hearne wearing the watch when he died? Was it still ticking on his wrist when his heart stopped beating? Or maybe he took it off before he died, lost it somewhere in the Quarter, and it was just by luck that Mother found it. Yes, maybe it was just a coincidence, I told myself.

I sharpened a bookbinding knife and cut a deep square in the center pages of a water-damaged copy of *A Passage to India*. I put the watch in the hollowed-out slot and locked the book in the glass case at the back of the shop where we kept the repair materials. Patrick had lost his key ages ago.

I walked through the Quarter, tossing the square cutouts of *A Passage to India* in waste bins along the way. I spotted Frankie across the road and whistled to him. He sauntered over on his spidery legs and fell into step next to me.

"Hey, Josie. Whatcha got for me?"

"I don't have anything. Actually, I'm wondering if you've got something for me. Do you know where my mother was on New Year's Eve?"

Frankie stopped. He pulled a pack of cigarettes from his shirt pocket, bouncing it until a white stick of tobacco appeared. He snatched it with his lips. "This info's for you?" he asked, lighting his cigarette.

"Oh, I see. You've already talked to Willie?" I asked.

"I didn't say that."

"Well, yes, it's for me. And I won't say anything. This is between us."

Frankie stared at me, cigarette hanging from the corner of his mouth. A group of tourists approached with a camera, pointing at a nearby building. Frankie grabbed my arm and pulled me to the edge of the sidewalk.

"Your mom's run off with Cincinnati, Jo."

"I already know that, Frankie. That's not what I asked. Where was she on New Year's Eve?"

He looked up and down the street, blowing smoke out of the corner of his thin lips. "She was at the Roosevelt, having a couple Sazeracs."

"And then?"

"Drinking with some tourists."

"What tourists? Where? Was she at the Sans Souci?" I asked.

"Whoa." Frankie put his hands up. "I didn't say that. Look, I gotta go. And, Jo, I'm in the business of information"—he leaned in close—"but I'm no stoolie."

I opened my purse and took out my wallet.

"Keep it. Word is that you're puttin' together a college fund."

"Where did you hear that?" I asked.

"I hear everything, Yankee girl." Frankie grinned, gave an exaggerated bow, and strode away.

I walked back to the bookshop, stopping to look in the window of Gedrick's. They had dresses on sale for $9.98. I wished I could have worn something new and fashionable to the Lockwells' party instead of looking like a sad waif. Mrs. Gedrick stepped out of the shop to empty a dustpan in the street. Her shoulders perked to offer a greeting, then she saw it was me and emptied the dirt into the gutter with a scowl. When I was twelve, I came down with a flu so bad I was nearly delirious. I tried to walk by myself to Dr. Sully's and got as far as the Gedrick's shop. I collapsed, throwing up red beans and rice all over the sidewalk. Mrs. Gedrick kept insisting that we call my mother. I knew Mother would be furious if we bothered her. So I told her to call Patrick's father, Charlie. When Charlie arrived, Mrs. Gedrick wagged a finger at him, saying, "Shame on the parents, whoever they are." I remember driving away in the back of Charlie's car, looking at the wreckage that was my life in red beans and rice on the sidewalk. There wasn't shame on my parents. The shame was all on me.

I turned onto Royal Street and saw Cokie standing next to his car, parked at the curb.

"Hi, Coke."

"Willie sent me to pick you up," he said.

A ripple of fear pulsed through me. Willie knew about the watch.

"She wasn't back when I left this morning," I told him. "She had an appointment."

"I know. But she back, and she got Mariah packed. She ready to go."

"Go where?"

"She told me to come and get you, says you two are going out to Shady Grove for a couple days."

"But what about the house?" I asked.

"She say Dora and Sadie take care of the house."

Shady Grove was Willie's cottage in the country, three hours outside of New Orleans just past Yellow Bayou.

"Well, I don't know, Coke," I told him. "I have to work at the shop."

"She told me come and get you, that she ready to leave in an hour. I was happy to come find you. I got somethin' I think you want." Cokie reached in the window of his cab and then handed me a newspaper. It was a copy of the *Commercial Appeal*.

"Cornbread, he still drivin' the truck route between here and Tennessee. He picked this newspaper up when he was in Memphis."

A large headline blazed across the front page:

F. L. HEARNE, JR., ARCHITECT, DIES. STRICKEN ON TRIP TO NEW ORLEANS.

"There's all sort of information on your rich Memphis man in that article," said Cokie.

"Thank you! Thanks so much, Coke."

Cokie smiled wide. "Sure. But don't be tellin' Willie I gave it to you. Hurry up, now, she's waitin'."

I ran down to the shop, wondering what to tell Patrick. I saw him through the window, at the counter with a customer. I folded the newspaper and put it under my arm.

"Hey, Jo," Patrick called out as soon as I walked through the door. The man at the counter turned around—tall, dark, and gorgeous.

"Hi there, Josie," he said.

I looked at the handsome man.

"Ah, you don't recognize me? Well, it was dark, and you were in your nightgown."

I felt a rush of heat beneath my cheeks. "Oh, yes, you work at Doubleday's shop."

"That's right," he said, extending his arm for a handshake. "James Marshall."

I shook his hand, wishing I looked better, cringing at the thought of this gorgeous man seeing me in my nightgown.

"Cokie came by for you," said Patrick.

"I know. Willie is insisting I go to Shady Grove with her for a few days. I could argue, but you know how she is when she wants to go to Shady Grove."

"That's fine," said Patrick quickly. He smiled an odd smile.

"It is? Are you sure you can manage?"

"C'mon, Jo, I think I can handle it. I'll be fine."

I hadn't expected such an easy acceptance. "And what about Charlie? Will you two be all right?"

"Who's Charlie?" asked James.

"My father," said Patrick. "We'll be fine, Jo. Just go."

"Shady Grove—sounds nice," said James.

"It's out in the country, quiet," said Patrick. "Hey, Jo, have you finished the December bookkeeping yet? I want to wrap up the year-end accounting."

"And the inventory," added James.

"Oh, right. And when did you last take inventory?" asked Patrick.

I looked from James to Patrick. "Yes, December's done. Why do you need an inventory?"

"Just trying to stay on top of things for the New Year. Is that Cokie I see waiting for you out there?" asked Patrick.

I nodded and made my way to the back staircase, stopping quietly to peek at E. M. Forster, ticking behind the locked glass.

SEVENTEEN

Willie would be steaming. She had been waiting nearly two hours. But I hadn't planned to leave town and had things to prepare. I also spent time reading the newspaper article about Forrest Hearne. The story said that Mr. Hearne was a former Vanderbilt player, had come to New Orleans with three other men, that all three planned to attend the Sugar Bowl, but none of his friends were with him when he died. He was a member of the Lakeview Country Club and on the board of several charitable organizations. It also reported that Forrest Hearne's wife was in shock over her husband's death. He had called her earlier that evening from New Orleans and was in perfectly fine form. Marion. I remembered him mentioning her name when he purchased the book of Keats. I hid the newspaper article beneath the floorboard near the cigar box of money.

Cokie's cab slowed to a stop. "I got to find a parking spot. Willie don't like me takin' up the driveway. I'll put your bag in the Cadillac." I got out of the car. "You need help with that stacka books?" asked Cokie.

"No, I've got them."

"Jo, you really gonna read all those out at Shady Grove?" asked Cokie.

"Every one of them." I smiled and closed the door of the cab. I walked down the narrow drive toward the garage at the back of Willie's house. As I approached, I heard Evangeline's giggle at the back door.

"Sorry I was so early this time," said a man's voice. "But I just had to see you."

"Come back soon, Daddy," said Evangeline in a childlike voice. I crept past the edge of the house just as Evangeline slipped back through the screen door in her pigtails. I stopped to shift the stack of books.

"Oh, I'll be back soon, baby," said the man, putting on his hat and tightening the knot in his tie. My mouth fell open. It was Mr. Lockwell, Charlotte's uncle.

He stepped into the drive, so giddy he nearly bumped right into me.

"Mr. Lockwell," I whispered.

He looked at me and then at the back door. "Uh, hello." Recognition dawned slowly. The lines across his forehead twitched. "I know you, don't I?"

"I'm Jo—Josephine, a friend of your niece, Charlotte."

His feet shifted. "What are you doing here?"

My breath caught somewhere in the back of my throat. I looked down at the stack of books in my arms. "I'm delivering an order of books to Willie Woodley . . . she loves to read. I work with Patrick in the bookshop. Do you come here often?" The question escaped before I thought better of it.

"N-no. Look, I'm in a hurry," he said with a disgusted and condescending tone, as if suddenly I was polluting his space like the Gedrick's sidewalk.

I saw the shift in attitude. I was just a sad waif from the Quarter, someone he could wave away with his handkerchief like a foul smell. Anger began to percolate. My eyes narrowed.

"Oh, okay," I challenged, "because I heard that girl call you Daddy and then you said you'd be back soon, so I thought maybe you come here often."

Mr. Lockwell stared at me, a mixture of panic and irritation on his face. "I have to go. Good-bye, Josephine. I'll tell Charlotte I saw you in the street." He grinned at his dig and started down the drive.

I should have let him go.

"Mr. Lockwell," I called out.

He turned at the sound of his name and put a finger to his lips. "Sshh—"

"I thought you might like to know," I said, following him toward the street. "I'm going to be applying to Smith."

"That's nice." He continued walking.

"And I was hoping you could write a letter of recommendation for me."

"What?" he said.

"A letter of recommendation, to include with my application to Smith. A letter from one of the most successful men in the South would be a great help. Shall I stop by your home next week to speak to you about it?"

"No," he said. He dug through his blazer and thrust a business card at me. "You can call me at my office. Don't call my home. I . . . I really don't come out here often."

And with that, he quickly ran down the drive toward the street.

"What's wrong with you?" said Willie. "You're gripping the damn steering wheel like you're trying to break it. I asked you to drive so I could relax, but how am I supposed to close my eyes when you're hunched over the wheel like a madman?"

I leaned back and loosened my grip on the wheel, watching the gray pavement roll under the headlights through the fog. My fingers ached. The interior of the car was dark, except for the glowing light of the radio dial, tuned to a country station playing Hank Williams. What was I thinking? What if someone had seen me? I had confronted Charlotte's uncle and blatantly dangled his deceitfulness right in front of his face. It was my pride. My pride took over when he looked at me like a piece of trash. But what if he went back and told Evangeline, and Evangeline said, "Oh, don't worry, she's just a hooker's daughter," and then he told Mrs. Lockwell, and Mrs. Lockwell told Charlotte?

I hated New Orleans.

No, New Orleans hated me.

"Dora told me you want to go to college," said Willie.

"What?"

"You heard me. And I think it's a good idea."

I looked over at Willie's dark silhouette in the passenger seat. "You do?"

"You're smart, Jo. You know how to make the most of a situation. You'll do well at Loyola. Hell, you might even get in at Newcomb."

My fingers hooked around the wheel again. "But I don't want to go to college in New Orleans, Willie. I don't want to go to college in Louisiana. I want to go out East."

"What are you talking about? Out East where?"

"In Massachusetts."

"What the hell for?" said Willie.

"For an education," I told her.

"You'll get a fine education at Loyola or Newcomb. You're staying in New Orleans."

No, I wouldn't stay in New Orleans. I wouldn't spend the rest of my life cleaning a bawdy house, being leered at as the daughter of a French Quarter prostitute. I'd have nice friends like Charlotte and socialize with people like Forrest Hearne—people who thought better of me than gutter trash.

"You're salted peanuts," said Willie.

"What? What's that supposed to mean?"

"You're salted peanuts, and those people out East are petits fours. Don't be cliché, thinking you're going to be Orphan Annie, who winds up in some kind of castle. You're salted peanuts, Jo, and there's nothing wrong with salted peanuts. But salted peanuts aren't served with petits fours."

Willie agreed with Mother. She thought I wanted a fairy tale, when I was destined for nothing more than a crummy life skirting the New Orleans underworld.

"I'll pay the tuition for Loyola or Newcomb," said Willie. "That was your plan all along, wasn't it, to threaten to leave so I would pay for your damn college here?"

We didn't speak for the rest of the drive.

EIGHTEEN

The days unfolded slowly out at Shady Grove. Willie's cottage sat on over twenty peaceful acres. You could breathe deeply without fear that something putrid, like urine or vomit, might slip into your nostrils. In the summer, I didn't wear shoes for days at a time. I'd kick my flats off in the grass the moment we arrived, and they'd sit on the front porch until we left. The winter was mild this year, more wet than cold. I'd need to build the fires, but not for warmth—just to dry the cottage out a bit. An old friend bought Shady Grove for Willie. She'd never tell me who it was, or what happened to them, just that she got the better end of the deal.

New Orleans was full of noise all hours of the day and night. But the countryside was so quiet. You could hear sounds at Shady Grove that the din of New Orleans swallowed whole. The cottage wasn't secluded, but the closest neighbors, Ray and Frieda Kole, were over a half mile away, and we never saw them. Ray and Frieda were terrified of the dark. They slept during the day and sat locked in a rusted Buick in their back field at night, with the ignition and headlights on, ready to run if the boogeyman ever showed up. Willie wasn't interested in neighbors or socializing. She said she came to Shady Grove for peace and quiet, to get away from people. She even wore a cotton dress and a rose shade of lipstick at the cottage, instead of her usual red.

I took long walks each afternoon, reading while I made my way two miles down the dirt path to the crossroads at Possum Trot. Willie had barely said a word to me for three days. The silence gave me more time to think about Mr. Lockwell, Forrest Hearne's watch, Smith, and Mother. All four made me nervous. I was relieved when Willie finally started talking.

"Get my guns. Let's go shoot," she said.

I got the golf bag from the trunk of the Cadillac. Six years ago, one of the tricks lost a set of golf clubs to Willie in a poker game. She had me pawn the clubs and put her rifles and shotguns in the green leather bag. Frankie and I often joked that Willie had become an excellent golfer. I set up the cans on the back of the fence.

"You want to use the shotgun?" asked Willie.

"No, I'll just use my pistol," I told her.

"Suit yourself. Give me the shotgun."

I was ten when Willie taught me how to shoot. I once forgot to put the safety on and fired the gun accidentally. Willie whipped me so hard I ate my dinner standing up that night. But I never forgot the safety again. "Be in control of your piece, Jo. The minute it takes control of you, you're dead," Willie would tell me.

I blew the first can off the fence. "Nice shot," said Willie.

"It's easy—just pretend it's Cincinnati," I told her. I thought about Cincinnati saying I was like Mother and took another shot.

She laughed. "Trouble is, I got a lot of Cincinnatis. Don't know which one to choose. Has Patrick figured out that Cincinnati's the one who robbed his house?" Willie blew a loud shot and missed the coffee can. She rarely missed.

"No. And I pray he doesn't. He told me he saw Mother near the Roosevelt Hotel with a guy whose suit didn't fit him. He still has no idea who Cincinnati is. It's all my fault," I said, moving down a few steps to the next can. "I was always telling Mother what beautiful things Charlie had. I should have known when she asked me about his house out of the blue like that. If you could have seen it, he took everything, Willie, not just the expensive things, but Patrick's bronzed baby shoes, and even a pack of cigarettes on the counter."

"I'm still surprised he didn't get that expensive piano somehow."

"He probably tried. Maybe that's when Charlie came home and . . ." I dropped my arms. "Who could do that to a man like Charlie?"

Cincinnati had beaten Charlie so badly he was in the hospital for over a month. When Patrick came home and found Charlie in a puddle of blood, he was sure his father was dead.

"Made it easier for me to shoot Cincinnati when he beat your mother," said Willie. "And come on, you know burning him with that hot coffee was more for Charlie than for your mother."

"Patrick thinks the robbery and beating is what set Charlie crooked," I said, firing another can off the fence.

"Nope. He was already touched in the head when Cinci robbed the house. Your mother knew that. She had seen Charlie at the bookstore and said he was talking ten sides of crazy. She gave Cincinnati the tip he'd be an easy target. She went with him, you know. I still wonder if Charlie saw her."

I stared at Willie. Charlie had been as good to Mother as he had to me. He was always patient with her and tried to steer her straight. Sure, my mother would stuff something in her brassiere in a department store dressing room. I knew she'd hustle drinks from tourists and steal tips from tables. But to stand by and watch Cincinnati do that to Charlie?

"No, she couldn't have actually been there," I told Willie.

"Oh, yeah, your mother's real helpful that way," said Willie.

Pain surged at my temples. I held my pistol out to Willie. "Give me the shotgun." As soon as it was in my arms, I began firing, pumping shell after shell. When the cans were gone, I started blowing holes in the fence.

"Stop! That's my fence, you idiot!" yelled Willie.

I lowered the gun and looked at Willie, trying to catch my breath.

"Nice round," said Willie. "What do you think those East Coast petits fours would say about that?"

I nodded. "Pretty salty."

We drove to the nearest town for milk and eggs. I stared at the sunlight gleaming off Mariah's hood and thought of Mother telling Cincinnati all about Charlie and Patrick's house. Who could deliberately take advantage of a poor man like Charlie? And Charlie had done so much for us before falling ill.

Willie paid the store owner to let us make a phone call. She rang the house to check in. I heard the warble of Dora's voice through the receiver but couldn't make out the words.

"Tell 'em to come by tonight at ten. I can be back and ready by then," said Willie. "Call Lucinda and have her bring a couple girls with her. No, of course not the redhead. I don't need another catfight. Okay. All right. We'll leave as soon as we can."

Willie hung up the phone.

"Six johns from Cuba. They came by last year and dropped nearly five grand in four hours at the house. Dora said she put them off as long as she could, but they're going back to Havana tomorrow. We have to go."

I nodded and followed Willie out of the store and back to the car.

"Oh," said Willie, stopping next to Mariah, "Dora said that Patrick's called a bunch of times for you. He says it's important."

NINETEEN

"Take my bags to my room and then get out of here," ordered Willie, handing me her things.

Girls in evening dresses paraded in front of Willie for approval. She checked their fingernails, looked at their jewelry, and asked if their brassieres and panties matched. They all wore a smear of glossy lipstick. Prostitutes had patent-leather lips, all except Sweety, who always blotted her lips.

"Welcome back," said Dora, dressed in apple green satin with a huge bow that looked like a melted rainbow.

"What the hell is that?" said Willie.

"Something special for the rich Mexicans that are coming," said Dora. She twirled around for Willie.

"They're Cubans, not Mexicans! Go change into your velvet gown. You're a prostitute, not a piñata, for God's sake." Dora sighed and started up the staircase. "Where's Evangeline?" asked Willie.

"Sulking. Her big spender hasn't been by in a while," said Dora.

Mr. Lockwell. Maybe he really was scared to come back. But what if his appetite for pigtails trumped his fear of humiliation? I had to get that letter from him as soon as possible.

"What, are you just gonna stand there and gawk?" Willie asked me. "I said drop my bags and get out. Vacation's over."

I carried my suitcase, heavy with books, back to the bookshop in the dark. I watched for Cokie, hoping he might drive by and give me a ride. But he didn't. Cars whizzed through the street, and music spilled out from the windows and doorways of each building I walked by. Cast-iron balconies sagged like sad, rusted doilies. I passed Mrs. Zerruda scrubbing her stoop in brick dust to ward off a hoodoo hex. Somewhere behind me a bottle broke on the sidewalk. Shady Grove felt a million miles away.

The bookshop was locked. The sign said CLOSED, but the lights were on. I made my way up the stairs to my apartment. A package leaned up against my door. My heart leapt when I saw Charlotte's name on the return address. Taped to my door was a note from Patrick:

Please come to the house.
It's Charlie.

I pounded on Patrick's door and leaned over the railing to look in the front window. "It's Jo!" I yelled.

The door flew open, and Patrick stood barefoot, clothes filthy, his face a wreck.

"Patrick, what is it?" I asked. I heard a yell from inside the house.

"Hurry." He pulled me inside and locked the door behind me. The smell stopped me, as if I had smacked into a wall of rotting food and filthy diapers.

"Oh, Patrick," I said, plugging my nose, "you have to open a window."

"I can't, then they'll hear him. Jo, he won't stop. It's never been like this. He won't snap out of it. He has no idea who I am. He's terrified of me and won't stop screaming. He only sleeps a few minutes at a time. I'm worried they're going to haul him off to Charity. I haven't slept for days, I—I . . ." Patrick's chest puffed up and down in desperate breaths.

"It's okay," I told him, taking his hands. Patrick's bloodshot eyes had sunk into deep wells of gray. The skin around his nose and mouth was mottled with red blemishes. What had been going on?

"Have you tried playing the piano?" I asked.

"The usual songs don't work."

"Have you given him the medicine?"

"I did, but now it's gone and I can't find it. I think he flushed it down the toilet. It's all my fault."

"Slow down, Patrick. Where is he?"

"In his room. If he sees me, he'll go into complete hysterics."

I passed the kitchen and spotted crusty plates stacked on the counter. I walked up the stairs slowly, listening. The old wood groaned underfoot as I reached the top and was immediately answered by a blistering yell from behind Charlie's door.

"See! I told you," whispered Patrick from the foot of the stairs.

"Shh." I waved at him to be quiet while moving my face near the doorjamb. "Charlie, it's only me. May I come in?" No response from behind the door. I put my hand on the cool glass knob. "I'm coming in, Charlie." Still no response. The door creaked as I pushed it open and peeked inside.

The room was destroyed. The drapes had been torn from the windows, contents spilled from drawers, the floor covered in clothes, soiled sheets, shoes, the typewriter, dirty dishes, and cups.

The smell. I gagged and pulled my head back into the hall for a breath. I told myself I had seen worse, but I wasn't sure I had. I steadied my grip on the door, took a breath, and walked in the room. Charlie sat in his underwear on a bare mattress, wild-eyed, clutching the Valentine box.

"Lucy?" he whispered.

"Hi, Charlie," I began.

"Lucy, Lucy! Lucy!" he continued to whisper, rocking back and forth. It was more than I had heard him say in months.

I nodded, fearful that any disagreement might set him off. I picked up the pillow from the floor and placed it on the bed, which resulted in several rounds of Lucys.

"Time to rest, Charlie," I told him. I smoothed his hair away from his eyes and nudged his shoulders down toward the pillow, trying to smile instead of gag.

He lay down and looked up at me, gripping the pink heart-shaped box against his chest. "Lucy."

I thought about trying to take the box but didn't want to push my luck. I began sorting through the items on the floor, finding horrible surprises under each towel or piece of clothing I picked up. Some things were not salvageable.

I worked for over an hour, placing things outside his door and tying up items for the trash in sheets. Once Charlie closed his eyes, I crept out of the room and shut his door.

Patrick was sitting in an armchair near the window in the living room, staring off with a blank face.

"He's lying down, but I don't know how long he'll stay that way," I told him. Patrick said nothing. "Patrick?"

"Lucy—Lucille—is his aunt. She's been dead for over fifteen years."

"He needs his medicine."

"I don't know what he did with his medicine. The druggist is closed now," said Patrick, still staring into a void.

"I'll call Willie. She'll arrange something through Dr. Sully."

Patrick nodded, silent.

"It'll be okay, Patrick. Once we get the medicine, it will be all right."

He turned to me, almost angry. "Will it? Or will it just continue to get worse? Just the sight of me makes him go mad, Jo. I couldn't restrain him, couldn't bathe him. He acted like he despised me, like I was going to hurt him."

"He's sick, Patrick."

"I know. He needs professional help, a hospital. But I can't bear to have him treated like a lunatic in Charity's mental ward. He's not crazy. Something's just . . . wrong. He changed after that beating."

"I'll call Willie about the medicine."

Patrick pointed to the telephone on the floor near the hallway. Willie would be furious that I was bothering her when the Cubans were there. I said I was calling about Charlie and was surprised how quickly Willie came to the phone. I told her everything.

"Poor sack." Willie sighed. "I'll handle the meds. It might take a couple hours because it's so late, but I'll send Cokie by."

I hung up the phone and started to clean the kitchen. Patrick's voice came from over my shoulder.

"It's my fault, Jo. I left him."

"You leave him every day. Generally he's okay when he's locked in his room."

"But I left him at night."

"You left him on New Year's Eve, and he was fine."

"No, I left him for longer than usual."

"Where were you?" I asked, rinsing a plate.

Patrick glanced down at his feet. "I had some business."

"Buying dead people's books? Well, now you know that you can't be away that long. So stop feeling bad about it." I sounded like Willie.

Patrick looked up at me, serious. "I don't know what I'd do without you, Jo, you know that?"

I laughed. "You'd survive."

"No, I don't know if I would." He took a step closer. "Jo, we can tell each other anything, right?"

I looked at him. "What do you mean?"

He moved in close. "Just what I said. If I were to tell you something, I wouldn't want it to scare you away."

My pulse began to jog. I looked from Patrick to the sink. "I can't believe you're saying that. Think about the things I tell you about Willie's. That doesn't scare you away. Oh, and talk about scary, before I left for Shady Grove, I ran into John Lockwell leaving the house after a date with Evangeline. She was in pigtails and her schoolgirl outfit."

"No!" said Patrick. He stepped back from me.

"Yep."

"Did you hide?" he asked.

"Hide? No, I told him I had a book delivery for Willie. I asked if he came to Willie's often. At first he was rude and tried to brush me off. So I chased him down the driveway to Conti, told him I was applying to Smith and that I wanted a written recommendation from him."

"You what?"

"Yep, and I told him I'd call or come by his house to get the letter if that was more convenient. He put two and two together real quick. He doesn't want me telling his wife or creepy kids that I ran into him at a brothel, now, does he?"

Patrick looked elated. "Jo, you're a genius! Do you think he'll give you the letter?"

"He told me to call him at his office. I think I'll just stop by." I wiped my hands on the dish towel and turned to face him. "So, see? I tell you everything." I took a breath. "What did you want to tell me?"

Patrick paused, taking in my face. He smiled gently. "I think that's enough for one day. You never cease to amaze me, Jo."

Patrick was sound asleep on the couch when Cokie arrived with the medicine.

"Oooeee, smells like dead muskrat in here," whispered Cokie, pinching up his face.

"Not as bad as it did smell. I just opened the windows." I wiped the kitchen counter clean and hung the damp dishrag over the faucet.

"Willie had Sadie package up some groceries, too," said Cokie. He handed me the bag.

"Have you been workin' dominoes?" I asked him. I always knew when Cokie was gambling because his fingertips were dusted with chalk.

"Yeah, me and Cornbread been playin'. How bad off is Mr. Charlie?" asked Cokie.

"Pretty bad. He needs this medicine."

"Dr. Sully sent two kinds. One is only to use if he gets real *real* bad."

I walked into the living room, looking at the two bottles. Patrick was snoring, but not like Charlie upstairs. Charlie was sawing, pulling loud rips with each breath. Patrick's breathing purred, his upper lip puffing out when he exhaled. I set the two medicine bottles in front of him on the coffee table and pulled a quilt up to his shoulders. I started to leave, but suddenly looked at him, bent down, and kissed him on the forehead.

TWENTY

The contents of Charlotte's package lay neatly arranged on my desk—the Smith catalog, brochures, and application. Charlotte had included a tattered copy of Candace Kinkaid's sequel, *Rogue Betrayal*, with an inscription that teased, *To my dear friend Jo. May your heart ever swell with rogue desire. Fondly, Charlotte.* She also sent the Smith College photograph that she had mentioned at the party. I propped the small picture up on my desk.

My head felt heavy and I longed for a nap. I had gone to Willie's an hour early in order to check on Charlie by breakfast. Charlie had calmed down and agreed to take his medicine. He no longer spoke and just sat in the chair by the window, clinging to the pink heart-shaped box. I worked in the bookshop all day until Patrick arrived in the afternoon. We had agreed he would work for just a short time while I saw to my business, the business with Mr. Lockwell.

I looked at myself in the broken mirror hanging on my wall and sighed at the girl staring back at me. I had chosen a dress I felt was my most professional for an office visit and wished I had appropriate gloves to match. But I didn't have gloves. The color had faded from the dress after years of washing and wear. My shoes were scuffed. Hopefully no one would notice. I blotted my lips with a tissue.

812 Gravier Street. Everyone knew the address. It was the massive white-domed Hibernia Bank Building. Mr. Lockwell's office was on the eighth floor. As the elevator climbed, my stomach fell. I replayed Mr. Lockwell's condescending tone in my head, the little scoffing sound he made through his nose in Willie's driveway. I thought of Willie's shotgun in my arms, fierce and strong. Holes in the fence, I told myself. Salted peanuts.

The elevator doors parted, revealing polished hardwoods and a well-dressed woman at a reception desk flanked by potted ferns. I had expected a hallway with offices. Mr. Lockwell had the entire floor. The woman inspected me thoroughly as I stood a foot outside the elevator doors clutching my purse.

"This is the eighth floor," she said.

"Yes." I nodded, taking a step closer. "I'm here to see Mr. Lockwell."

Her thin eyebrows rose. "Do you have an appointment?"

"I'm a friend of the family. He's expecting me. Josephine Moraine," I said, realizing I was speaking louder and faster than intended.

The woman picked up the phone. "Hello, Dottie. I have a Josephine Moraine here for Mr. Lockwell." She paused and stared at me while speaking. "She says she's a friend of the family and that he's expecting her."

Ten minutes passed, then twenty, an hour. I flipped through

a *LIFE* magazine on the table, pretending I was interested in the article on President Truman. The receptionist alternated filing her fingernails and answering the telephone, throwing glances my way occasionally and shaking her head. I sat stiffly on a chair, becoming angrier with each minute. I approached the desk. "Perhaps I'll just visit Mr. Lockwell at his house this evening. Could you ring back and see if that might be more convenient for him?"

She called back, and within an instant, the doors swung open and Mr. Lockwell appeared in a starched shirt and tie. "Josephine, so sorry to keep you waiting. Charlotte will have my head. Come on back."

Mr. Lockwell guided me into a large corner office. The room was five times the size of my entire apartment, with tall gleaming windows overlooking the city. He closed the door and walked behind his broad mahogany desk. "I was just about to have a drink. Join me." He gestured to a long sideboard filled with decanters, glasses, and an ice bucket.

"No, thank you."

"Oh, come on, now. I'll call Dottie in to mix us up a couple of martinis."

I set my purse on the chair and walked to the table. "Shaken or stirred?"

He seemed amused. "Stirred. Dirty."

I mixed his cocktail, feeling his eyes searing through my back.

"Whoa, now that's a drink!" he exclaimed, taking a sip and sitting down at his desk. "How long have you been making martinis?"

"I just learned," I told him.

"I wish you could teach Lilly to make a real drink. Sure you won't join me?"

I shook my head and took one of the chairs in front of his desk. "I know you're extremely busy." I pulled a piece of paper from my purse with the address of the Smith registrar on it and pushed it toward him on the desk. "The letter can be brief. Just a recommendation to include with my application."

Mr. Lockwell leaned back in his chair, not even glancing at the paper. "Oh, so you're serious about this, are you?"

"Quite."

He took another sip of his martini and loosened his tie a bit. "Did you tell my niece that you ran into me the other day?"

"No, I haven't had the opportunity yet."

"Well, young lady, I don't really know you, and I can't write a letter of recommendation for someone I don't know." He eyed me carefully. "Maybe you should consult your family about this recommendation. Perhaps your father?"

I feigned a sad expression. "Unfortunately, he's no longer with us."

"Oh, no?" He took a swig of his martini. "Well, where is he?"

"I believe you know what I mean."

"I know what you mean," he said, leaning over the desk toward me, "but I don't believe you. You're trying to hustle me, kid. You're slick witted. I smelled something wasn't right when you and your fella came to my home. Richard and Betty are still arguing about your piano-playing friend. I've seen him before, sitting in the back of the cathedral in the middle of the day."

"You've seen Patrick at the cathedral?" That was surprising.

"Yes, we sinners frequent the cathedral," he said sarcastically. He stared across the desk at me. "So, are you proud, poor, or both? My niece, Charlotte, loves to feed strays, but generally they at least have a decent pair of shoes."

A tight burning flamed within my chest. I shifted forward and folded my hands carefully on his desk. "Well, it was such a fortunate coincidence to run into you and your friend with the pigtails when I was delivering books. I had hoped to ask you—or Mrs. Lockwell—for a recommendation anyway," I fired back.

He engaged, moving his bishop closer to my queen. "Oh, yes, delivering books. I stopped by your bookshop in the Quarter. Twice. It was closed."

"Family illness." I nodded. "But I know that Mrs. Lockwell loves to read. I'd be happy to bring some books by for her." I put my hands back in my lap.

We sat in silence across from each other, me clutching my purse, Mr. Lockwell perspiring.

"If I write you a recommendation and for some reason you get in, next you'll ask me for money. That's how this works, right?"

Genuine shock pushed me back in my chair. I had never, ever intended to ask Mr. Lockwell for tuition money. "I assure you, Mr. Lockwell, I do not want your money."

"Right. You think this is my first rodeo?"

"I simply want a strong recommendation from you, a name that the application board might recognize and respect."

"Because your father's no longer with us," he said with mock pity. "I imagine your mother's no longer with us either, huh? You're taking this Cinderella story to Smith?"

"Really, this is not about money. I want to go to Smith. Charlotte has sent me all the application materials. I had excellent marks in school."

A clock on the wall chimed. Mr. Lockwell drummed his fingers against the leather inlay on top of his desk. I looked past his hands to the bureau behind him. Silver frames. Family pictures.

"You know, I just might tell my wife about the whole thing. You see, a business associate asked me to meet him for a drink at Willie's, and when I got there, I didn't want to stay and insisted we move the meeting to a bar in the Quarter. I'll tell Lilly. After all, that's what happened."

I hadn't thought of that. "You can absolutely tell her that, Mr. Lockwell, if you like."

"What I'd like is to never see you again."

I had him. I could close it.

"Then this works well for both of us. Your glowing recommendation will get me into Smith—all the way across the country—and you'll never hear from me again. Ever."

He lit a stub of a cigar from a Waterford ashtray on his desk and drained the remaining liquid from the glass. "Ever, huh?" I could practically see the thought bubble above his head. It had Evangeline dancing around in her short plaid skirt. "Maybe I can put something together," he said. He pulled the piece of paper with the registrar's information toward him.

"I'll wait for it. That's Moraine, *M-o-r-a-i-n-e*."

"What, do you expect me to type it up myself? I'll come up with something and Dottie will prepare the letter."

"Two copies, please. I'll come by tomorrow."

"No, I'll have them sent by the bookshop when they're ready.

You won't need to come back." He raised his eyebrows and his glass. "And make me another one of these before you leave. Damn good."

As I turned to leave Mr. Lockwell's office, he stood near the window, fresh drink in hand. "Bye-bye, now, Josephine," he said with what I thought might be a smile. He didn't offer to walk me out. I made my way down the elevator to the lobby of the building, exhaling a mixture of relief and happiness as I walked through the door to the street.

"Miss Moraine."

Someone touched my elbow, and I turned. It was a police officer.

"Detective Langley would like to ask you a few questions. Come with me, please."

TWENTY-ONE

I sat, humming, on a cold metal chair in the hallway of the police station, staring at the gray tile floor. It reminded me of the floors in my grade school. When I was bored, I used to stare at them, imagining they were a cloudy vat of water and with a secret password, the seam in the tile would open and suck my desk straight down into the abyss. I'd have to hold on, I'd be moving so fast, my thick hair blowing a tangled tempest behind me. I didn't know what the abyss was, but I was sure that something better than New Orleans was under the school's gray tile. The police station floors didn't feel at all promising. Filmy residue from a dirty mop had painted circular shadows near the legs of each chair. Whoever cleaned the station was lazy. You always moved chairs to mop properly.

A clatter of hacking and high heels stopped in front of me.

"Well, hey there, Josie girl. Your momma's not here, is she?"

Dora's sister, Darleen, teetered in front of me, the left side of her neck speckled with either hickies or a beating.

I shook my head. "No, she's not here."

"Thanks for waiting, Miss Moraine." A pudgy man with a receding hairline leaned out of a doorway nearby. Darleen raised her eyebrows and then quickly walked away, the exposed nails from her worn stilettos tapping against the tile. I walked into the office.

"Detective Langley," he said, extending his arm for a handshake. His palm felt moist and fat. "Have a seat."

The windowless office was nothing like John Lockwell's. Stacked file boxes lined each wall nearly to the ceiling, and piles of folders rose up around the detective on his desk. The air was thick with hot breath and nicotine. No photographs. The detective pulled a file folder in front of him and took a swig from a coffee mug that hadn't been washed in months. I could see a caffeine skin on the inside of the cup.

"We're lucky we caught up with you. Your friend from the bookstore told us you were running errands on Gravier Street," said the detective.

I nodded. I had seen Frankie and Willie have conversations with the police. They always listened intently and spoke very little. I intended to do the same. Willie used to have a police contact who covered for her in exchange for time with Dora. He was fired and Willie no longer had an inside cop.

"I don't know if you're aware, Miss Moraine, but a gentleman from Tennessee died of a heart attack at the Sans Souci on New Year's Eve," said the detective. He waited for a response.

"I read about it in the papers," I told him.

He nodded and held up a picture of Forrest Hearne.

Handsome, sophisticated, kind Forrest Hearne. He was smiling in the photo, his teeth perfectly aligned like squares of clean chalk.

"Mr. Hearne's checkbook register shows that the afternoon prior to his death, he made a purchase in the bookstore where you are employed. Do you remember anything about him?"

I clasped my hands together so they wouldn't tremble, thinking of Forrest Hearne's check crisply folded in the cigar box under my bed. "He . . . said he was from Memphis and was down for the Bowl."

The detective didn't look at me. Instead, he stared down at the file, sparked a match, and lit a cigarette. He held up the pack, offering one.

"No, thank you."

He stuffed the pack in his shirt pocket. "What did he buy?"

"Keats and Dickens," I said.

He made a note on a dog-eared pad in front of him. "That's the title of the book?"

"No, those are the names of two writers. He bought a book of poetry and a copy of *David Copperfield*."

The detective continued writing and yawned. His tongue was stained the color of mustard. My shoulders relaxed slightly. This man was what Willie called a Paper Joe, not someone actively pursuing a case, just getting notes for the record. He certainly wasn't the chess match John Lockwell had been.

"Okay, did you notice if he was wearing any jewelry? The widow reported that the deceased had an expensive watch."

An icy rod shot through my nerves and into my throat. The

watch. Of course she noticed that it was gone. Under the engraving *F. L. Hearne* on the back were also the words *With Love, Marion.* It was obviously a gift. An expensive gift. And now she wanted to know where it was. *Tick, tock, tick, tock*—the sound pulsed through my head.

"Did you notice a watch, Miss Moraine?" asked the detective.

"Yes. He was wearing a watch."

"How do you know?" asked the detective.

"I noticed it when he was writing his check."

The detective flipped the photo of Forrest Hearne up toward him. "This fella looks like a society guy. Nice watch?"

"Mmm-hmm. Gold."

The chair groaned as he leaned back. He yawned again and ran his hand through the thin plumes of hair he had left. "Okay. So you can confirm that he had the watch when he bought the books?"

"Yes."

"And what time was that?"

"I don't recall the exact time. Late afternoon."

"Anything else? Did he appear sick to you?"

"No, he didn't appear sick."

"Marty." An equally disheveled man leaned in the doorway. "Shooting over in Metairie. The guys out there are saying it's one of Marcello's guys."

Sleepy Detective Langley suddenly perked up. "Any witnesses?"

"Two. Both talkin'. How much longer ya gonna be?"

"I'm done. Just let me grab some coffee, and I'll be down.

Thank you, Miss Moraine. Sorry to interrupt your day, but the gentleman's family is concerned about the watch and some cash that's missing. They keep contacting us. I'll show you out."

"That's not necessary. It sounds like you have pressing business. I'll show myself out." I gathered my purse and left his office and the station as quickly as possible.

The family's concerned about the watch. Of course they were concerned. How far would his wife go to find it? The strands of anxiety in my stomach were now firmly tied in knots. I felt like I might be sick. How did the watch end up in a man's sock in my mother's bedroom? I could have just told the detective I had found the watch and was happy to give it to him for Mrs. Hearne. But then he might have questioned why it ended up at Willie's, he'd question Willie, and she would find out I had the watch and hadn't told her. Besides, Willie was always saying she didn't want any problems.

I knew what to do.

TWENTY-TWO

I ran my thumb over the letters etched in the gold. I saw it on his wrist and heard his deep voice. *Good luck at college, whichever one you choose,* and *Happy New Year. It's gonna be a great one!* He had no idea. He seemed well, full of hope. *David Copperfield.* I barely knew him, yet something in me clung to the watch, and I wanted desperately to keep it. But I couldn't.

I put on my sweater, dropped the watch in my purse, and left my apartment.

The cold air hung damp and a misty rain fell softly in the dark. I should have brought an umbrella, but I didn't want to turn back. I knew if I did, I might lose my nerve. So I continued down the sidewalk on Royal toward St. Peter. The cloudy sky turned the streets into a wet black maze. Generally, I could watch for shadows behind me on the pavement, but tonight there weren't any, just a slick of black. Doors slammed and voices echoed between the buildings. A man yelled at his son about the trash, and a soprano sang a beautiful aria from somewhere above me.

"Psst. Hey, girl."

An old man in rags and carpet slippers peeked out from one of the doorways in front of me. I clutched my purse and stepped off the sidewalk into the street. He began to follow me, croaking nonsense.

"Hazel is under the table." He giggled from a foot behind.

I quickened my pace and heard the sudden halt of his slippered footfall. It was replaced by an eerie singing.

"Thou art lost and gone forever, dreadful sorry, Clementine," he crooned.

Maybe I should have waited until daylight. My hair was wet and I began to shiver as I passed Dewey's soda shop. It glowed warm and pink. I was nearly to the corner when I heard door hinges creak behind me.

"Jo!"

I turned. Jesse was jogging toward me.

"Hey, Jo. Where ya goin'?"

I opened my mouth, then closed it again. Where was I going? What could I tell him? I looked down at Jesse's denims, cuffed wide over his black motorcycle boots, and tried to think. "I'm . . . meeting a friend."

"Kinda late, isn't it?"

I nodded, wrapping my arms around my wet sweater.

"Wanna warm up for a second?" He motioned with his head toward the soda shop.

My eyes pulled to the happy pink glow on the corner. "Well . . ."

"Aw, come on, Motor City. It'll be quick. You're shivering."

I looked down St. Peter into the darkness. "Okay, just real quick."

I fixed my hair in the ladies' room and tried to blot myself dry with the thin handkerchief from my purse. When I returned, a cup of hot cocoa sat on the counter next to Jesse. I slid onto the vinyl stool. Jesse's soda glass was empty.

"Have you been here long?" I asked him.

"I was just about to leave and then I saw you. I had to get out of the house. My granny was driving me crazy. She's tryin' to plant a hex on our neighbors to make them move. They're loud and keep her up at night."

"Really? What's the hex?"

He rolled his eyes and pushed the hot cocoa closer to me.

"Oh, come on, Jesse. Tell me. I don't believe in that stuff anyway."

I didn't believe in it, but I did have a gris-gris bag in my purse that Willie's witch doctor insisted I carry.

"Nah, it's just crazy stuff," he said, trying to wipe what looked like motor oil from his fingers with the napkin.

"Oh, and I don't understand crazy?"

He smiled. "All right, then." He spun toward me on his stool and planted his boots on opposite sides of my legs. He leaned in close. I smelled his shaving tonic and tried to steady my face, which seemed to be pulling toward the scent.

"She has this spell she swears works to get rid of people. She finds a dead rat, stuffs its mouth with a piece of lemon dipped in red wax. She pours a teaspoon of whiskey on the rat, wraps it in newspaper, and then puts it under the neighbor's porch." He raised his eyebrows.

"I haven't heard that one." Jesse was funny and surprisingly easy to talk to.

"She's really superstitious, but that's New Orleans."

"Yeah, that's New Orleans." I shook my head.

He tipped his soda glass slightly, watching the last of the liquid crawl up the side. "But would you ever leave?"

I looked up. Jesse was staring at me. "I mean, do you ever think of leaving New Orleans?" he asked.

Did he know? I wanted to tell him yes, but it didn't feel right. He already knew about Mother. Perhaps that was why he brought it up. I stared down at the counter. "So are you the first one in your family to go to college?" I asked.

"Yeah. My dad's still in the pen. He talks about getting out, but I know that's just talk."

"What's he in for?"

"Gambling . . . and other stuff. He's never been out for more than a couple months before he gets arrested again," said Jesse.

"Your dad isn't tied with Carlos Marcello, is he?" I thought about Detective Langley saying one of Marcello's men had been involved in the shooting out in Metairie. I wished it had been Cincinnati.

"Aw, heck no. Marcello's the big time. If you're tangled with him, you don't end up in jail, you end up dead. My dad's just your average Crescent City crook. This town will eat you up if you're not careful. But I won't be here forever. After all, do I really seem like a flower salesman?"

"Well, hello there, Jesse!" Two attractive blondes linked arm in arm approached us at the counter.

"Hey, Fran," said Jesse over his shoulder, though still keeping his eyes on me. "Do you like flowers, Motor City?"

"My mom loved the roses she bought from you last week," said the girl, nudging closer to Jesse.

"I'm glad." Jesse turned to them and spoke in a mock whisper. "Now, if you'll excuse me, ladies, I'm kinda busy, trying to woo this gal here."

I laughed, trying not to snort hot chocolate through my nose.

"Doesn't look like she's interested," said Fran. Jesse's face clouded.

I slid off the stool. "How rude of me. Please, have a seat. We don't need two stools." I pulled myself onto Jesse's lap. The blondes stared. I slung my arm over his shoulder and gestured toward the vacant stool.

"Is that car running yet, Jesse, or are you still riding the Triumph?" asked Fran.

"Still riding the motorcycle, but the Merc's comin' along."

"It's gonna be fantastic," I said, swishing Jesse's straw against the soda residue in his glass. "High-pressure heads, dual carburetors."

All heads snapped to me.

"Jo's originally from Detroit," said Jesse. "The Motor City."

"How cute," said Fran, boring holes through me with her stare. "Jo from Detroit and Jesse from Dauphine."

"Actually, I'm from Alabama," said Jesse.

"But that doesn't sound as good," said Fran.

"I think that sounds real good." I lowered my voice to a whisper. "After all, girls, you know what they say about boys from Alabama." I nodded slowly.

Fran's mouth dropped. She had two fillings on the right side. Her friend started to giggle uncontrollably. Fran pulled her toward the door.

I watched the girls saunter away in their expensive coats and pink lipstick. As soon as they were out the door, Jesse started laughing.

"Impressive. High-pressure heads, huh?" he said.

"I read about it in a hot-rod book we had in the shop."

"It's a game for them," he told me. "Slummin' with Jesse."

"What do you mean? She seemed interested in you." I looked at Jesse. He wasn't stylish or sharp like Patrick. He was rugged, quietly mysterious. Jesse had blue eyes, spicy brown hair, and a deep scar near his right ear. Despite an injury to his foot when he was young, he had played baseball in school.

"Come on. They're not interested. They're just flirting with a guy from the Quarter so when they get older, they can say that they once played the other side of the tracks."

"Yeah, telling stories while they drink highballs at their bridge parties."

"Exactly," said Jesse. "They'll talk about the time they went slummin' in the Quarter—"

"With the handsome flower vendor."

"Who ruined their reputation forever," he whispered in my ear.

Jesse's warm mouth near my ear made something quiver in my stomach. A nervous feeling took over and I jumped down from his lap. "Sorry, I'm probably breaking your legs." I sat down on my stool and smoothed my skirt.

"Don't worry. A handsome flower vendor can handle it." Jesse looked at me.

"What?" A flush of heat pulled across my cheeks.

"You said 'with the handsome flower vendor.'"

"No, I didn't."

"Yeah, you did, and now you're blushing." Jesse grinned. "But don't worry. I know you didn't mean it. You were just playin'." Jesse fiddled with the napkin under his soda glass. "The friend you're meeting tonight, it's the guy from the bookstore, right?"

I was so warm and comfortable, I had forgotten all about it. The watch. The detective. The lie to Jesse. I wished I could tell him the truth, but what would I say? *Actually, Jesse, I've got to run. I've got a dead man's watch in my purse, and his widow and the police are looking for it. You know how these things are, with your dad in jail and all.*

I just nodded. "Yes, I'm meeting Patrick. I should probably go." I opened my purse.

"No, I've got it, Jo. Please."

"Thank you, Jesse." I smiled.

"How 'bout I walk you there," he said, putting the money on the counter and standing up. "It's dark."

"Oh, no. I'm fine."

He nodded, and his smile faded. "Sure. Great to see you, Jo. Have a good night."

"Good night, Jesse. Thanks again for the hot chocolate."

I walked down St. Peter and then over to Eads Plaza, trying to decide where I would do it, where it might be the darkest, and where no one would see me. The drizzle had stopped, but the sky was still black and thick with foamy clouds. A rat nibbled on wet trash in the street. It stopped and stared at me. I thought about Jesse's granny stuffing its mouth with a lemon. I crossed the road and made my way down to the edge of the riverbank. My shoes slipped on the wet gravel, and I stumbled, nearly falling. I pretended to walk casually, glancing over my shoulders to see who might be around. A couple stood kissing near the water's edge. I walked past them, hoping they would leave.

The wind blew, and the tarty smell of the yellow Mississippi lapped against my face, lifting the ends of my hair. I heard the cry of a saxophone down the bank and could see the twinkling lights of the steamboat *President*, with all the paying guests making merry. I stood and stared out at the water, wondering how far I'd have to throw the watch so it wouldn't wash back up onshore. I should have tied the watch to a rock, to make sure it would sink and stay lodged at the bottom. Something behind me crunched and I spun around.

I squinted but saw nothing through the black. I thought of all the tales of ghosts on the Mississippi, of Jean Lafitte and the headless pirates who haunt the riverfront. I turned and faced the water. I opened my purse.

I reached in and grasped Forrest Hearne's watch, telling myself to throw it into the river. Somehow I imagined I could feel the inscription *With Love, Marion,* stinging my fingertips, begging me not to throw something so full of beauty and affection into the muddy Mississippi. That's what had happened to Forrest Hearne on New Year's Eve, though, wasn't it? A beautiful man was stolen, sucked down into the muddy filth of the Quarter.

The words of Dickens hovered in my head:

I have in my heart of hearts a favorite child. And his name is David Copperfield.

The watch was now burning my hand. I looked out to the water and thought of Forrest Hearne and his kindness, Mother and Cincinnati, Willie, the girls, Patrick, Charlie, Jesse, and Cokie.

And I started to cry.

TWENTY-THREE

The doors opened and I stepped inside. "Eighth floor, please."

The elevator operator slowly turned to me.

My hands went cold. "Mother?"

Her face was gray and lifeless, her mouth ringed with scabs. She slowly shook her head and laughed. The laugh I hated.

"Oh, no, baby girl," she hissed. "No eighth floor for you."

She grabbed the handle and jammed it forward. I felt the elevator drop and plunge violently. We were falling and Mother was laughing wildly. The scabs on her mouth cracked and began to bleed. Trails of blood ran from her mouth and down her neck, soaking into her buttercream Orlon uniform. I screamed.

And that's how I woke up. Screaming.

The screams were still bouncing inside my head as I cleaned at Willie's, still echoing between my ears as I walked back to the bookshop. Every few minutes, the screams would be mingled with the ticking of Forrest Hearne's watch. I had returned it to its hiding place in the shop.

And Mother. I couldn't erase the vision of her ghoulish face, the blood. I worried that something had happened to her on the road. I wished she'd write and then I wondered why. Things would be simpler without Mother in New Orleans, simpler without me wrapped in the shadows of her black heart and childish mind. But I wished I'd hear from her anyway.

I changed out of my cleaning clothes and walked downstairs to the shop. The door was open, and Patrick was unloading a box of books at the counter. He moved slowly, and his shoulders frowned.

"How's Charlie?" I asked.

"The same."

"You okay?"

"Yeah, just tired. Did the cops find you yesterday?" asked Patrick.

"Of course they did. You told them I'd be on Gravier Street. Why did you tell them where I was?"

Patrick eyed me, confused. "I figured you'd want to help. I know you thought Mr. Hearne was a nice guy, just like I did. Don't you want to find out what really happened to him?"

"It's not any of my business. What do I know about Mr. Hearne? I've only been interested out of curiosity."

Patrick shrugged. "And? How did it go with Mr. Lockwell?"

"I told him I was there on your behalf, that you wanted his daughter's hand in marriage."

"Sure, then you can marry the kitten-killing brother, and we'll be one happy family. But seriously, what happened?"

"He made me wait over an hour, so I told the receptionist that I'd just visit him at home. He then appeared instantly and escorted me to his office, which, for the record, is larger than this store and has a full bar."

"Of course," Patrick said.

"So I made him a couple martinis, and after a bit of uncomfortable conversation, he agreed to write the letter."

"Wow. So you did it. That's great," said Patrick.

I nodded and motioned to the boxes on the counter. "What'd you get?"

"Yves Beaufort died. He had a large collection of Victor Hugo that Charlie always wanted. I have to go back for the rest, but I'm dreading it. When I arrived this morning, the widow was in a black negligee. Said it was her mourning attire. She told me she would give me a discount if I fixed her sink."

"Ew. Isn't Mrs. Beaufort near eighty?"

"Eighty-two and doesn't look a day older than ninety-five. And what do I know about plumbing? The things I do for Victor Hugo, huh?"

The door opened and Frankie sauntered into the shop. He put his hands on his hips and looked around.

"Frankie! You finally came to buy a book."

"Hey, Yankee girl." He folded a stick of pink chewing gum into his mouth, smelling the foil wrapper before crushing it and shoving it into his pocket. "Not looking for books, just looking for you." He nodded to Patrick. "Hey, Marlowe, how's the old man doin'?"

"He's swell, thanks," said Patrick.

"So, Jo, I heard that you were at the clink yesterday. Everything all right?" asked Frankie.

"Darleen told you?"

"I didn't say who told me. Everything all right?"

"Yeah, everything's fine, Frankie."

"They askin' about your momma?"

"No, why would they be asking about Mother?" I said.

"They were asking about the guy who died on New Year's Eve," said Patrick. I looked at him and furrowed my brow. He didn't need to volunteer any information.

Frankie looked from me to Patrick, his jaw working the gum. "The guy from Memphis. Right. The cops come here, too?" he asked Patrick.

Patrick didn't respond. Frankie looked at me.

"Forrest Hearne bought two books at the shop the day he died. They asked me if I thought he seemed sick when he was at the store. I told them that he seemed fine. That's it."

Frankie leaned on the counter and spun one of the books toward him. "Victor Huge-o."

"It's pronounced Hugo," said Patrick. I had to stifle a laugh. Mispronunciation was one of Patrick's pet peeves.

"Oh, yeah? I knew a guy named Hugo once. Still owes me a ten spot." Frankie flipped open the book and began riffling through the pages.

"Please, the spine. It's very old," said Patrick, carefully taking the book. "Can I help you find something else?"

"Nah," said Frankie, standing up and cracking his knuckles. "So, Jo, got anything Willie should know?"

He looked at me in that typical Frankie way. It was impossible to know what he knew, but I had to assume whatever he did know he told Willie, and Willie paid him handsome for it.

Guilt crawled over me again. I should have told Willie about the watch. I had never kept anything like this from her. But Frankie couldn't know I had the watch. The only thing I could be sure of was that Frankie knew more than I did.

"No, I don't have anything for Willie. I'll let you know if I do," I told him.

"Yeah?" He smiled and cracked his gum. "And will ya let me know how long you've been seein' Jesse Thierry?"

Patrick spun around. "You're seeing Jesse Thierry?"

"I'm not seeing Jesse Thierry," I said.

Frankie grinned. "No? Word on the street is that you were sittin' in his lap last night and he was whispering in your ear."

I hated this town. Who was watching me? I stared at Frankie. Had he told Willie?

"Where did this happen?" said Patrick.

"I'm not a gossip man, Marlowe—I'm an information man." Frankie held out his hand for payment.

"Stop! You're not selling information on me. It was at the soda counter at Dewey's, and it was just a joke. Jesse's a friend."

Frankie put up his hands, surrendering. "I don't have a problem with it. Jesse's a good guy. The girls love him something crazy. See ya, Yankee girl." Frankie walked to the door. I followed him out onto the street. I couldn't stand it. I had to know.

"Say, Frankie, have you heard anything about Mother?"

"She's been seen here and there. You know, Jo, you should stay close around Willie."

"I do stay close to Willie."

"She's always had your back, and you should have hers too."

Frankie cracked his gum, gave me a salute with his long hand, and walked off down Royal.

I knew that Willie was Frankie's biggest benefactor. So it only made sense that he stayed close to her and brought her info. But what was he implying by saying I should stay close to Willie? Patrick motioned to me through the window to come back in the store.

"You know, now it makes sense," said Patrick. "Jesse comes by the store a lot, but he doesn't buy anything. He just gets grease on the books. Isn't he from some hillbilly town in Arkansas?"

"Alabama, and he doesn't get grease on the books. You're making that up."

"Well, I guess he seems nice enough. He's always smiling. Did you ever notice that?" said Patrick.

"No, I never noticed that."

"Do you like him?"

"He's just a friend," I said.

Patrick nodded. "He's got good teeth." His thoughts reversed. "Hey, I ran into Miss Paulsen yesterday."

Miss Paulsen was a professor at Loyola and a lady friend of Charlie's. I had never met her, but Charlie once confided that he thought she was looking to develop their close friendship into a long-term commitment. She hired Patrick as her aide in the English department one year.

"Miss Paulsen went to Smith," said Patrick.

"She did?"

"Yeah, I completely forgot about that. Anyway, I told her about you, and she said she would be happy to answer any questions you might have. She's stopping by the shop later this week to pick up a book I ordered for her. You can speak to her then," said Patrick.

"Oh, Patrick, thank you!" I made an awkward attempt to hug him because it seemed appropriate. He stood surprised, then put his arms around me and rested his chin on my shoulder.

TWENTY-FOUR

I had read the materials so many times, I practically had them memorized.

> *It is the aim of the Board of Admissions to have its entrance requirements flexible and thus make it possible for able girls to come to Smith from various types of schools and all parts of the country.*

I looked at the word *able*. Able to meet the stringent requirements? Able to be accepted? Probably able to afford it, which I couldn't.

> *The Board of Admissions attempts to select from the complete list of candidates those students whose records of character, health, and scholarship give evidence of their equipment for college.*

Character. I knew I was one, but they wanted me to have one.

Health. Besides the occasional red beans and rice incident on the Gedricks' sidewalk, I was healthy.

Scholarship. The one B in Mr. Proffitt's class was going to haunt me. I could still feel his sticky mothball breath steaming over my desk. Did he eat rotten sweaters from his attic? "You must apply yourself, Miss Moraine," he would say in his whispery tone. "You must seek the soul of the equation." The soul of the equation? I wasn't convinced that calculus had anything close to a soul. But I should have pretended and joined Mr. Proffitt for a meal of sweater vests. That B would dent my application.

Admission is based on the candidate's record as a whole, the school record, the recommendations, the College Board tests, and other information secured by the college regarding general ability, personality, and health. All credentials should reach the Board of Admissions before March 1 if the student wishes to have her application considered at the April meeting by the Board of Admissions.

Before March. It was already February. Mardi Gras approached on February 21, and the parties and balls were already under way. Willie would be keeping the house open longer each day to cash in on the "high-time hoopla," as she called it. She had extra seasonal girls arranged and two rooms reserved at the motel nearby. The girls would work in shifts, taking time to bathe and sleep a few hours at the motel in between. I'd still clean in the morning, but it would take longer, and there were always errands during Mardi Gras.

I stared out the window from the counter of the bookshop and watched the passersby. John Lockwell would also be busy during Mardi Gras. When I was in his office, I saw a photo of him with Rex, one of the oldest Mardi Gras krewes. If I didn't get the recommendation letter before Mardi Gras festivities started, I wouldn't get it at all.

Residence

Smith College has the policy of placing groups of students from each of the four classes in houses of its own. Each house has its own living room, dining room, kitchen and is supervised by the Head of the House.

The "Head of the House." It sounded like Willie. I looked at the return address from Charlotte. She lived in Tenney House.

Expenses

Tuition fee $850

Residence fee $750

Books $25–$50

Subscriptions and dues $24

Recreation and incidentals $100

Enough. I slid the stack of papers under the counter. Looking at the expenses made my stomach churn. Nearly two thousand dollars. Eight thousand dollars for four years. My life savings in the cigar box was less than three hundred dollars. Sure, I always had seven cents for the streetcar and a nickel for a soda, but two thousand dollars for one year? Willie said she'd pay for Newcomb or Loyola, but they were a third of the cost of Smith. I would apply for financial assistance and scholarships. They'd be my only hope. Somehow I had to turn the salted peanuts in the cigar box into petits fours.

I stared out the window. A woman in a smart suit crossed the street toward the shop. I estimated her to be in her midfifties. People naturally parted from her course as she made her way to the door. Literary fiction. I put my thumb on the counter, signaling to Patrick, who wasn't there. Habit.

"Good afternoon," I said as she pushed through the door.

The woman cut a path straight toward me. She placed her pocketbook on the counter and smiled. It was a polite smile, but reserved, as if her teeth desperately wanted to peek out, but she wouldn't let them. Her hesitation indicated appraisal. Her head tilted slightly as she looked at me. The hair at her temples was pulled tightly toward her bun. The skin was stretched like flesh-colored taffy.

"Miss Moraine?"

I nodded.

"I'm Barbara Paulsen, chair of the English department at Loyola. Patrick Marlowe was my aide for a year."

"Oh, yes. It's a pleasure to meet you. Patrick tells me you went to Smith."

"Indeed." Her head tilted again, this time in the opposite direction. Full evaluation. "And he tells me you're applying. You're quite late, you know. Most girls apply before their senior year of high school."

"Yes, but I'll make the March deadline."

"Patrick said your grades are strong. And your extra-curriculars?"

I stared at her.

"You do have extracurricular activities for your application? Achievement awards?"

I shook my head and continued shaking as she sprayed me with student council, language club, social committee, and all the other affiliations that any girl applying to an East Coast school would have.

"My extracurricular was limited. I had to work several jobs during school," I explained. Limited? More like nonexistent.

"I see. What other forms of employment did you have besides working here at the bookstore?"

She was asking if I could afford it, which I couldn't. I looked at the hair tearing at her temples and tried to formulate a safe answer. "I work as a housemaid in one of the homes here in the Quarter."

Miss Paulsen didn't react with the shock or horror I expected. She seemed to appreciate my candor and fiddled with the strap on her pocketbook. "Patrick explained that your father is absent. What about your mother, dear?"

Mother? Oh, she's in a dusty motel in California right now, cooling herself with a cold Schlitz in her cleavage.

"My mother . . . cleaned homes as well," I told her. "She's pursuing employment out of state at this time."

Silence ticked between us until she spoke. "Charlie Marlowe and I are old friends. Patrick was one of the best students I've ever had. He's not the writer his father is, but he knows literature, and I think he'd make an excellent editor. I've always encouraged him in that direction but—" She stopped and waved the topic away with her hand. "What I'm saying is that I have the utmost respect for Patrick, and he seems to have the utmost respect for you." Confusion dangled from the end of her sentence.

"Patrick and I have been close friends for a long time," I explained.

"Are you dating him?" The words came out quickly, too quickly, and she knew it. And there was something else pulsing behind her question. Not jealousy exactly. Some sort of curiosity? "Not that it's my business, certainly," she added.

"Oh, I don't mind the question. We're just friends," I assured her.

"I've just always wondered why he stayed in New Orleans. Everything's okay with his father?"

"Perfectly." I smiled.

"Good. I'd like Charlie to visit my writing class again this year."

I imagined Charlie at the head of the lecture hall in his underwear, clutching the heart-shaped box to his chest.

"Well, you'll need some strong recommendations for your application. Unfortunately, I won't be able to write one for you. I've already written one for a girl at Sacred Heart, you see, and that recommendation would be diluted if I were to write another one. But I do encourage you with your application, Miss Moraine. These exercises, no matter how futile, build character."

Futile. She was telling me it was useless. That I was useless.

"I believe you have a book for me?" she prompted. "I paid in advance when I ordered it."

I had seen the book—*Le Deuxième Sexe* by a French author, Simone de Beauvoir. Patrick had ordered it from a press in Paris. He said it was an analysis of women. I took the keys from my pocket and walked toward the bookcase. I opened the glass door and pulled the book from the shelf. I felt a warm shadow behind me. Miss Paulsen was inches from my back.

She pointed over my shoulder. "*A Passage to India*. What edition? I'd like to see that as well." She held out her hand.

TWENTY-FIVE

I was a liar.

I'm sorry, Miss Paulsen. *A Passage to India* is currently under restoration. No, Patrick, I don't know who Mother was with near the Roosevelt Hotel. Yes, Jesse, I'm going to meet Patrick tonight. No, Willie, I didn't know Mother had left for California. No, Detective Langley, I didn't find Forrest Hearne's watch under my mother's bed, a bed in a brothel with a bullet hole in the headboard.

It went on. Each lie I told required another to thicken the paste over the previous. It was useless, like when I learned to crochet and made a long string of loops. Being useless builds character, Miss Paulsen had said. Perhaps she was home now, drinking a weak Earl Grey from last night's tea bag, massaging her taffied scalp.

I sat on my bed, staring at *A Passage to India* in my lap. How foolish of me to keep the book downstairs in the shop. But the pieces still didn't fit together. If Forrest Hearne hadn't come to

Willie's, then how did the watch end up in Mother's room? If Mother knew about the watch, she certainly wouldn't have left it. No, it would have been quite the complement to Cincinnati's wardrobe of death. And Frankie said Mother had been at the Roosevelt Hotel on New Year's Eve.

I crawled under my bed and pulled back the loose floorboard. I wrestled my hand through the opening, retrieved the cigar box, and inserted the book in its place. I made room for the box of money in the bottom of one of my desk drawers. Two things volleyed in my head:

Mr. Hearne hadn't thought I was useless.

Someone who had been with Forrest Hearne had been at Willie's.

Preparations for Mardi Gras swelled. People celebrated the oncoming festivities. For fourteen days, I carried John Lockwell's business card in my pocket, vowing to call and inquire about the letter. For fourteen nights, I lay in bed, certain I could hear the telltale watch ticking under the floorboard.

Willie's house was filthier each day as Mardi Gras approached. I arrived at five A.M. and saw cars parked deep in the belly of the long driveway. Willie rarely allowed cars in the drive. She said it was an excuse for cops to look at the house. Fortunately, the police became more lax around Mardi Gras.

The girls worked late and slept late. Evangeline had settled into her new room. It no longer smelled like Mother. Willie was exhausted, but I didn't dare deviate from our normal schedule. I held the coffee tray and tapped the bottom of her door with my foot.

"That better be my coffee, and it better be hot."

I pushed through the door and found Willie sitting up in bed, surrounded by bulging stacks of cash.

"Shut that door. I don't need the girls seeing this green. They'll ask for a bonus—like I don't know they're all pocketing extra on the side as it is. Do I have 'Stupid' tattooed on my forehead?" She dropped her hands in her lap. "Well, what do you have?"

"The usual Mardi Gras leftovers." I emptied my apron pockets on her bed. Single cuff links, silk ties, lighters, party invitations, hotel keys, and a bulging money clip.

Willie reached for the money clip and counted the contents. "That's the Senator's. Seal it in a plain envelope and give it to Cokie. Have him deliver it to the Pontchartrain Hotel. That's where he's staying. We're lucky he was with Sweety and not Evangeline. What else?"

"Evangeline's pillowcases are torn."

"Yeah, she had the scratcher last night," said Willie.

"Speaking of Evangeline," I began carefully, "I noticed she's got some new jewelry in her box."

"It's not stolen. She's got a big man."

"Someone new?" I asked.

"No, he comes by every once in a while." Willie placed a tall stack near the end of the bed and continued sorting. "Three thousand. Bring me a warm washcloth. This cash is filthy."

"Evangeline's new date is a jeweler?" I called from the bathroom.

"Nah, he's a developer from Uptown. Builds hotels and shopping centers. I don't like him. He's got a twisted need for power. But he throws cash like rice."

I stood at Willie's bedside and cleaned her hands with the warm cloth. She leaned back against her pillows and sighed.

"Willie, your hands are swollen. What happened?"

"They're yeasty. Too much salt." She pulled her hands from my grasp and quickly gathered up the bills, stacking and rubber-banding them by denomination. "I cleared three grand just last night. If this keeps going, it'll be the best season yet. The safe is open. Put these in and bring me the green box from the bottom shelf."

Three thousand dollars. Willie earned a year of tuition to Smith in one night. I placed the stacks in the safe next to the other rows of cash and grabbed the green box she requested. The word *Adler's* was etched in gold on the top. I knew Adler's. It was an upscale jewelry store on Canal. Everything was beautiful and expensive. I had never set foot in Adler's, but I sometimes looked in the window. I handed the box to Willie.

"Shall I tell Sadie about Evangeline's pillowcases?" I asked, gathering up two glasses from Willie's desk.

"Cut the act. You're not thinking about pillowcases right now," said Willie.

I sucked in a breath. I put the glasses back down on the desk so she wouldn't see my hands shaking.

"You may think some things slide by me, Jo, but they don't. I've been in this game a long time, and my mind is like a trap."

I nodded.

"Stop hiding near the desk. Come here," she barked. I approached her high bed.

"Here." She thrust the green box at me. "Open it."

The top creaked and popped open on its hinges. Wrapped

across a white bed of satin was a beautiful gold watch. The words *Lady Elgin* curved in a soft arc across the face. It was the female companion to Forrest Hearne's watch.

She knew. This was her way of telling me she knew. I drew a breath. I couldn't look at her.

"Well?" she commanded.

"It's beautiful, Willie. Do you want me to put it on you now? I know you hate small clasps."

"Me? What are you talking about? Don't you have something to say, idiot?"

The jig was up. "Willie, I'm sorry—"

"Shut up. I don't need to hear it. Take the watch and say thank you. You think your good-for-nothin' mother will remember? No. But don't go expecting something every year. Eighteen is a milestone. And don't show the girls. They'll just start whining about a trip to Adler's, and I need them to be focused tonight. Valentine's Day is always a doozy. Don't forget to pull the decorations from the attic. Why are you just standing there? What, you need to hear me say it? Happy birthday. There. Now, get the hell out."

My birthday. I hadn't forgotten, just thought others would. I backed up toward the door. "Thank you, Willie. It's beautiful."

"Well, take the glasses. Just because you're eighteen doesn't mean you can fall down on the job. And remember something else, Jo."

"What?"

Willie stared at me. "You're old enough to go to jail now."

TWENTY-SIX

By the time I finished cleaning and pulled the Valentine decorations from the attic, the girls were in the kitchen having coffee.

"Happy birthday, sugar!" said Dora. "Sweety reminded us last night."

"You mean happy death day," said Evangeline. "The madam she's named after died on Valentine's Day."

"Can you imagine dyin' on Valentine's Day?" said Dora. She twisted her long red hair on top of her head and stuck a pencil through it. "There's somethin' so sad about that. But y'all know I'm gonna kick it on St. Patrick's Day, ride out in a coffin lined in green satin."

"Did Willie give you anything for your birthday?" Evangeline asked, rubbing her palms across her thighs.

"Vangie, Willie don't give birthday gifts—you know that," said Dora. "You're just fired up about presents because you think your big man might bring you a Valentine's gift."

"A big man? Do you have a new boyfriend, Evangeline?" I asked.

"Mind your own business," she snapped. She swiped the pencil from Dora's hair and stomped out of the room.

John Lockwell had Evangeline. I didn't have my letter.

I shot a quick glance over my shoulder, making sure I was alone. I dialed RAymond 4119. There was a click, then the double ring.

"Good morning, the Lockwell Company."

"Good morning. Mr. Lockwell, please." Was my voice shaking? I coughed into my hand. I pictured the receptionist, filing her nails and rolling her eyes.

"Hold the line, please."

"Mr. Lockwell's office."

I took a breath, trying to sound pleasant, calm. "Hello, Dottie. How are you? This is Josephine Moraine phoning for Mr. Lockwell."

Silence. "Is Mr. Lockwell expecting your call?"

Absolutely not. "Yes, he is, thanks."

"One moment, please."

More silence. Sal walked by carrying a king cake. I pointed to the phone and mouthed, "For Willie." Sal nodded.

The voice on the line swayed deep and thick. "Let me guess—you want me to be your valentine."

I looked down at the receiver. "No, Mr. Lockwell, this is Josephine Moraine, Charlotte's friend."

He laughed, then hacked some late-night cigar miasma from his lungs. "I know exactly who you are. You're lucky you caught me. I'm not usually in the office this early, especially around Mardi Gras. I had to come in to sign a check. Closed a big deal. Why don't you come over and make me one of your martinis to celebrate? Hell, I'm still drunk from last night."

"I'm calling to follow up on the recommendation letter. I've got to send in my application soon." It came out exactly as I had rehearsed it in my apartment.

"Have you gotten some new shoes yet?"

"Excuse me?"

"You've got nice ankles, but those beat-up—whatever they were—make your legs look dumpy. You need some heels. High heels."

My palm tightened around the receiver. "What I need is the letter."

"Well, come over here in a nice pair of heels, and I'll give you the letter," he said. I heard a creak and a tap. I saw him leaning back in his red leather chair, putting his feet on the bureau in front of all the framed pictures.

"Give me the letter, and I'll make you a martini," I countered.

"Nope." He chuckled. Maybe he really was drunk. If so, I needed to take advantage of it.

"Be here at six thirty," he said.

"Three thirty."

"Six," he said. "Bye-bye, Josephine."

It was a game to him. Just a little game. It was silly, really. Then why did I have such a sick feeling inside?

TWENTY-SEVEN

Next to my dull exterior, it appeared newer than a new pair of shoes. The gold was so shiny it looked ridiculous on me. She'd had the watch engraved on the back: *Jo is 18.—Willie.*

With all that was going on around Mardi Gras, she still remembered my birthday. And I was keeping something from her, breaking what was most important to Willie—trust. I was relieved to see Cokie's cab pull up to the curb outside the bookstore. He walked through the door carrying a cardboard box and started singing and dancing.

"I'd rather drink muddy water than let you jive on me. Josie girl, it's your birthday, so don't you jive on me."

A birthday serenade from Cokie was tradition. It still made me blush.

"I don't think Smiley Lewis would appreciate you turning his song into a birthday tune," I said.

"What you talking about? Smiley would be honored. He's

gonna record that song one day. I'll tell him to play it that way just for you tonight. Happy birthday, Josie girl." Cokie smiled from ear to ear.

"Before I forget"—I slid the envelope across the counter—"Willie wants you to drop this off at the Pontchartrain."

"All right, then. Now that we got business behind us, let's talk about the business of your birthday. I see you got Willie's gift. But who wants a big ol' mess a gold when you can have this?" Cokie set the floppy box on the counter in front of me.

I loved Cokie's birthday gifts almost as much as I loved Cokie. Never fancy, but always meaningful. And he always claimed it was a puppy.

"Now, be careful when you open it so he don't jump out," warned Cokie.

"You've fed him already, though, right?" I asked.

"Sure did. I fed him early this mornin'."

I pulled back the flaps and peeked in the box. An aluminum thermos with a red plastic top. A map.

Cokie bounced with excitement. "That's brand-new from Sears. The ad says it'll keep your drink hot for near a whole day. You can even put soup in it, it says. But you'll need to put coffee in it."

"I will?"

"Sure you will. How you gonna make it over thirty hours with no coffee?"

"Thirty hours?"

Cokie put the box on the floor and brought out the map. "I got it all figured out. Even talked to Cornbread, and he confirmed the route." He spread the map out on the counter in front of us. "See, we here." He pointed to New Orleans on the map. "Now, follow me." His dusky finger traced along a line he had drawn with a red pen. "First you'll go through Mississippi, then Alabama, then on up through Georgia."

My eyes jumped ahead. The red ink ended abruptly in Connecticut. "Cokie, you did this?"

"Me and Cornbread. He knows the routes from truckin'. I got the idea from Willie. Sometimes when I'm drivin', she talks. She ain't even talkin' to me, she's just talkin', like thinkin' out loud. Well, she was hotter than blue blazes because you told her you want to go to some fancy college out East. She go on, sayin' you're too salty for those schools, and I said, 'Why not? Maybe those schools need a little spice. They'd be lucky to have Josie girl.' Ooh, she got mad and said gettin' into those schools is political and you ain't got the politics to get in and so on. But you know what? I think you can do it. My only worry is how you'll get up there. So I talked to Cornbread. He said I could try to take you in the taxi, or maybe he could find you a rig route and you could ride up with a trucker. And then we charted it out. But I wasn't sure which school you gonna pick—'cuz they all gonna want you—so we stopped the trail in Connecticut. Over fifteen hundred miles. That's some long road." He patted the top of the thermos. "So you'll need coffee."

He smiled wide. He was so certain, his belief so absolute.

"Josie girl." The smile faded from his voice. "Why you cryin'?"

I shook my head, unable to speak. I reached for the thermos and cradled it against my chest. Tears rolled down my face.

"Aw, you shouldn't be cryin' on your birthday." He pointed to the map. "Where is it?" he asked softly.

"It's Smith College in Northampton. Near Boston."

"All right, then." He pulled the red pen from his pocket and continued the trail from Connecticut into Massachusetts. "Boston. There." He looked at me. "Why you frettin', Jo? You not sure?"

I inhaled my tears in order to speak. "I'm sure I want to go, but I'm not sure it's possible. Why would they accept me? And if they did, how would I pay for it? I don't want to get my hopes up only to be disappointed. I'm always disappointed."

"Now, don't let fear keep you in New Orleans. Sometimes we set off down a road thinkin' we're goin' one place and we end up another. But that's okay. The important thing is to start. I know you can do it. Come on, Josie girl, give those ol' wings a try."

"Willie doesn't want me to."

"So what, you gonna stay here just so you can clean her house and run around with all the naked crazies in the Quarter? You got a bigger story than that."

I held up the thermos. "And hot coffee for the journey."

Cokie started to shuffle and sing. "I'd rather drink muddy water than let you jive on me. Josie girl, you goin' to Boston, so don't you jive on me."

I hugged the thermos.

"All right, I better get to the Pontchartrain, or Willie will have my hide," said Cokie. "I got somethin' else." He reached in his back pocket and pulled out a thin piece of newspaper, torn at the edges. "Cornbread got back from Tennessee. He gave me this. The rich man's family ain't satisfied. Apparently his watch and money were stolen, so they suspicious. They wanna do their own autopsy." He laid the piece of newsprint on the counter.

TENNESSEAN'S DEATH SUSPICIOUS

The body of Forrest L. Hearne, Jr., 42, will be exhumed in Memphis on Monday for autopsy. Hearne, a wealthy architect and builder, died during the early morning hours of January 1 at the Sans Souci nightclub in New Orleans. Hearne and his two friends had traveled to New Orleans to attend the Sugar Bowl football game January 2. Hearne reportedly left Memphis with $3,000, but no money was found on his person when he died. The deceased was also missing his expensive wristwatch and Sugar Bowl tickets. Hearne's death was attributed at the time to a heart attack. Dr. Riley Moore, Orleans Parish coroner, said Hearne collapsed in the club and was dead when the ambulance arrived.

"Josie." Cokie moved toward the counter. "You okay? You're grayer than a bottle of rain, girl."

TWENTY-EIGHT

"You really have to go tonight?" said Patrick. "I thought maybe you could come over for your birthday, say hello to Charlie."

"Yes, I have to go. He's going to give me the letter."

"Why don't I go with you? Maybe it'll look more serious if I'm there."

I liked the idea of Patrick coming. Then I thought about what Mr. Lockwell had said. High heels. He wouldn't appreciate Patrick being there. And I knew better than to tell Patrick about his comment.

"Let's meet up later at the Paddock. Smiley Lewis is playing tonight. Could you come after Charlie goes to sleep?" I asked.

"The Paddock's so grimy. Besides, I can't leave Charlie for too long. He's been acting up. Miss Paulsen called asking to talk to him. She said she came by. You didn't tell her about him, did you?"

"Of course not. I'd never do that."

"Promise me you won't tell anyone, Jo."

"I promise! I love Charlie just as much as you do," I told him.

"Some of the neighbors are suspicious. I told them that he's completely absorbed in writing a play and sometimes reads it aloud, acting the parts."

"That was smart. He did spend thirty-five days inside writing once," I said.

"Yeah, but I don't know how long they'll buy it. I like Miss Paulsen, but she's pretty nosy. And her brother's a doctor. All we need is for her to get a look at Charlie and call for a straitjacket."

"Don't say that. Have you written to your mom yet?" I asked.

"I had told her about the robbery and the beating, but she doesn't know how bad it's gotten." Patrick shuffled some papers on the counter. "Say, Jo, I keep forgetting to ask, do you have that inventory report? The accountants need it for taxes."

"Your accountant is part of the Proteus Krewe for Mardi Gras. He's not thinking about tax season right now."

"I know, but I want to have it in advance. I'm tired of always doing things last minute. And I hate to ask, but do you think you could do me a favor and stay with Charlie for a couple hours tomorrow night? I've got some books coming in around dinnertime, and I want to turn them around and deliver. We could use the money."

"Sure, I'll stay with Charlie."

"Thanks, Jo. Jeez, now I feel bad. Your redneck Romeo, Jesse, gets you flowers for your birthday, and I can't even go with you to the Paddock."

"Flowers?"

"You didn't see?" Patrick rolled his eyes. "Step outside and look at your window."

I walked into the street and looked up toward my apartment. Balancing in the wrought-iron window box was a bouquet of pink lilies. How had Jesse gotten them up there?

I had never received flowers and didn't own a vase, so I propped them in a glass on my desk. The fragrance quickly filled the small space. Staring at the lilies, I felt a mix of happiness and apprehension. Unless it was Cokie, gifts from men weren't free.

I put on the same dress I had worn to Lockwell's office before. It was the only nice dress I owned. I tied a red scarf around my neck onto my shoulder, trying to make the outfit look different, and combed my hair over to the side to tame the puff from the humidity. For some reason, my hair always looked best right before bed, and what good was that?

I looked down at my feet. Pretty shoes for a letter. Sex for a string of pearls.

Was there a difference?

TWENTY-NINE

My heels echoed across the deserted marble floor of the lobby. Six o'clock on Valentine's Day and so close to Mardi Gras, everyone was out chasing hearts. When I reached the eighth floor, the reception desk was empty. A trickle of perspiration slid between my shoulder blades in a single stream and landed at the base of my spine. I grabbed a magazine from the reception area table and fanned my face. The temperature outside was only seventy, but I had tried to walk fast. I lifted my arm and fanned the orbs of sweat in my armpits. Was I hot or nervous?

"Now, that's the best use of that magazine I can think of."

I looked up. A man in a gray suit with a briefcase stood near the reception desk.

"I think they reduce the cool air after hours. Are you here for someone?" he asked.

"Mr. Lockwell." I nodded, adding, "I'm a friend of his niece."

"I think he's back in his office. Big day for him. Another nice deal. I'd show you back, but I'm late to meet the wife for dinner. Go on through."

I walked by the rows of desks toward Mr. Lockwell's mammoth office. Each step was more difficult and my toes began to cramp. This was a mistake. Mr. Lockwell's voice rose in volume as I approached. He was giving dates and dollar figures. Large sums. He said the deal was signed today and his attorney had just left the office with the contract. I stood outside the door. I heard him hang up the phone and knocked on the door frame.

"Come in."

The office was a haze of cigar smoke.

"Well, hello, Josephine." Mr. Lockwell grinned and walked around his desk toward the door. His greedy eyes immediately locked onto my feet.

My stomach twisted. I felt the taste of humiliation rise in my throat. He stared at my feet. "What the hell are those?"

"They're called loafers. Brown loafers."

"I know what they're called, but that wasn't the deal," he said.

"Show me the letter first."

"Show you the letter?"

"Yes. Show me the letter and then I'll show you the high heels."

He leaned back against his desk. "Is that the only dress you own?"

"This isn't about the dress. This is about the letter."

"And the shoes," he added.

"Yes, and the shoes. So, show me the letter."

"Oh, I'll show you mine if you show me yours? I love that game."

I swallowed hard and stared, trying to keep from throwing up.

He ran his hand through his hair, a habit from his youth, no doubt, before his hairline began its slow retreat at the temples. His fleshy midsection challenged the buttons on his dress shirt. He wasn't ugly, but if he picked a flower, I was fairly certain it would die in his hand. Mother might find him attractive. For some, a bloated bank account improved a man's features.

"Well, you see, Josephine, today was one of those great days, but great days are often really busy days. So I don't exactly have the letter."

I nodded. "I figured that was likely. That's why I didn't sashay in here wearing the shoes. That would be called a negative ROI."

"ROI? Return on investment?"

"Exactly, a bad investment of my time and self-respect, not to mention money, on a pair of shoes I'd never wear. Durable goods, Mr. Lockwell." I motioned to my feet. "Practical and high yield."

"Jesus, I should hire you. Are you looking for a job?"

"I'm looking for a college education. Smith. Northampton."

Mr. Lockwell laughed, pointing his finger at me. "You're good, Josephine. You just may have earned your letter. And with a little spit shine, you could earn a lot more, if you know what I mean." My face must have conveyed my disgust. He rolled his eyes. "Or you could work in an office. Are you eighteen?" he asked.

"As a matter of fact, I am."

"Why don't you come by on Friday?" he suggested.

"I'm not interested in a job. I know you're a busy man, Mr. Lockwell. In the interest of time, why don't you give me a sheet of your letterhead? I'll type up the recommendation and bring it by for your signature. Discreet and effortless."

He crossed his arms over his chest. "You know, I really want you to work for me."

"A diploma from Smith would make me a more desirable hire."

"Honey, you're already a desirable hire... in a dirty Cinderella kind of way. Call me John."

"On second thought, Mr. Lockwell, give me two sheets of letterhead. Best to have a backup."

THIRTY

Once I fed a new ribbon into Charlie's typewriter, it worked without issue. Charlie sat across from me at the kitchen table in his stained undershirt, staring at the typewriter. I spoke to him as if he understood everything. My biggest fear was that the old Charlie was in there somewhere trying to communicate, but a synaptic disconnect made his behavior erratic. Some responses were still there. If you put him in front of the steps, he'd walk up or down. But then it was hard to get him to stop. There were moments when his eyes flashed with clarity or when his head turned at conversation. But the sparks were gone as quickly as they came.

"Lockwell's a real piece of work, Charlie. He thinks he's the cat's pajamas because he has money. He has a picture of himself framed in his office. If he didn't have a family pedigree, he'd be a hustler in the Quarter. You know the type."

I pecked at the keys on the typewriter.

"Okay, this is what we've got." I rolled the cylinder to move the paper up off the print bracket. "You ready, Charlie?" Charlie stared at the typewriter, silent.

> *To the Attention of the Director of Admissions:*
> *It is with great pleasure that I write this letter of recommendation for Miss Josephine Moraine.*

I peeked at Charlie. "I put Josephine because that's what he knows me as. Long story. I put Josie on the actual application."

> *I became acquainted with Miss Moraine through my niece, Charlotte Gates, who is currently a freshman in good standing at Smith College. Miss Moraine is of sharp intelligence, strong moral fiber, and possesses an impressive work ethic. While most girls her age might pursue extracurricular activities that are social in nature, Miss Moraine has dedicated herself to the pursuit of knowledge and enlightenment through literature.*

A warble came from Charlie. I looked at his face but couldn't decipher the expression as one of laughter or pain. "I know, the word *enlightenment* is a bit much, but I'm trying to make Lockwell sound evolved."

> *Since her early teens, Miss Moraine has invested her time and talents running one of the most reputable bookstores in the Vieux Carré of New Orleans, owned by celebrated author Charles Marlowe.*

I winked at Charlie.

> *During her tenure at the bookstore, Miss Moraine has developed a cataloging and inventory system, and assists with commercial buying, antiquarian acquisitions, and restoration. In addition to working at the bookstore, I understand that Miss Moraine is employed as a personal assistant to one of the families in the French Quarter.*

Charlie's chair creaked with comment.

"What? Willie's is kind of a family, isn't it? Wait, I'm almost done."

> *Considering her scholarly and professional merits, I have offered employment to Miss Moraine within my corporation. I have been informed, however, that she prefers to pursue a college degree at a fine institution such as Smith, where she may benefit from both an environment of integration and education. In closing, I ask the Board of Admissions to please favorably consider the application of Miss Josephine Moraine, as I believe she would be a true asset to the college.*
>
> *Sincerely yours,*
> *John Lockwell, President*
> *The Lockwell Company, Ltd.*
> *New Orleans, Louisiana*

"It's not perfect, but I think it's pretty good." I pulled the paper from the typewriter, folded it, and put it in the envelope in my purse.

Charlie continued to stare at the typewriter.

"Hey, would you like to type something?" I put a blank sheet of paper in the typewriter and moved it across the table in front of Charlie. His stare floated from the typewriter to my face.

"Come on, Charlie, type something. Do you want me to help you?" I knelt next to him and raised his hand toward the typewriter. When I let go, it tremored and hovered for a moment over the keyboard and then fell to his lap.

"Almost. Let's try again." I lifted his hand, but this time it fell straight back into his lap.

I took my glass into the kitchen, and that's when I heard it. A swift, sharp attack on the keyboard. One letter, with conviction. I spun around and ran back into the room. Charlie sat motionless in front of the typewriter. I peered over his shoulder.

B

"Keep going."

He didn't move. I crossed in front of him to look at his face. There was sadness in his silence.

"Come on, Charlie Marlowe. I know you're in there. Type another letter."

Something was short-circuiting, making his inner lights flicker like the electricity in a storm. Was it the medicine? The medicine dulled everything and made him nearly comatose. I decided I would hold off on giving him his medicine to see if the faint lights got any brighter.

We sat at the table for over an hour. I read a book. Charlie did nothing, but I noticed he fidgeted and looked around a bit more. Patrick was late. He said he wouldn't be gone long. Where was he? I snapped the book shut.

"You know what? I'm gonna give you a haircut."

I found scissors in the kitchen and wrapped a large towel around Charlie's shoulders. He raised his hands and pulled it off.

"Oh, so you're moving now. I shouldn't have taken the typewriter to your room. Maybe I could have gotten another letter out of you." I put the towel back on his shoulders and walked to the kitchen to get the comb from my pocketbook. "You know," I called to him over my shoulder, "I should have done this a long time ago. You never would have let your hair grow this long." I filled a bowl with water to wet the comb and poured myself another sweet tea. "What I'd love to do is shave that white beard. You never wore a beard."

I walked back into the dining room. "You're going to feel like a new—"

Blood. Everywhere.

On the table. On the floor. All over Charlie.

His face was covered in it. He moved the scissors from his face to his forearm and began to slice a trench.

I dropped the bowl of water and ran to him, cutting my own fingers as I wrestled the large scissors from his hand.

"Oh, no. Oh, no. Oh, no." I couldn't stop saying it. Charlie reacted to the fear in my voice and started bucking in the chair. Blood spilled from a slice on his forehead. I grabbed the towel, swiping at the blood to see the wounds. His forehead, his ear, the side of his neck. Charlie continued to resist my efforts with the towel. We struggled. I heard Willie's voice: *Don't be an idiot and panic. Pull yourself together.*

I took a deep breath and stepped back. I started humming. Charlie stopped bucking. I continued humming and once again picked the towel up off the floor. I walked behind Charlie and put my arms around him, humming in his ear and examining the wounds. I applied pressure to his forehead and neck while holding him. If he lost any more blood, we'd be in trouble.

I heard the key in the lock.

I called out before he entered the room. "Now, Patrick, it looks worse than it is. It's just a couple cuts."

Patrick screamed. Loud. The kind of scream that hurls out of you when you see a loved one spilling red. The color slid from his face, quickly replaced by a ghost I didn't recognize.

"Be quiet!" I snapped. "Do you want the neighbors to come running? I was going to give him a haircut, and when I went for my comb, he went for the scissors."

"There's . . . so much blood," said Patrick.

"It's coming from the slice on his head. I'm putting pressure on it now. Do you have a first-aid box?"

Patrick shook his head.

"Give Charlie his medicine."

Patrick just stood, staring.

"Patrick! Listen to me. Give Charlie his medicine."

"More medicine?" said Patrick.

"I didn't give it to him."

"What? How could you forget?"

"I didn't forget. I wanted to see if his clarity would increase without it."

"Oh, Jo, how could you be so careless?" Patrick ran to the kitchen and came back with Charlie's medicine. His hands shook as he gave his father the meds.

"He has to have his medicine, or he goes crazy. That's why we got him the meds in the first place."

"I'm sorry, but it really seemed like he was coming out of the fog. I was going to ask you, but you were over two hours late. Where were you?"

"Don't play doctor, Jo. He needs the medicine," said Patrick. "Thank God he didn't hit an artery."

"He'll need stitches," I said. I looked at Charlie. What had I done?

"He can't see a doctor. They'll take him to the mental ward immediately. How will I explain that my father carved himself up with scissors?"

"Willie knows people. I'll call her. Things happen at the house, and she takes care of them."

We got Charlie to the couch. I called Willie, and she said she'd send Cokie over with the first-aid kit. She said Dr. Sully was out of town, but she knew an army doctor who had seen a lot of action during the war. She'd give him a credit at the house, and he'd probably come running over to stitch Charlie up.

So we waited.

Patrick alternated watching the clock and watching Charlie. I cleaned the cuts on my fingers and tried to scrub the blood off the chair and the floor. You had to get at blood early, preferably with peroxide, before it set. I sat on my knees, raking the scrub brush over the spot. Maybe it would fade with time. Most homes in the Quarter had bloodstains anyway.

Cokie arrived within an hour. He took one look at me and reached for the wall to steady himself. "Josie girl," he breathed. "Lord, you look like a butcher. You all right?"

I looked down at my blouse and pants. Cokie was right. I was one big smear of blood.

"I'm fine. Hurry, bring the first-aid box in here."

Cokie gasped when he saw Charlie. "Oh, Mr. Charlie, what you gone and done to yourself? Jo, this looks bad. Willie's sending an army doctor she knows. Maybe you best wait on the first aid until he gets here." Cokie looked at Patrick. "You okay, buddy?"

"I can at least wrap up his head. That's what's bleeding the most." I set to work on the bandage.

Twenty minutes later, there was a knock at the door.

"The neighbors are probably all looking out their windows, trying to watch the show," lamented Patrick.

"Don't you worry about those neighbors," said Cokie.

Randolph was a young army doctor who had seen a lot of action in France during the war. Randolph was also drunk.

"Would you like a cup of coffee?" I asked.

"Nah, coffee makes me jittery. That's not good for sewing. I'll splash some cold water on my face," he said, and went into the kitchen.

"Oh, great," whispered Patrick.

Randolph came back and opened his bag.

"Do you have a license to practice?" said Patrick.

"If you wanted to interview physicians, you would've taken this old dog to the hospital. Since you're not at the hospital, I'm thinkin' you don't have options. I'm probably your best bet right about now. Slap me across the face."

"Excuse me?" said Patrick.

"You heard me. Slap me across the face. Hard. It'll sober me up."

Patrick hesitated. Cokie stared.

"Oh, for cripe's sake. Do I have to slap myself?" yelled Randolph.

I cracked him across the cheek. Just like he asked. My hand stung.

The doctor shook like a wet dog and then set to work, asking what medications Charlie was on. He took out a bottle of chloroform.

Patrick was right. The neighbors would be talking. Could we really tell them that the cast of Charlie's play included an army doctor, a quadroon cabbie, and a girl covered in blood? Charlie Marlowe never wrote horror, but somehow horror was writing Charlie Marlowe.

THIRTY-ONE

The men finally carried Charlie up to bed. I followed, taking his shoes and shirt. They laid him down and propped up his head with pillows.

The doctor looked around the room, his gaze stopping at the set of industrial locks on the bedroom door.

Patrick watched him carefully. "Thanks, Doc. Much appreciated."

"He'll be out for a while. You better get some sleep while you can. But I suggest you stay in here," said Randolph.

"I'll stay with him. You get some sleep," I told Patrick.

"You can go home. I think you've done enough for one night." Patrick stared at me, his face a mix of fury and fear.

"Patrick," I whispered, trying not to cry.

He put his hand up and shot a glance at the doctor.

Randolph turned to Cokie. "I believe I have an IOU waiting for me. Willie said you'd take me to her house."

Cokie nodded. "Come on, Josie. You ride with us to Willie's, and I'll take you home from there."

"I want to stay. I need to help with Charlie."

"I'm fine, Jo." The slight tremor in Patrick's voice made my heart ache. He wasn't fine. None of this was fine. And it was my fault. Within a few short months, his father's sanity had crumbled. Patrick had become a full-time nurse. He was willing, generous, and completely unqualified to heal his father, but desperate to allow him this lapse of dignity in private.

"I saw the piano downstairs. Do you play?" Randolph asked Patrick. He nodded.

"Music has been known to calm some of these guys. Their brain locks into it, and it shuts off some of the other reflexes. Just make sure it's slow and pretty."

Patrick turned to Cokie. "You should go out the front door, since your cab is in the street. You two can go out the back."

"Josie girl, you can't go out like that. You look like you been working the ax for Carlos Marcello. Patrick, give the girl some clothes." Patrick left for his room. Maybe Sadie could help me get the blood out.

Randolph gestured with his head toward Patrick's room. "Is he okay? Seems like he's about to blow."

"He's mad at me. I turned my back on Charlie and he cut himself. It's my fault."

"Now, don't go blamin' yourself," said Cokie. "He should've been home with his father instead of runnin' round the city with his friends."

"He was delivering books. He has to keep money coming in," I said.

I rolled and belted the denims to make them fit and tucked the shirt in. I could smell Patrick on the clothes—a frosty pine scent—and somehow it was comforting. Cokie drove us to Willie's. It was approaching midnight and the streets popped with Mardi Gras excitement. Cokie and Randolph talked about the war. Randolph predicted that US troops would soon be in Korea. I hoped he was wrong. We didn't need another war.

Cokie's cab pulled into Willie's driveway.

"Go to the side door," I told Randolph.

"What's the new password?" he asked.

"Mr. Bingle sent me."

Randolph went in through the side door as instructed. I got out of the car for some air, staying in the shadows so Willie couldn't see me through the windows. Music and laughter spilled from the house and almost covered the sound of male voices arguing.

"Cokie, is someone back there?" We walked down the drive.

John Lockwell's Lincoln Continental was parked in back of the house. The hood was propped open. Lockwell stood in his shirtsleeves looking at the engine and talking to another man.

"I'm telling you, John. Just leave it, and we'll tow it in the morning."

"Are you crazy? I'm not having my car towed from a whorehouse for the world to see. I told Lilly I'd be home by one A.M. tonight. Her friends have her convinced there's a murderer in the Quarter."

"You need a ride, sir? My car's in the driveway," offered Cokie.

"No, I need to drive my own car," he insisted. I stepped out from behind Cokie.

Mr. Lockwell threw up his hands. "What are you doing here?"

"I was taking a walk. I live nearby." The numbers flipped on the rotating counter of lies.

"Well, unless you can fix my car, you don't need to be here," he said.

"I know someone who can fix your car," I said.

"You do? How quick can you get him here?"

I turned to Cokie. "Can you take me to Jesse's?"

"Sure, but no tellin' if he'll be home," said Cokie.

"I'll be right back." I turned and started jogging down the drive with Cokie. But then I stopped. "Wait, Coke." I turned around and marched back to Mr. Lockwell.

"I have the best mechanic in the Quarter, and I can get him here pronto."

"Then why are you standing there? Go!" said Mr. Lockwell.

I reached into my purse and grabbed the envelope. "This will save time. I'll have you sign the recommendation now."

"You've gotta be kidding me."

I shook my head. I took the sheet out of the envelope and unfolded it against the driver's-side window. "Sign here."

Lockwell stood and stared.

"I'll have your car fixed, and this will be done." I pointed to the signature line.

"What's this all about?" asked his friend.

Mr. Lockwell's voice dropped. "Did you fool with my car, just to get this letter?"

"Of course not!"

He grabbed my wrist. "You better have a mechanic. If you're hustlin' me, kid, I swear I'll find you and you'll be sorry."

"Josie, you okay?" called Cokie.

"I'm fine," I called back.

Lockwell moved closer. "Did you hear me? You'll be sorry."

I nodded.

Mr. Lockwell took a pen from his shirt pocket. "God, I can't even read this. It's too dark back here." He looked at me. He looked at the car. He scribbled his signature. "There. Now, hurry."

"Come on, Cokie." I took off down the driveway with the letter and jumped in the cab. I held up the piece of paper. "Cokie, don't tell Willie about this."

"Josie, what are you up to? This is crazy. You don't even know what's wrong with his car. Maybe it can't be fixed. Maybe Jesse don't have the parts. It's after midnight. Maybe he's asleep. Maybe he's not even home. Then what you gonna do? That man is waitin', and he don't want to be messed with."

I stared at the signed letter. I didn't want to be messed with either.

Lights were on at Jesse's. I ran up and pounded on the door. The hinges creaked. A woman peeked out.

"What do you want?"

"Good evening, ma'am. I'm a friend of Jesse's. Is he home?"

"Go away, it's too late to be out. Nothing good ever happens after midnight," she hissed.

"Who is it, Granny?" The door swung open. Jesse stood

shirtless in his jeans, holding a bottle of milk. The bottle was sweating. So was his torso.

"Hey, Jo." Jesse looked at my clothing and raised an eyebrow.

"Jesse, I need a favor."

It took less than ten minutes for Jesse to start the engine.

"You got a card, kid?" Mr. Lockwell said from the window, between pulls on his cigar.

"A card?" Jesse asked.

Lockwell threw a green bill at me from the car. It hit my knees and landed on the driveway. "You're lucky he was able to fix it. Get yourself a dress. I want to see some high heels, Josephine." He drove away.

Jesse stared at his boots.

"It's not what it sounds like," I said, kicking the money away from my feet.

Jesse looked up. I saw his eyes float over my shoulder toward the house. A rich man in back of a brothel threw money at me and told me to get a pair of high heels—I knew exactly what it sounded like. I didn't want Jesse to think of me that way.

"Looks like he's pretty well-to-do."

"He's my friend's uncle." That sounded bad too. Jesse knew Willie's girls were called nieces. "Jesse, can I tell you something?"

He nodded.

"I asked Mr. Lockwell to give me a recommendation for college. He didn't want to, but I convinced him." Oh, that sounded even worse. "Wait, it's not like that, either. I know he comes here to Willie's, and he gave me the recommendation so I wouldn't tell my friend's aunt, his wife." I reached in my purse and pulled out the envelope.

Jesse's face brightened. "So you've put the pressure on the nasty goat, huh? Well, in that case, you've earned it." Jesse grabbed the money and flicked it to me.

I laughed. Lockwell was a nasty goat. "You take the money. You fixed the car."

He grabbed his toolbox, and we started the walk home, back down the driveway.

Jesse talked about cars and dirt racing. After a few blocks, his voice became nothing but a warble of sounds in my ear. So much had happened. Charlie, Patrick, Lockwell, and Willie—I saw her staring out the window as Jesse and I left her driveway. Had she seen me talking to Lockwell? Had she seen him sign the recommendation? When was she going to break open the game and admit she knew I had Mr. Hearne's watch? Jesse stopped walking, and I realized we were at the bookshop.

"You haven't heard a thing I've said."

"Yes, I—no, I haven't. I'm sorry, Jesse. I'm just so tired."

"Okay, tired girl, let me tell you a secret."

I didn't need any more secrets. I had enough of my own. I looked up at Jesse.

"Uh-huh. There you are, all tired, standin' in your boyfriend's clothes, but here's the secret." Jesse moved in close. "You like me."

"What?" I moved my face from his, trying to restrain what felt like a smile tugging at the corners of my mouth. My body seemed to react involuntarily around Jesse. It made me nervous.

"Yep, when you were in trouble, you went running, but not for your boyfriend. You came runnin' for me." Jesse backed away slowly, smiling. "You like me, Josie Moraine. You just don't know it yet."

I stood at the door, watching him step backward. He nodded and smiled his Jesse smile. He did have nice teeth.

"Oh, and Jo?" he called from halfway down the street. "You're welcome for the flowers."

Jesse turned and walked away, his laughter and toolbox fading into the darkness.

THIRTY-TWO

I was late. Two hours of sleep was worse than no sleep. I felt queasy, and the pressure behind my eyes from crying had turned into a headache. I had cried about Charlie and how my negligence nearly killed him. I cried about letting Patrick down. I cried about lying to Willie, manipulating Mr. Lockwell, not being forthright with Charlotte. I cried about Mr. Hearne's death and the pathetic fact that I clung to a dead man's watch because a respectable person had felt I was decent and not useless. I cried about lying. If I poured all the lies I had told into the Mississippi, the river would rise and flood the city. I cried about forgetting to thank Jesse for the flowers and cried even harder that he thought I liked him. Did I like him? Sometimes it felt as if I was trying really hard not to like him. It was all worse than wrong.

Fat Tuesday approached. Willie's house would be a fat disaster. The thought of sweeping up sin made my head throb. I walked into the house and smelled it right away. Bourbon.

Someone had spilled it. Not a glass, but a bottle. That would be a half hour. There was something else. Wine. I hoped it wasn't red. That would be forty-five minutes, maybe more. I couldn't be certain. I wasn't certain of anything anymore, except that New Orleans was a faithless friend and I wanted to leave her.

Sadie wrenched my arm, yanking me into her wiry frame as soon I stepped into the kitchen. She sobbed, making groaning sounds into my shoulder and then began unbuttoning my blouse.

"Sadie, stop. What are you doing?" I pushed her away, hard.

She looked at me, her brows twisted in confusion, her face swollen with crying. She reached into the sink and held up my blouse from the night before.

I had forgotten my bloody clothes in Cokie's car. He had left them for Sadie. The poor woman probably thought I was dead.

"Oh, Sadie, no. I'm fine. Really." I opened the neckline of my blouse and held my arms in the air, showing her both sides. "I'm not hurt."

Sadie collapsed into a chair and kissed the cross hanging from her neck.

I sat down at the table to try to calm her. She was in a pool of prayer so deep she didn't even respond. That's when I caught sight of the headline on the table.

MEMPHIS TOURIST'S DEATH DECLARED MURDER

I grabbed the paper.

Tennessee state officials have declared that knockout drops given in the Sans Souci on Bourbon Street killed Memphis tourist and former football star Forrest Hearne. Jefferson Parish investigator Martin Langley confirmed to the New Orleans *Times Picayune* that an autopsy in Memphis confirmed the cause of death. Hearne, a beloved and successful Memphis resident, died in the Sans Souci during the early morning hours of New Year's Day. The death was initially ruled a heart attack, but the victim's wife became suspicious when she realized several items were missing from her husband's person, including cash and an expensive wristwatch. Examinations of the body were performed in Tennessee by a Memphis coroner and later confirmed by a Louisiana state chemist. Both tests revealed unmistakable evidence of chloral hydrate. The drug, often referred to as a "Mickey Finn," is tasteless, colorless, odorless, and fatal in large doses. The Memphis chief investigator bitterly assailed the city of New Orleans for the lack of diligence local administration showed in the initial ruling of cause of death. *The Memphis Press-Scimitar* further reported that administering knockout drops to

tourists of visible affluence is a widespread practice in the French Quarter, where the nightclub is located. Evidence in the case will be turned over to the New Orleans city police department.

Forrest Hearne hadn't died of a heart attack. Someone had slipped him a Mickey.

I knocked on Willie's door, hoping she'd be in the bath or too tired to talk.

"Come in."

Willie looked as tired as I felt. A pad of onionskin paper was balanced on her lap. She always recorded the night's receipts on onionskin. It could be burned, swallowed, or flushed if the cops came by.

"God, I need that coffee. I feel like a bag of smashed assholes."

It sounded like she had swallowed a handful of rusty nails. "I'm sorry. I was late this morning, Willie. I haven't even been upstairs yet. But I'll hurry." I set the tray on the bed.

"Sit down, Jo."

I turned Willie's desk chair toward the bed and sat down.

"Cokie told me what happened last night. He was so proud of you, said you were great in the pocket. Really brave. Randolph told me the same thing, said it was practically a slaughterhouse scene, that Patrick was about as useful as a rubber crutch, but you took control. I saw the welt where you knocked Randolph across the face." Willie laughed.

"He was drunk, said he needed to be slapped to sober up. And poor Charlie was just lying there covered in blood. I was so scared, Willie."

"Of course you were. Hell, I'd be scared, too. Cokie said you thought it was your fault. That's the stupidest thing I ever heard. Charlie's obviously more pickled than any of us knew. I set up a trade with Randolph. He's going to check on Charlie every couple days for a line of credit with Dora."

"Thank you, Willie."

"Now, Randolph can't write prescriptions—he's got problems of his own. I'll still have to get those from Sully. But at least he can monitor and let us know what he needs."

"The neighbors are probably becoming suspicious," I said.

"Tell them Charlie's in Slidell visiting a friend. I don't want him in the mental ward with all the nut jobs," said Willie. "Charlie's a dignified man. Always helped me when I needed it. Randolph says the outbursts will pass, and he'll go quiet."

"You mean his fits will pass?"

Willie took another sip of her coffee. "Cokie also told me that you fixed Lockwell's car."

"I didn't. Jesse Thierry did."

Willie nodded. "Well, you sure made Jesse look like a hero. But I guess that's why you did it. You've been seen around town together. You like him."

She stated it as fact, just like Jesse did. It annoyed me. And who had told her I was seen with Jesse? It had to be Frankie.

"Jesse's a friend, Willie, nothing more. He talks about cars and dirt racing."

"Oh, right, and you're on your way to becoming a Rockefeller. I forgot."

"I didn't mean it like that."

"Well, don't worry. There are lots of nice girls who will be happy to take your sloppy seconds. Hell, the Uptown women gawk at him like he's sex on a stick. Jesse's a good kid, even if he's too lowbrow for you."

Willie had a way of making me feel ashamed of myself without even trying. I watched her unfold the newspaper. She looked at the headline, then at me, then back at the headline. She coughed and continued reading. "So, someone slipped the Mick too fat. Killed him, eh?"

I nodded.

Willie read aloud from the story. "'*The Memphis Press-Scimitar* further reported that administering knockout drops to tourists of visible affluence is a widespread practice in the French Quarter, where the nightclub is located.' Such crap. They're painting us all as thieves! Next we'll be voted the most dangerous city, and that'll grind tourism to dust."

Willie slapped the paper down in fury. She got up, lit a cigarette, and began pacing in front of the bed, her black silk robe flowing loose around her.

She pointed at me with her burning cigarette. "This is gonna get bad, Jo. People will demand a cleanup in the Quarter. This fella was high cotton. Every Uptown wife is going to see this and think of her own husband. They'll lock 'em down. The police will turn up the heat. They'll be on the house like a bitch on a bone. Business will suffer."

"Do you think they'll catch the person who did it?"

Willie didn't respond. She paced, sucking nicotine. She stopped and turned to me. "Don't you talk to anyone. If someone comes asking questions, you tell them you know nothing. You come straight to me."

"Who would ask me questions?"

"The cops, idiot."

I looked down into my lap.

"What, they already came around?"

I nodded. "Like I told you, Mr. Hearne came into the shop and bought two books the day he died. The police wanted to know what he bought and if he seemed unwell. I told them that he bought Keats and Dickens and that he looked fine."

"What else?" Willie took a hard pull on her cigarette. I watched the paper burn back.

"That's it."

"Well, that's plenty. They could call you to testify." She spun around toward me. "Was Patrick there? Did he see Hearne?"

"Yes."

"Patrick will take the stand. Not you."

"Willie, what are you talking about?"

"Shut up! Get out and get to work. You're late. Dates will come knocking early, wanting a fix before Mardi Gras. And put some cold water on your face. It's fat from all your boo-hooing. You look like Joe Louis in the twelfth round."

THIRTY-THREE

I slept through Mardi Gras.

I used Patrick's fan from the shop to mask the noise. We always complained that fan was loud, but on the floor next to my bed, it was perfect. I slept for fourteen hours, not waking once, not even to think about the Smith application.

I had mailed it the day before Mardi Gras, including a crisp ten-dollar bill for the application fee. I often thought about opening a bank account and loved the idea of having printed checks, but Willie didn't trust banks or bankers in New Orleans. She said they were the wildest men in the house, and she wasn't going to let them pay her with her own money. She also didn't want anyone tracking her earnings.

The clerk at the post office said the envelope would arrive in Northampton by February 27. She had looked at the address on the envelope, looked at me, and gave a pitiful smile. She was probably thinking, "Oh, you're not really trying to get into

Smith College, are you? I heard they're hiring at Woolworth's on Canal."

Charlotte's most recent postcard was dated February 15, and it arrived on the twentieth.

The front of the card framed a large, beautiful building covered in snow. The caption running along the bottom said *Built in 1909, the William Allan Neilson Library at Smith College contains 380,000 volumes and adds 10,000 annually.*

I flipped the card over, reading Charlotte's tiny writing yet again.

> *Dear Jo,*
>
> *Have you mailed your application? I hope so! Aunt Lilly says Mardi Gras is in full swing. I'm so envious of all the fun you must be having. I showed all the girls the postcard you sent from the Vieux Carré. The flying club has an aerial tag match with Yale this weekend, and next week our congressman will meet with the Progressives. Can't wait for you to join us. Write soon.*
>
> *Fondly,*
> *Charlotte*

I wanted to join them, to work on something important and meaningful.

"Hey, Motor City."

The voice filtered in from outside, followed by a whistle. I peeked out the window. Jesse nodded from across the street, standing in front of his motorcycle. I opened the window and leaned out. The street was covered with remnants of celebration. Trash Wednesday, they called it.

"Did you get some sleep?" he called up. "I didn't see you out."

"I slept through the whole thing."

"You hungry?"

I was starving. "Are you going to the cathedral to get your ashes?" I asked.

Jesse laughed. "I'm from Alabama, remember? Baptist. Salvation by grace. Let's go find a muffuletta."

We sat on a bench at the edge of Jackson Square. A good night's sleep had helped. My mind had cleared, and the earth no longer shifted beneath my feet. Jesse's head lolled against the bench, his eyes closed, the sun baking the comfortable smile on his face. It was nice not talking. Somehow Jesse and I could have a conversation without saying a word. I closed my eyes and leaned back, trying to bring the orange shadows behind my eyelids into focus. Birds chirped, and a breeze rolled over my arms. We sat that way for a while, cleansing ourselves of the chaos that had been Mardi Gras, content with the lunch settling in our stomachs.

"Jess?"

"Mm," he replied.

I kept my eyes closed and felt my body relaxing further into the bench. "I did something."

"That's never a good intro."

"For some reason, I want to tell you about it," I said.

"Okay. Start tellin'."

"Back around the New Year, I met a girl, Charlotte, from Massachusetts. She came into the shop, and we got on really well. We had never met before, but it was like she knew me completely. I felt so comfortable with her. Have you ever met someone like that?"

"Yep."

The clouds shifted, and the glow of sun brightened on my face. "But she's from a really wealthy family, a good family, and she's a freshman at Smith College in Massachusetts. She even flies a plane. Charlotte kept telling me that I should apply to Smith. I know it sounds ridiculous, me being able to go to a prestigious school like that, but she sent me all the information."

Suddenly, the insanity of the whole thing came into focus, and I nearly laughed.

"But for some reason, I began to want it, really badly. I told Willie, and she was mad. She said I had to go to school here in New Orleans, that I was out of my league trying to get into a college like that. Well, that made me want it more. So I did it, Jesse. I applied to Smith in Northampton. I told you I convinced that lout John Lockwell to sign a recommendation. I sent the application the other day. I'm scared to admit it, even to myself." My voice dropped. "But I really want this."

I felt a shadow glide over my face as the sun slipped behind a cloud. I took a deep breath and exhaled, feeling the weight of secrecy lift off of me and onto the breeze.

"Crazy, that's what you're thinking, right?" I said.

"What I'm thinking?" His voice was close.

I opened my eyes. Jesse was inches from my face, blocking

the sun. I felt his breath on my neck and saw his mouth. My body jerked with panic and my fists leapt to my chest.

Jesse pulled back immediately. "Oh, Jo, I'm sorry. I didn't mean to scare you," he said softly. "You . . . had something in your hair." He held up a piece of a leaf.

Confusion flooded the space between us. I tried to explain. "No, it's just . . ."

Just what? Why was I whispering? I knew Jesse didn't want to scare me. Yet my knuckles were clenched, ready to fight him off. I felt ridiculous, and he seemed to know it.

"Wouldn't it have been funny if you had popped me one?" He laughed and ran his hand through his hair. "Well, not funny, but you know what I mean."

Jesse leaned back on the bench and put his hands in the pockets of his leather jacket. "Okay, you asked what I was thinking. What I'm thinking is"—he turned to me and smiled—"you better get yourself a winter coat, Motor City. It's cold in Massachusetts."

I barely heard him. Jesse's aftershave lingered all around my face. I was suddenly aware of how close we were sitting on the bench and was consumed with wondering if his hands were warm or cold in the pockets.

"How much does a school like that cost?" he asked.

"A lot," I said quietly.

"How much is a lot?"

"For tuition, residence, and books, it's close to two thousand dollars per year," I told him.

Jesse blew a low whistle.

"I know, it's crazy."

"It's crazy, but it's just money. There's lots of ways to get money," said Jesse.

We walked up St. Peter to Royal, back toward the shop. Neither of us spoke. We moved through the afterbirth of celebration, kicking cans and cups out of the way, stepping over pieces of costumes that had been abandoned through the course of the evening. Jesse grabbed a string of milky glass beads hanging from a doorway. He handed them to me, and I put them over my head. The day had a peace about it, like Christmas, when the world stops and gives permission to pause. All over the city, Orleanians were at rest, asleep in their makeup, beads in their beds. Even Willie's was closed today. She'd spend the whole day in her robe, maybe even have coffee with the girls at the kitchen table. They'd laugh about the johns of the prior night. Evangeline would complain, Dora would make everyone laugh, and Sweety would leave midafternoon for her grandmother's. Did Mother miss it? Was she thinking about New Orleans, about Willie's, about me?

"Looks like you've got an eager customer." Jesse motioned to the bookshop.

Miss Paulsen stood with her face to the window, peering inside.

"Hello, Miss Paulsen."

She turned toward us on the sidewalk. "Oh, hello, Josie." She looked at Jesse. Her eyes unashamedly scanned him up and down.

"This is Jesse Thierry. Jesse, this is Miss Paulsen. She's in the English department at Loyola."

Jesse smiled and nodded. "Ma'am."

Miss Paulsen stiffened. "I'm also a friend of the Marlowes'." She addressed the comment to Jesse. "I've been trying to reach them for quite a while now. I've been to their house, but no one answered."

"Well, I better get going," said Jesse.

I didn't want him to leave, to abandon me with Miss Paulsen, who would demand answers to too many questions.

"Nice to meet you, ma'am." Jesse backed away. "See you, Jo. It was nice."

Miss Paulsen shot me a look as Jesse walked across the street. Her shoulders jumped when he fired up his motorcycle. I could see Jesse laughing. He revved the engine again and again, until Miss Paulsen finally turned around. He waved and took off down Royal.

"Oh, my." Miss Paulsen touched her coiled bun, leaving her hand on the nape of her neck. "Is that boy in college?"

I rubbed my arm, still feeling Jesse against me. "As a matter of fact, he is. Delgado. Is there something I can help you with, Miss Paulsen?"

"Indeed there is." She folded her arms across her chest. "Enough is enough. What's going on with Charlie Marlowe?"

THIRTY-FOUR

We had agreed upon the story. Charlie was out of town, helping a sick friend in Slidell. So that's what I told her. The lie came out so easily it frightened me. I used to feel sick to my stomach when I heard Mother tell a lie. How can you do it? How do you live with yourself? I used to wonder. But here I was, lying to Miss Paulsen and smiling while doing it. I even added details about Charlie possibly acquiring a bookstore in Slidell. Patrick and I had never discussed that. I made that up all by myself.

Patrick hadn't come to the shop in days. When I stopped by the house, he was always at the piano, playing endless melodies for Charlie. Something had changed. A curtain had fallen between us. It made me want to cry. I'd give my special knock and then let myself in with my key. Patrick would turn slightly from the piano, see it was me, and then turn back around. He communicated with his father through Debussy, Chopin, and Liszt. He'd continue playing, sometimes for hours. I'd bring groceries, straighten up the house, and he'd remain seated at the piano. We wouldn't exchange a word. But as soon as I'd walk out onto the stoop to leave, I'd hear the notes stop. He was speaking to Charlie through the music. He was ignoring me through it.

I was happy to see him come through the door of the shop. I couldn't speak freely because a customer was browsing one of the stacks. Patrick and I had worked together for years, but today the space behind the counter felt cramped. We maneuvered around each other awkwardly and had lost our comfortable rhythm.

"Hi." I tried to smile at him. I put my hand on the counter, signaling mystery.

Patrick looked down at the woman, shook his head, and gave me the sign for cookbook.

It was the most we had communicated in over a week. I had repeatedly apologized about what happened with Charlie. I knew he heard me, but he hadn't responded. His simple cookbook signal filled me with joy.

"Charlie?" I whispered.

"Randolph's there. I have to run a few errands."

I pulled out a stack of mail and handed it to him. "I sorted the bills and checks. I figured you'd be going by the bank."

He nodded.

The woman came to the register with the new *Betty Crocker Cookbook*.

"I was so sure she'd choose Agatha Christie," I said after she left the shop.

"She desperately wants to read mysteries," said Patrick. "But she had to buy the cookbook because her angry husband is demanding hot meals as soon as he drops his briefcase at the door. She's miserable in the marriage—so is her husband. He drinks to escape, she cries in the bathroom sitting on the edge of the tub. They never should have gotten married. She's even more miserable now that she bought the cookbook instead of Agatha Christie. She feels trapped."

I looked out the window and watched the woman standing motionless in the street. I played through the scenario Patrick had created and could suddenly see her throwing the book in a trash bin, shaking her hair out, and running to the nearest saloon. Two young men crossed the street toward the shop looking at us through the window. I pegged one to buy the Mickey Spillane novel. The other boy looked familiar. It was John Lockwell's son, Richard.

"Jo." Patrick tugged at my arm, pulling me into him. I felt his hand slide under my hair, and suddenly he was kissing me. By the time I realized what was happening, he had stopped.

"Patrick." I was so shocked I could barely say his name. My hand rested on his shoulder, not in a fist. I had let him kiss me and didn't fight him off.

He quickly looked out the window. "I'm sorry, Jo," he whispered.

His face was so close to mine, drawn with pain.

"Patrick, I'm sorry, too, I—"

He didn't let me finish. He kissed me quickly, grabbed the stack of mail, and left the shop.

I leaned against the counter to steady myself, filled with a mixture of shock, confusion, and Patrick's toothpaste in my mouth. I touched my lips. Was it an "I'm sorry" kiss or an "I'm sorry I didn't do this sooner" kiss? I couldn't tell. But I hadn't resisted and was more bewildered than fearful.

I finalized the inventory that Patrick had requested and sorted a new shipment of books. I was distracted and shelved things in the wrong place. I put the new best seller *Confessions of a Highlander* by Shirley Cameron in the travel section instead of in romance. I caught my mistake and scolded myself. I moved it to the register display, hoping a regretful housewife would buy it instead of a cookbook.

I kept returning to the same conclusion. Patrick and I made sense. We were comfortable. We had known each other a long time. We loved books. He was smart, talented, stylish, and very organized. He had seen all my ghosts. There wouldn't be any uncomfortable explanations or risk of rejection when Dora hooted at me in the street, when Willie insisted I go with her to Shady Grove, or when Mother resurfaced, begging for a sirloin for the black eye that Hollywood had given her. Patrick would take a Greyhound from the station on Rampart to visit me at Smith. On Christmas Eve, he would be waiting at the station in his blue peacoat when my bus pulled in late at night. We'd listen to music together, I'd give him cuff links for his birthday, and we'd spend Sunday mornings drinking coffee and combing the obituaries for dead books.

I smiled. Patrick didn't scare me. It made sense.

The bell jingled. Frankie walked into the shop, peering between the stacks.

"Wow, twice in the same month. Let me guess—you've been dreaming of Victor Hugo?" I asked.

Frankie looked around. His hands twitched. "You alone?" he whispered.

"Yes."

"You sure?" he asked, chomping on his gum.

I nodded. The ever-present humor was absent from his voice. A shadow rolled through my stomach.

"Your momma's on her way back."

I let out the breath I was holding. "Already? Why am I not surprised?" I slid a book into its proper place. I had to ask the question. "Is Cincinnati coming with her?"

"Don't know. I told Willie, and she told me to come and tell you."

"How did you find out?"

"I have a source over at American Telegram. They saw the message transmitted."

"Mother sent Willie a telegram?" That seemed odd.

"No, the telegram was sent last night from the Los Angeles police chief to one of the head detectives here in New Orleans. They delivered the telegram to his house last night, all private."

"I knew Cincinnati would get her in trouble. So he's been arrested, and now she's coming back."

"It's not Cinci. Your momma's the one in custody."

"What?"

Frankie nodded. "Telegram said, 'Louise Moraine in custody on way to New Orleans.' My leak in the detective's office said that they've been hunting her down."

"What for?"

Frankie blew a small bubble and looked out the window.

"What for, Frankie?"

His gum snapped just as the words came out of his mouth.

"The murder of Forrest Hearne."

THIRTY-FIVE

I ran to Willie's, my stomach bouncing in my mouth the entire way. Yes, Mother was stupid. And greedy. A murderer? I didn't want to believe it. The thought scared me too much. Echoes of all her rotten promises came floating at me from the jar of shame, and with each step I took, I heard the ticktock of Forrest Hearne's watch—the watch I had found under her bed.

I crept in through the kitchen door. Dora sat with her emerald dress hiked up around her thighs, bare foot on the kitchen table. She was painting her toenails a pearlescent shade of pink. She took one look at me and opened her arms.

"Oh, sugar, come to Dora. I'd get up, but I'd ruin my hooves."

I walked into Dora's arms. She squeezed me into what felt like pillows. "Now, I've read a couple crime novels, hon. Nothin' has been proved yet. Willie said they're just callin' her in for questioning."

"But why?"

"Because she offed a rich guy, stupid," Evangeline said as she walked into the kitchen.

"Now, Vangie, hush," scolded Dora. "Louise didn't off anyone. She was just at the wrong place at the wrong time." Dora turned to me. "When police questioned people, someone said they saw her having a drink with the rich man on New Year's Eve."

"Mother was drinking with Mr. Hearne?"

"Was that his name?" asked Dora.

"Yeah," said Evangeline. "Forrest Hearne."

"Ooh, now that's a sexy name. Was he somethin' to look at?" said Dora.

"Picture in the paper looked all that. Said he was an architect and rich," reported Evangeline.

"Now, why didn't he come to the *maison de joie* to see the queen of green?" said Dora. "If he did, he wouldn't be dead."

"Dora, stop," I said.

"Oh, sugar, I'm sorry. I'm just sayin' that you shouldn't worry yourself. After all, the police are questioning everybody now, aren't they?" Dora raised her eyebrows slightly. Her sister, Darleen, had seen me in the police station.

"I guess." I nodded.

She nodded back. "I'd be more concerned that Cincinnati might be comin' back with her," said Dora.

"Well, Louise is gonna have to stay up in the attic," said Evangeline. "That room is mine now. I finally got the stink out."

I got up to find Willie. Evangeline grabbed my arm at the door.

"Stay away from John Lockwell," she whispered. An asterisk of spit shot through her teeth and onto my chest. She stared at the bubble of saliva. "Oh, look." She grinned. "It's raining."

I knocked on Willie's door.

"You shouldn't be here" was the reply.

I walked in anyway. Willie sat fully dressed for the evening in her traditional black. Her hair was pulled up higher than normal, anchored with two diamond-encrusted fleur-de-lis combs. The black book sat open in front of her on the desk.

"I'm getting as bad as Charlie," she said over her shoulder. "Last week I wrote down that Silver Dollar Sam likes Seven and Seven." She made a correction. "It's Pete the Hat that likes Seven and Seven."

Willie's black book was a card catalog. She listed each customer with a code name, what girl they liked, service preference, even what they drank and what card game they played. Silver Dollar Sam was really a car salesman named Sidney. But he had a tattoo of a silver dollar on his back. There was just enough information in the book for Willie to use it as an insurance policy. If anyone gave her trouble, she had a visit record she'd offer to share with his wife or mother. Before the action started each night, Willie would examine the list of any advance reservations. She'd make sure to remember their favorites while making it all seem natural and unrehearsed.

Willie appeared completely calm about the news of Mother. She always said she could make tea in a tornado. Her ease relaxed me.

I picked up a tube of Hazel Bishop lipstick from her bed and blotted some color onto my lips and cheeks. "So, what do we do?" I asked.

Willie turned a page in the book. "We've already discussed this. You won't speak to anyone. You stayed in on New Year's Eve. You saw nothing. You and your mother are estranged. When she gets back, you'll go out to Shady Grove. You'll be out of town for a while."

"By myself?"

"What, you want Cincinnati to go with you?"

"No, but won't it look strange if I'm suddenly out of town?"

"Oh, are you so important that everyone will notice? You said the police already asked you questions and you answered them. All the locals know your mother, and they know better than to mess with me and mention your name. No one will say anything."

"But who will clean the house in the mornings?"

"What, Cinderella, you're gonna miss your scrub brush?"

I leaned against the post on Willie's bed. "No, I'm going to miss you, my wicked stepmother."

Willie put down her pen and turned in her chair. "How do you know I'm not your fairy godmother?"

We stared at each other. I looked at Willie, dressed in all black, with chianti lips and eyes that would send a snake slithering back into its hole. I suddenly burst out laughing.

"Okay," I said. "You're the wicked stepmother with the fairy godmother heart."

"I'd rather be like you," said Willie. "Cinderella with the stepmother heart."

Ouch. Was she joking? She acted like she considered it a compliment.

She turned back to her book. "Cokie will take you out to Shady Grove."

"He's just going to leave me out there, Willie?"

"You won't need a car. You can walk to the grocer if you need to use a phone."

"But what if something happens?"

"Salt the peanuts. I'm not worried. You're a good shot. I'll tell Ray and Frieda to watch the road for cars. You know they're wide-eyed at night. Now, unless you want some old lech to pull the petals off your daisy, you better get out of here."

I walked out to the street just as Cokie was dropping off a customer.

"I'd drive you, Josie girl, but I got to pick up a group of conventioneers and bring 'em over."

"That's okay, Coke. Did you hear I'm taking a trip?"

"Sure did. Willie don't want you around for your momma to drag you into nothin'. She goin' tell your momma that you're in Slidell, helpin' Mr. Charlie." Cokie scratched at the back of his scalp. "Jo, I gotta ask you. How did you know that one of the wheels was off this thing? From day one, you were pushin' me about the coroner's report. Did you know somethin' 'bout that Tennessee man and your momma?"

"No, I just . . . liked him. He came into the shop. He was so kind and treated me with respect. He inspired me, Coke. I don't know many men like that."

Cokie nodded. "Well, looks like we'll be breakin' in that thermos on our trip to Shady Grove."

He drove off to pick up the conventioneers. I started the walk back to the shop, thinking about the watch. I had to get rid of it. I could throw it in a trash bin. I could take it out to Shady Grove and hide it. A car passed me. I heard the brakes hiss and the transmission shift into reverse. The shiny Lincoln Continental backed up and stopped in front of me.

"So did you get into Smith yet?" John Lockwell flicked his cigar ash out the window.

"I'm waiting to hear."

"Still don't know what that letter said."

"It was very complimentary . . . and well written," I assured him.

"I hope it mentioned your martinis."

"No, but it mentioned my auto repair connections."

"Running like a timepiece now. Would you like a ride? Charlotte would consider me a horrible uncle if I didn't pick up her friend. Come have a drink with me. I have a private apartment in the Quarter now. More discreet."

"No, thanks. I have plans."

Lockwell smiled. "Maybe some other time." He pointed his finger at me. "There's something about you, Josephine. And I like the lipstick."

He pulled away. I wiped my mouth with the back of my hand.

THIRTY-SIX

I sat on my bed with the cigar box in my lap. I looked at Mr. Hearne's check. Would his wife notice that it hadn't cleared? If I put it through now, the cops might notice the transaction and come asking questions. I looked at his signature, confident, elegant. My mind traced back to Mother in the Meal-a-Minit, pulling the wad of cash out of her purse, bragging about going to Antoine's for dinner. They were certainly a pair. Cincinnati in a dead man's suit, Mother in a dead man's wallet.

I had put the check in the floorboard with the watch. I'd take them both out to Shady Grove to get rid of them. That should have been foremost on my mind. But it wasn't. I had spent the whole morning thinking of Patrick, wondering if he would come by the shop. He didn't. I'd have to wait to see him when I stopped to see Charlie. I watched the clock, counting the minutes until closing time. I had washed my hair and set it last night. I kept looking in the mirror and had changed my blouse twice. Suddenly I wanted to impress Patrick, look good for him.

Miss Paulsen stopped by the shop, snooping once again. I told her that I was going out to Slidell to visit Charlie and would bring back a full report. She wrote a note to Charlie and insisted upon sealing it in an envelope for me to give him. I then sold her the Shirley Cameron book and we discussed her friend from Smith who wrote historical fiction. She thought we'd get along. Miss Paulsen was interesting and kind when she wasn't being a detective.

A letter arrived from Charlotte asking if I had received word on my application. She also mentioned that her cousin Betty Lockwell had been writing to her about Patrick, asking for another introduction. Charlotte found Betty's crush funny. I found it annoying. I threw the letter in my desk drawer, locked the door, and headed out.

As I walked, I rehearsed what I would say when I saw Patrick. I wanted to seem comfortable, not let on how giddy I'd felt all day about the kiss. I'd let him take the lead. I listened for the piano when I arrived at the door, but the house was silent. I put my key back in my pocket and knocked.

The door opened. "Hey, Jo. Come in." Patrick was barefoot, wearing a pressed shirt and feeding a belt through the loops of his slacks. His hair was still wet.

"You look nice," I said, hoping for a return compliment.

"Thanks. I'll be right back. Gotta get my shoes." He ran upstairs.

Something smelled good. I wandered into the living room toward Patrick's piano. I ran my fingers over the word *Bösendorfer* and then dragged my hand silently over the keys. *Liebesträume* by Franz Liszt sat on the music rack. I looked at all the notes and marveled at how easily Patrick was able to turn little black dots into beautiful music.

"I made croquettes," he said as he came back down the stairs. "I used the recipe from the same Betty Crocker cookbook the doomed housewife bought."

"What does it mean?" I asked, pointing to the sheet music.

Patrick moved up behind me and looked over my shoulder. "*Liebesträume,* it's German," he said.

"I know it's German, but what's the translation?"

Patrick closed the sheet music and set it on top of the piano. "It means *Dreams of Love.*"

Was he blushing? "Oh," I said, not wanting to reveal the internal smile beaming through my chest. "How's Charlie?"

"He's been sleeping a lot. Nearly twenty hours a day. I have to wake him up to eat."

"Do you think it's the medicine?" I asked.

"I don't know. I'm going to ask Randolph." Patrick pulled a plate from the cupboard and handed it to me. "I was looking for an extra pillow for Charlie in his closet. I found his manuscript on the top shelf."

"Did you read it?"

"I feel bad saying this, but yeah. I know he'd want me to wait until it's finished. But I was dying to read it. And you know what? It's really good. I wish he could have finished it."

"Well, you never know. Maybe he will when he gets better," I said.

We sat at the kitchen table to eat. I had hoped we would eat in the dining room, but that may have seemed too formal. I kept telling myself to stop thinking of the visit as a date. I had eaten with Patrick hundreds of times. But I couldn't help it. Once I left for Shady Grove, I didn't know how long it would be until I saw him. We started eating, and I told him about Mother.

"Whoa. Jo, that's crazy," said Patrick.

"I know it's crazy. Dora says they want to ask Mother some questions because someone reported that they saw her with Mr. Hearne."

"What does Willie say?"

"Willie's making me go out to Shady Grove." I looked at Patrick. "I don't know how long I'll be gone."

"Well, that makes sense. She doesn't want your mother to drag you into the drama."

"I don't know how long I'll be gone," I repeated. "We may have to close the shop."

"I'll figure something out," said Patrick. "You could probably use the vacation. Take a bunch of the new books you've been wanting to read."

We finished dinner, exchanging random small talk. I debated every other minute as to whether I should bring up what had happened in the shop.

"Say, Jo, can I ask a favor?" said Patrick. "Remember James from Doubleday? It's his birthday, and his girlfriend is throwing a party tonight. They invited me, and I really wanted to make an appearance but . . ."

"But you need someone to stay with Charlie."

Patrick nodded. "I'd take you to the party, but Randolph is busy tonight and can't come by."

"Of course I'll stay with Charlie."

"Aw, thanks. I won't be long."

I cleaned up the dishes, and Patrick went upstairs to check on Charlie. He came down in a blazer and tie.

"You look nice. And you smell nice, too." It smelled like new cologne.

"Glad you like it." He started toward the door, stopped, and walked back to me. He placed his hands on my shoulders and kissed me quickly. "Thanks, Jo. I'll be right back."

The door banged shut. I hadn't noticed it in the bookstore. His lips were cold.

He wasn't right back. Hours passed. I read magazines, dusted the piano, and then finally wandered upstairs to check on Charlie. I paused at the closed door of Patrick's bedroom, resisting the urge to go in and peek around. Instead, I went into Charlie's room. He was sleeping, a sheet pulled neatly over him. The room was clean and orderly. Medicine bottles lined the top of his dresser next to a sheet of instructions from Randolph. I opened the window a crack near the desk to get a bit of air circulating. The piece of paper was still in the typewriter. I did a double take. There was another letter.

BL

I sat on the edge of Charlie's bed. The pale skin around his wounds was stained blood orange from Mercurochrome. I pulled back the sheet slightly. Charlie was hugging the pink Valentine box. His color was weak, and his gray hair still shaggy.

"Oh, Charlie," I whispered, "what's happened to you? I just wanted to give you a haircut. I'm so sorry."

His eyes flickered open and locked on me. And for the briefest moment, he smiled. It was the same smile he gave me when I was eight years old hiding in his bookshop, the smile he gave through the front window when I was outside sweeping the sidewalk. It was the smile that said, "You're a good girl, Josie."

I brushed the wisps of hair from his eyes. "I love you, Charlie Marlowe. Do you hear me? We're gonna figure this out." But he was already back to sleep.

I woke to the smell of coffee. A blanket was tucked around my shoulders on the couch. The curtains in the living room glowed a pale shade of peach. The sun was coming up. I made my way into the kitchen. Patrick stood at the counter, still in his blazer and tie.

"Did I wake you?" he said.

"I can't believe I fell asleep. Is Charlie okay?"

"He's fine. Sorry, I was later than I expected." Patrick hadn't been to bed but didn't look tired.

"Fun party?"

"Yeah, but I was the music monkey. They had me playing piano all night long. I've played enough jazz to last a lifetime." Patrick turned and smiled. "Jo, guess who was at the party."

"Who?"

"Capote."

"Truman Capote? Did you tell him you loved his book, and you've been selling it like crazy at the shop?"

"We only talked a short bit. Mostly about Proust. He has the strangest voice, Jo, and he's so small. He's only twenty-five or twenty-six but was talking circles around the literati. The only person who could keep up with him was that eccentric Elmo Avet."

"Willie knows Elmo. She calls him the Queen Bee, but she loves the antique furniture he sells her. Sounds like quite the birthday party."

"I made you some coffee. You're leaving this morning, right?" he asked.

I nodded.

"We'll miss you," said Patrick, pouring a cup of coffee.

"I'll miss you too. You can reach me through Willie. She'll be leaving messages for me with the grocer. And of course you can write. I left the address on the counter. Oh, I almost forgot. Miss Paulsen came by the shop."

Patrick turned around, his face wrinkled with fear. "Again?"

"Yes. I told her I was going to Slidell to visit Charlie. She gave me a note for him." I pulled the sealed envelope out of my purse and handed it to Patrick.

He tore it open and read it. He handed it to me.

You were never one to write mysteries, and now you've become one.

Send a letter from Slidell, or I'll know this is all a lie.

Worried—Barbara

THIRTY-SEVEN

I loved Cokie's cab.

But we weren't in Cokie's cab. We were riding in Mariah, and Cokie's smile pulled clear across his face.

"Pour me another drip from that thermos, Josie girl. See, this is fine drivin'. One day I'm gonna get me a big black Cadillac like this, whitewall tires and all, that's right."

"This car attracts too much attention. We should have taken your cab. I love your cab. It's so comfortable."

"My cab's a good girl. If she could talk, oooeee, what she seen. Now, this ain't the route to Northampton. That's north through Mississippi and up into Alabama. Cornbread say it's better to drive as soon as the sun comes up and pull off before the sun goes down. I agree. You'll stay with Cornbread's cousin in Georgia, and he has an old aunt in Virginia if you need to stop there."

"It's so sweet of you to plan, Coke, but I haven't been accepted yet."

"You'll be accepted. I know it." Cokie nodded repeatedly. "You have to be."

He turned to me from the wheel. "You got to get outta here, Josie. New Orleans is fine for some people, real good for a few. But not for you. Too much baggage that'll pull you down. You got dreams and the potential to make 'em real. I bet you latched onto that rich man from Memphis 'cuz he fit your idea of a daddy. And I agree, ain't no way you could turn out so good unless the other half was something fine. So you'll be accepted, and you'll do us all proud. You'll sure do me proud."

We passed the three hours talking. Cokie told me stories about his parents. His father was a white man from Canada who settled in New Orleans. He had a wife and kids and had taken up with Cokie's mother on the side. He died before Cokie's third birthday. Unlike me, Cokie had been close with his mother and got teary just talking about her. He loved her deeply and said she always did right by him. She died when he was sixteen. He said it made it impossible to find a wife, because he wanted a woman with the qualities his momma had. Any woman I'd suggest as a potential mate he'd reject with a scoff and comments that made me laugh so hard I nearly wet myself.

"Well, why not Bertha?" I asked.

"Now, Bertha's nice, but she too old. I like a girl where her skin fits a little better."

"And Tyfee?" I tried.

"Tyfee? You gotta be kiddin'. She only got three toes and sweats like a dog crappin' peach seeds. And she's always dyein' that gray hair of hers with coffee grounds. Looks like dirt. No, thank you."

Tyfee only had three toes. Who knew?

Cokie was picky about a mate but seemed to know exactly what he wanted in a woman. It made me think about Patrick and our awkward good-bye. He'd hugged me hard and long, like he'd never see me again. But he didn't kiss me. He just stared, his eyes full of silence. I couldn't tell if he was upset about me leaving or upset about Charlie.

We arrived just before lunch. Cokie stopped at Ray and Frieda Kole's. He felt the hood of their car.

"It's cold. They've been asleep awhile," said Cokie.

Poor Ray and Frieda. I wondered what made them so scared of the dark.

Cokie set a box from Willie on their porch. It had a pot of Sadie's gumbo, a carton of cigarettes, a bottle of muscatel, and a letter from Willie instructing them to keep an eye on me.

We pulled down the long tree-lined drive to Shady Grove.

"Now, Jo, you make sure you keep your ears wide. It's nice and private down here, but that can also be trouble. You scream out here, no one's gonna hear you. Not even Ray and Frieda. They're a mile away."

"You're acting like there's bears out here or something."

"I'm not talkin' 'bout no animals. I'm talkin' 'bout criminals."

I laughed. "No one wants to rob Shady Grove. There's nothing here but furniture and old dishes." Shady Grove was the picture of peace. A small Creole cottage with a deep front porch surrounded by moss-draped oak trees.

Cokie set the parking brake. "Now, Josie, I'm not foolin'.

This business with your momma is serious. There's lotsa people who don't want her back in New Orleans. Willie's smart pullin' you out of the sizzle, but even out here, you got to be ready. Some folk might be stupid enough to think they can get to your momma through you."

I got out of the car and pulled my small suitcase and a large box of books from the backseat. Cokie opened the trunk. It was packed with crates and boxes.

"Coke, this is half the pantry. I thought I was staying a week at most."

"Sadie been cookin' all night for you. You got plenty of supplies here." He pulled Willie's golf bag from the trunk. "Take this. You know I can't stand no guns."

I looked in the bag. "She sent all of them?"

"With extra rounds in the front pocket. She said she told you to bring your pistol."

"Isn't this a bit much?"

"Well, you never been out here alone. What if someone comes by?"

"Who, like Frieda Kole?"

"Like Cincinnati."

It came out and then he couldn't take it back. A chill pebbled across my neck. I heard his voice—*I'm gonna get you, Josie Moraine.* I pulled out one of the shotguns to examine what Willie had sent.

Cokie rubbed his forehead. "I shouldn't have said that. Now, Josie, I'm not sayin' that Cincinnati goin' be out here. Willie's worried that he and your momma might want you as a character witness for her, and well, Cincinnati is tied to some pretty bad folk."

"Like Carlos Marcello?"

Cokie looked on the verge of tears. Then I remembered Patrick hugging me so hard it hurt, like he was saying goodbye. Cokie sniffed and started carrying crates onto the porch. I grabbed his arm.

"What's really going on, Coke?"

"Your momma done got herself into trouble, Jo. A rich man wound up dead from a Mickey, and someone said she was with him."

"Who told the police that?"

"I don't know. If anything big happens, it will be in the paper. When you go to the grocery, you can pick one up. But make sure you take your pistol with you and case the house good and careful when you get back. Set some little signs for yourself so you know if someone been here since you left."

I lifted the shutters on the windows and pulled back the curtains. Cokie put the supplies in the kitchen.

"Now, don't worry your head. Willie just takin' precautions. You enjoy yourself out here. Get some rest and read all them books you brought. I'll be back in a sneeze to pick you up."

Mariah rolled down the thin drive, kicking dust around her rear. I stood on the porch watching, gripping Willie's shotgun.

THIRTY-EIGHT

I no longer wondered why Ray and Frieda were afraid of the dark. I was too.

Each night I walked down to their house at dusk and joined them in the car. I lay in the backseat and slept while they pretended to drive to Birmingham, Montgomery, and someplace new each night. I made them a big breakfast at sunrise and then walked the mile back to Shady Grove with my pillow. Each day at lunch, I'd walk to the grocer to check for messages and mail.

I loved Shady Grove and didn't miss New Orleans a bit. But I missed Patrick and wrote for updates on Charlie every day. A week passed, and I hadn't received a return letter from him. When I called Willie from the grocer's, she said Randolph had seen Charlie every day and that he had settled down and was sleeping a lot. She wouldn't tell me much about Mother, just that she returned, posted bond, and was staying at the Town and Country Motel. That meant she was with Cincinnati. Carlos

Marcello owned the Town and Country. Willie said she had sent Cokie out to Slidell to mail the typewritten letter for Miss Paulsen that Patrick had given her.

I tried phoning Patrick from the grocer, but no one answered.

I had just finished washing my hair when I heard the noise. It sounded like the rumble of an engine but then went quiet. I ran to the kitchen and grabbed the shotgun. I crept toward the front of the cottage and peered out the window. Nothing. I carefully pushed the screen door open with my bare foot. The hinges on the door complained, betraying my silence. I walked slowly out onto the porch, pointing the barrel of the gun in front of me at the drive. Something crackled on the side of the porch. I spun to my left, finger on the trigger.

"Whoa, easy there, now."

Jesse Thierry was standing next to his motorcycle by the side of the porch.

"I cut the engine on the drive and walked it down because I didn't want to scare you. Obviously that didn't work," he said.

I dropped the shotgun and let out a breath. "Look at you, locked and loaded, like Mae West of the Motor City."

It was hard to be angry when Jesse was funny. "I'm surprised to see you, that's all," I said.

"Hopefully it's a good surprise?"

"Sure. You drove all the way out here?"

Jesse took off his leather jacket and hung it over the seat of the motorcycle. "Weather's great, so it was nice. I ran into Willie in the Quarter yesterday and she gave me directions. She also said I have to report back to her." Jesse smiled. "So am I invited up on that porch, or are you still debating whether you want to shoot me?"

"No—I mean, yes, come up."

The words had barely come out of my mouth before Jesse jumped up and was at my side.

"I don't know how you do anything in those jeans," I told him.

"These? They're not tight, just shrink to fit. See, when you get a new pair, they never fit right, so you gotta get into a hot bath with 'em."

"You wear them in the bathtub?" I laughed.

"Yep. The hot water shrinks 'em to your body and then they fit perfectly."

"But you have to walk around in a wet pair of jeans all day."

"Just for one day." Jesse motioned to my hair. "Looks like you've been in the bath yourself." He settled into a chair on the front porch.

"I had just washed my hair, but then I had to go shoot someone. Do you want a cold drink?"

When I returned, Jesse was reading my book of Keats. We sat on the front porch playing cards and drinking iced tea. He said he'd seen Mother on Bourbon and that she looked thin and tired.

"That guy she's with looks rough, Jo."

"Cincinnati? He's worse than rough. He should be in jail. He's a task man for Marcello's crew. And my silly harlot of a mother adores him."

Jesse took another card. "I'll see your silly harlot of a mother and raise you a reckless alcoholic father. So reckless he wrapped his car around a tree. Killed my mother, busted up my foot, and scarred my face." Jesse put down his cards. "Gin."

"Oh, Jesse, I'm sorry. I didn't know."

"It's not your fault. It's not my fault. It's just the way it is. My foot's fine now. It's not like I'm three-toed Tyfee or something. But I'd never get into the service with it. How 'bout we play some poker?"

"Sure." I watched Jesse shuffle the cards, smiling at me. He said it wasn't his fault. I wished I could feel that way about Mother. I knew that I hadn't done anything wrong, but for some reason, I always felt guilty. Jesse dealt the cards to me, and I tried to remember all the poker hands.

"So," I said, "if you put my mother together with your father, that's a full house."

Jesse took a sip out of his glass, his eyes on me the entire time. "Sounds like a pretty empty house to me." He continued staring. "If the cops can pin it on your mom, it's a murder charge, Jo."

"I know. Willie's scared that they'll want me as a character witness. That's why she's hiding me out here."

"You feel safe?"

"I'm okay." Something inside of me wanted to admit to Jesse that I spent the night in the back of a rusted-out Buick on a fictional road to nowhere.

Jesse leaned back in the chair and looked out off the porch. "Gotta say, it's a beautiful hiding place. I wouldn't mind getting lost here at all. What's further down the road?"

"Want me to show you?"

THIRTY-NINE

I spread an undetectable layer of dirt on the front steps. That would allow me to see footprints or any trespassing while I was gone. I handed Jesse my pistol and asked him to put it in his leather jacket.

"Man, you're a regular Bonnie Parker."

"A dame that knows the ropes isn't likely to get tied up."

Jesse found that hysterical. "Did Willie say that?"

"Nope, Mae West. Now, how do I get on this thing in a skirt?"

Jesse wheeled the bike around. "I thought about driving the Merc out here, but I don't want you to see it until it's done. It's a great-looking car, Jo."

The clouds ran away and the sun burned overhead. Jesse explained how I should sit and where to put my feet. "Remember, keep your legs away from the muffler." He put on his sunglasses. "Now, you're gonna have to hold on to me. So try to control yourself, okay?"

"Very funny. Why don't I drive? Then you can be the one holding on."

"As much as I'd like that—and trust me, I really would—it's not a good idea. This is your first time on a bike." Jesse cranked up the Triumph, and I climbed on. I didn't plan to hold on to him, but as soon as the bike moved, I grabbed his waist. I could feel the laughter in his stomach. At the end of the driveway, I told him to take a left. We coasted down the road toward the crossing at Possum Trot. It was nothing like riding in a car. The sky was on top of us, and I could smell the leather of Jesse's jacket under the heat of the sun. The engine snarled. Jesse's left hand reached down and touched the top of mine.

"You okay?" he called out.

"Faster," I yelled back.

He responded, throwing the bike into gear and taking off, flying down the road like a bullet from a barrel. I had no choice but to hold on. I was terrified. And I loved it.

The air was all around us, blowing over my body, whipping through Jesse's hair and into mine. We pushed to the edge of recklessness, yet I felt safe. Safe from Cincinnati and safe from Mother. Riding with Jesse felt like letting a scream out of a bottle, and I didn't want it to end.

We finally approached the grocer. I squeezed his waist and pointed. He slowed down and pulled in.

I jumped off the bike.

"You okay?" asked Jesse.

"I loved it! My heart feels like it's gonna jump out of my chest. My skin is on fire."

"That's adrenaline. Sometimes I'll accelerate, feel that freedom in my face, and it's like I could ride forever." Jesse started to laugh. "Look at you."

"What?"

"You're smiling this huge smile, and your face is all flushed. Come on, I'll get you something to drink."

We stood next to each other at the soda cooler. I was still giddy from the ride and bumped him out of the way with my hip. He grabbed my arm and pulled himself back toward me.

"You better be nice, or I'll leave you out here," he whispered.

"Then I'll just walk back, like I do every day."

He looked surprised. "You walk all the way out here alone?"

"Every day. Me, myself, and I. Aren't you jealous?"

Jesse reached over and moved a piece of hair out of my eyes. "Yeah, I kinda am."

His hand lingered on my cheek. My eyes pulled to his.

"Hey, Josie. No messages today, but I got mail for you." The store owner handed me an envelope. I recognized Patrick's handwriting, turned my back to Jesse, and tore open the envelope.

> *Dear Jo,*
>
> *Sorry I haven't written sooner, but things have been busy. Charlie is sleeping a lot, but Randolph said that yesterday he walked around his room. I saw your mom on Chartres with some wiseguy. The cops brought the bandleader back from Baton Rouge for questioning, and he claimed he thought Mr. Hearne was asleep at the table, not dead. Capote threw a party before he left town and asked*

me to play piano. No mail from Smith yet. That's about all from here.

Miss you—Patrick

PS. Betty Lockwell has come by the shop twice. Write back and guess what she bought.

Jesse and I sat on the wooden steps of the small grocery, drinking root beer and throwing rocks at a tree. I imagined the tree was Betty Lockwell and nailed it, every single time. Each branch was an arm, a leg, then her head. Salted peanuts.

"So, how long have you been Patrick's girl?" asked Jesse.

I didn't feel like talking about Patrick, especially with Jesse. "I don't know," I told him.

I hurled a rock, taking out Betty's last remaining appendage.

"Does he kiss you right?"

I stopped and turned to him. "Excuse me?"

He gave me a smug smile. "That means no."

"And what about you? I'm sure you have lots of girlfriends."

"I'm not lonely. I don't have a girlfriend, though." Jesse took a swig from his bottle and leaned back on the steps. "That night at Dewey's, you said you were meeting your guy. I followed you. It was dark, and I wanted to make sure you were okay. You went all the way down to the river. He stood you up."

Jesse had followed me the night I took the watch to the river. "No, I—"

"Yeah, Jo, he never showed, and you started crying. And I stood there thinking, 'Man, this guy is so stupid.' So whatever upset you in that letter from him, just forget about it. You're moving on, and boy, Massachusetts has no idea what's coming for them. I bet you'll be the first Mae West they've ever had." Jesse drained the last of his root beer. "Come on, we better get going. I've got a three-hour ride ahead of me."

We drove back to Shady Grove, much slower on the return. I held on to Jesse and rested the side of my face on his back.

The dirt on the steps was undisturbed. The cottage lay quiet, asleep in an afternoon nap. We ate a sandwich on the porch in silence, staring at the shawls of Spanish moss blowing slowly back and forth from the branches of the oaks. Jesse returned my pistol, and I followed him back down the porch steps to his motorcycle.

"Oh, I almost forgot." He reached into his jacket and handed me a small card.

JESSE THIERRY
LUXURY AUTOMOTIVE SERVICE
TEL: RAYMOND 4001

"That guy Lockwell asked for my card, and I didn't have one. It got me thinking. Those Uptown guys could probably use a discreet mechanic, and I can charge handsome for it. I gave a card to Willie, and she says she can turn a lot of business my way. Sure beats selling flowers."

"That's a good hustle," I told him.

"We both got a little hustle, don't we?" He pulled on his jacket. "But I like to think we got more heart."

"I think it's great, Jesse. And you even have a telephone," I said.

"Nah, it's the neighbors'. They said they'd take the calls and come get me. Well, I'm gonna hit the road."

"Thanks for coming all the way out here and keeping me company."

"See ya, Jo." Jesse put on his sunglasses. "It was nice."

I sat on the steps and watched him drive away. I listened to the hum of the Triumph until it faded completely, replaced by a symphony of cicadas and bullfrogs. I sat until the sun dropped, then locked the door and began the walk down to Ray and Frieda's with my pillow.

We were on our way to Biloxi.

FORTY

Two days later, I received a postcard from Jesse.

> *Motor City. Mae West. Massachusetts.*
> *Jesse*

Part of me hoped Jesse would come back, but the other part of me hoped for another letter from Patrick. I finished the box of books. To appease my boredom, I cleaned the cottage several times over.

I stripped the bed in Willie's room, scrubbed the floors, washed the walls, and aired out the closets. I didn't dare reorganize anything. Willie wouldn't want me rummaging through her belongings. I did gently move the items in the drawers to wipe them. That's when I found the pictures. Tucked in the very back of Willie's top drawer was a yellowed envelope. Inside were three photographs.

The first was a tintype of a mature woman. She wore a long dark dress punctuated by a row of small buttons down the front. She stood with her arm resting on a column, her expression conveying the desire to beat the photographer with a wrench or some other blunt instrument. The word *Wilhelmina* was scratched into the back. I looked closely and thought I saw a shadow of Willie in her face.

The next photo had no name, just *1935* on the back. The man in the photo was incredibly handsome. I recognized the chair he sat in, but not the room. The chair was now Willie's chair in the parlor at the house on Conti.

The last photo was Willie, approximately ten years old, nestled in the crotch of a tree. Her hair poked out at all angles. Her face was abloom with mischievous happiness. Willie never spoke about her childhood. I stared at the picture, shocked that she had ever been a child at all. Somehow, I imagined Willie Woodley had been born with a rusty voice and street smarts to outwit any hustler. But here she was, a sweet child with a wide smile. What had happened to the Willie in the photo? I often longed to look at childhood photos of myself, but there weren't any. Mother never had my picture made.

I thought of the silver frames in Lockwell's home and office. They displayed his history for everyone to see. Willie had hers hidden in the back of a drawer. My history and dreams were on a list in my desk and, now, buried in the back garden.

The problem was taken care of. I had found an old praline tin in the kitchen. I wound life into Mr. Hearne's watch, set the time, and placed it inside the tin with his check. I could see

Forrest Hearne, hear his voice. He held out the check for Keats and Dickens, smiling at me, the watch peeking out beneath the shade of his shirtsleeve. Why didn't I wipe it clean of prints and just mail it back to his family? The address was on the check. His wife and children would cherish it. They would be so grateful.

I buried it near the crepe myrtle out back.

A horn blew. I recognized it immediately. I ran out onto the porch and watched as Cokie rolled up in Mariah. I jumped down the steps and threw my arms around him.

"It's so good to see you. Are you thirsty? Do you want something to eat?"

Cokie pulled from my grip. A solemn expression creased his face. "It's time to go back, Josie girl."

"Finally. I'm running out of food. Is Mother gone?"

Cokie hung his head. He spoke so quietly I couldn't hear him. "What did you say?"

He took a breath. "Mr. Charlie's dead."

I sat in the front seat of Mariah. My chest heaved. Warm tears slid down my face and onto my neck. Cokie said Charlie had taken a turn. Patrick and Randolph stayed up all night with him. Patrick was at his bedside, holding his hand, when he passed. Randolph called Willie. She and Cokie came over to help Patrick. Willie arranged for the undertaker, and the funeral would be tomorrow.

They all helped. Everyone was there. Except me.

Cokie brought the newspaper.

CHARLES MARLOWE—beloved son of the late Catherine and Nicholas Marlowe, brother of

the late Donald Marlowe, father of Patrick J. Marlowe, owner of Marlowe's Bookstore, author, aged 61 years and resident of this city for the past 39 years. Relatives and friends of the family are invited to attend the funeral, which will take place Wednesday, 11 o'clock A.M., at the funeral home of Jacob Schoen and Son, 3827 Canal Street. Interment in Greenwood Cemetery.

"You go ahead and cry, Josie girl. I done cried the whole ride down here. I know you wanted to be there. Now, your momma, she's still up to her neck, but Willie said you had to come back for Mr. Charlie's funeral."

"Of course I had to come back. This is wrong, Cokie. I should have been there for Charlie and Patrick. Willie had no right to keep me away."

"It's rough for Patrick, but I think he at peace. It was so hard for him, Mr. Charlie that sick and not bein' able to fix it."

Cokie drove me straight to Patrick's. He opened the door and I almost didn't recognize him. Grief had taken his face. He fell into my arms. Cokie helped me walk him back in the house and onto the couch. I put my arm around him and smoothed his hair.

"I'm so glad you're here," he said.

"Me too."

"He's gone, Jo. I knew it was bad, but . . . but I didn't think it would happen this quickly."

Sadie scurried around in Patrick's kitchen.

"Sadie's helpin' for tomorrow," said Cokie. "After the burial, folks will come here to eat. I'll be back in a bit. Now you take care, buddy." Cokie shuffled out the front door.

"Why do I have to entertain? My father just died," lamented Patrick. "I don't want to socialize."

"It's not entertaining. You're giving people the chance to express their condolences and comfort you." The words tasted sour. I agreed with Patrick. In New Orleans, sometimes death did feel more like socializing. And he knew better than anyone else. He frequented postmortem parties daily, trolling for books.

"Have you spoken to your mother?" I asked.

"We exchanged telegrams. She wants me to come to the West Indies, of course. But how can I? I have to throw a funeral party. I'm so grateful that Willie sent Sadie." He fell back and plopped his head into my lap. "Thank you, Sadie!" he yelled into the kitchen.

"She's mute, not deaf, Patrick."

He reached up and touched my face. "You don't know how happy I am to see you. I can't do this without you. You'll be with me tomorrow, right?"

"Every minute."

He ran his fingers across my cheek. "It's the strangest feeling. I'll be okay, feel strong, and then an hour later, something will happen and I'll completely break down. I feel ridiculous."

"You just lost your father." The word *father* caught in my throat. Suddenly I was crying, tears spilling everywhere. I pulled in breaths between sobs. "He took such good care of me. Who knows where I'd be if he hadn't given me the room above the shop."

Patrick pulled me down on the couch toward him. "I know, Jo. You lost him too."

We lay there, crying, until we both fell asleep.

FORTY-ONE

Funeral preparation was a surreal experience. Somehow, with the help of others, we got from face to face and place to place. But a thick, jellied haze draped about the day and distorted it into some kind of disturbing, slow-motion movie.

Miss Paulsen came as soon as she heard. She comforted Patrick and helped with the service arrangements. Willie spoke to the undertaker about Charlie's appearance. We all laced together—a brothel madam, an English professor, a mute cook, a quadroon cabbie, and me, the girl carrying a bucket of lies and throwing them like confetti.

Thanks to Willie, Charlie looked like himself again—sophisticated, literary. I borrowed a funeral dress from Sweety. Patrick asked Miss Paulsen to read a statement at the service. He didn't think he could do it. Miss Paulsen addressed the group in a poised manner, as she would her classroom.

"We are here today to honor the life and legacy of our dear

friend Charles Marlowe. His son, Patrick, has asked me to read a statement he has prepared." She cleared her throat.

"'I'm so grateful to all of you for your support during this difficult time. For most, my father's death probably came as a shock. In truth, my father had been suffering for several months, battling a degenerative brain condition. Although I know you must feel upset that you were not able to say your good-byes or extend offers of help, please know that the greatest gift you have given my father was the opportunity to endure this indignity privately. Those of you who know him know that he took pride in language, literary history, and professional appearance, all of which were lost to him in his final months.

"'My sincere thanks to Dr. Randolph Cox, Dr. Bertrand Sully, Willie Woodley, and Francis "Cokie" Coquard, all of whom helped my father in his final days. And I would never have been able to endure this dark journey without Josie Moraine. Josie was like a daughter to my father.

"'As many of you know, my father was a gifted author and bookseller. Fortunately, he lives on through his books. I know I will always take comfort in hearing his voice through his writing. Thank you all for coming today.'"

I was at Patrick's side the entire time. I turned and saw Willie and Cokie in the very back, Willie with her dark sunglasses, Cokie with tears streaming down his face. Willie approached me after the funeral. She looked tired and her ankles were puffy. She handed me a receipt.

"Here. I paid in cash. Tell Patrick everything's covered."

"Oh, Willie, I don't think Patrick would want you to pay."

"I don't care what he wants," said Willie. "It's what I want. I'll see you tomorrow. Get there early. The house is a pigsty."

"Aren't you going to the luncheon? Sadie prepared all sorts of food."

"I'm not going, and Sadie's not going either. What am I gonna do there, stand around eating ambrosia salad, talking about books? I've got a business to run. Elmo's bringing over a new bed frame. Dora broke hers last night. That girl should be in a sideshow, not a whorehouse."

Cokie waved to me as he left with Willie. He wouldn't be going to the luncheon either.

"Hi, Josie. Remember me?"

James from Doubleday Bookshop stood in front of me with a tall, attractive blonde.

"Yes. Hello, James. Thank you so much for coming. I know it means a lot to Patrick."

"This is my girlfriend, Kitty. I'll be coming to the house for lunch, but Kitty can't come. I wanted to introduce you," said James.

Kitty extended a gloved hand to me. She wore an expensive tailored suit with large pearl buttons. "Nice to meet you, Josie. Patrick's told us so much about you. He says you're like a sister. I'm so sorry for your loss." She gave me a smile. Her teeth were perfect, like Jesse's.

I nodded and they left. They looked like fashion dolls together. Perfect in appearance but plastic in attraction. Her words, "like a sister," scraped at me. Had Patrick really said that?

Very few went to the cemetery. Miss Paulsen said she couldn't bear it and instead went to the house to help prepare for the luncheon. Although she was upset, she said she understood why we had gone to such lengths to protect Charlie and found it very admirable.

Patrick stared at Charlie's grave. He looked solemn but beautiful in his dark suit. I looped my arm through his. "You take all the time you need."

We stood alone with Charlie for nearly an hour.

"There's so much I need to tell him. Things he didn't understand. But, no, there are Jell-O molds and pinwheel sandwiches waiting for us," complained Patrick. "It's payback for all the funeral luncheons I've gone to, hunting for books."

"Come on, you know Sadie doesn't make Jell-O," I told him.

The house was packed. The volume dipped when Patrick walked in, and people approached to again offer their condolences. I made my way in next to Patrick, and suddenly my feet stopped moving. In the corner. Near the punch bowl. I grabbed Patrick's arm.

Mother.

She wore a turquoise dress, much too loud for a funeral luncheon. Her hair was dyed a cheap shade of yellow, the roots dark and exposed. Her complexion was drawn and gray.

What was she doing here? I knew the answer. Food, free drinks, and—I couldn't help the thought—the opportunity to case the house. My eyes darted around for Cincinnati.

She cut straight for me, red nails wrapped around her punch glass.

"Baby girl!" She put her arm around me without actually

touching me and kissed the air near my cheek. I put my arms around her wilted frame. She recoiled at the contact.

"Mother, you're so thin."

"Dexedrine," she whispered. "It's a new diet pill that's being tested in Hollywood. It's workin' great. I think it'll be all the rage once it's approved. I can't believe there are so many people here. I mean, it's not like Charlie was somebody."

"He was very beloved, Mother. He was also a celebrated author."

"Well, book people, then. But they don't really count." She grabbed my wrist. "Where did you get that?" Her fingers quickly paraded over the gold watch from Willie. "That's fourteen carat. Let me try it on."

I gently pulled my arm away. "It was a gift."

Patrick turned around and stared at Mother. "Hello, Louise."

"Hi, there. I'm so sorry about your daddy. And how awful that he turned buck nutty like that. I've heard it can just happen"—she snapped her fingers—"like that. You poor thing, you must be so worried that it's in the blood. You could end up with it."

Patrick placed his hand on the small of my back and moved me closer to him. His face twisted with disgust. "You know, Louise, you've always been a piece of . . . work."

Miss Paulsen called Patrick over to her.

"He's turned bitter," said Mother. "Are you guys together? You little vixen, you're playin' two hands. I hear you're seeing Jesse Thierry too. Now, he's a dish. But if Pat's givin' you gifts like this watch, I'd stick with him mainly. There's bound to be more where that came from. But it's good to keep Jesse around too because he's the fun type."

I stared at Mother, desperately trying to figure out how we shared a genetic strand. But I knew we must, because despite her awfulness, there was a part of me that loved her somehow.

"I'm sure you've heard about all the garbage that's going on," said Mother.

"I did. Were you with that man from Memphis?"

"I wasn't with him, we had a drink together. It's not a crime to have a drink with someone." She drained her punch glass and set it in a planter. I picked it up.

"How did you meet him?"

"Oh, I don't even remember. Out and about. That night was such a blast it's all a blur." She leaned in close. "I have an alibi." She pronounced the word as if she'd rehearsed it.

"Was he a nice man?" I asked, needing to understand how my mother had intersected with Forrest Hearne.

"Nice? I don't know. He was rich. The kinda rich you know as soon as you see it. Hey, Cincinnati's in town, honey, maybe we can all go for dinner. He's pals with Diamond Jim Moran now. You heard of him? He's opening a restaurant here. He wears diamond everything, even his dental bridge has diamonds. I think Diamond Jim is single. Maybe we can all go on a double date."

Thankfully, Miss Paulsen approached, so I didn't have to respond to my mother's insidious suggestion. "Everything well, Josie?" she asked.

"Miss Paulsen, this is"—I paused, swallowing the lie that was about to take flight—"this is my mother, Louise."

"Lovely to meet you," said Miss Paulsen in her crisp tone.

"Mother, Miss Paulsen is a professor of English at Loyola."

Mother fished a wrapperless piece of chewing gum from her purse and started smacking on it.

"Oh, that's nice. I'm in from Hollywood. You've probably seen my picture in the paper."

"I can't say that I have," said Miss Paulsen. "Louise, your daughter is quite impressive. You must be very proud."

"Yeah, she's a real good girl. She just needs to learn to doll herself up more, classy-like. Did you know she's named after the classiest madam in Storyville?" She nudged my arm in pride. "Is there any vodka? I think I'd like a Bloody Mary." Mother wandered toward the kitchen.

There I stood, turned completely wrong side out in front of Miss Paulsen. A dignified professor, an alumna of Smith, and my filthy laundry flapping in her face.

She reached out and gently took my hand. "I think we understand each other very well now, Josie."

FORTY-TWO

Still no mail from Smith. I received another letter from Charlotte asking if I'd like to join her family in the Berkshires over the summer. I had no idea where the Berkshires were and had to look it up. It sounded expensive and would certainly be costly to get there. And then I'd need appropriate clothes, clothes that I didn't have and couldn't afford.

The door opened and Betty Lockwell sauntered into the shop with her sour-apple smile and rail-thin limbs poking out of an obviously pricey dress. I thought I had knocked her arms off back at the tree.

"Hello," she said, looking around the shop for Patrick. "Remind me of your name."

"Jo."

"That's right, Jo."

"Patrick's not here," I told her.

Her bottom lip pouted. "Oh, that's a shame. He recommended a book he said I'd like. But it was out of stock. Ted Capote."

"It's in now." I pulled the book from the display and handed it to her. She turned it over and saw the controversial photo of the nubile Capote, lounging on the back cover, staring into the camera.

"Wow, he's young. When will Patrick be here?"

"Perhaps you haven't heard, Betty. Patrick lost his father. The funeral was last week." I couldn't help myself and added, "He may go to the West Indies to see his mother."

"The West Indies? Well, that's no good."

John Lockwell burst through the door, his scowling son, Richard, in tow. "Come on, Betty, I told you we didn't have time. The car is running, and I'm burning gasoline." Mr. Lockwell saw me and stopped. "Well, hello there, Josephine. How are you?"

"How do you know her?" asked Betty.

I jumped in quickly. "I met your father when Charlotte invited me to your party." Mr. Lockwell gave me a grin. "I'm fine, Mr. Lockwell, how are you?"

"I'm just fine, too." He sauntered to the counter. "What's news?" He loved the secret elasticity between us. Richard watched, eating his fingernails near the door.

"No news on my end. How's business?" I asked.

"Better than ever. Lots to celebrate. Have you heard from Charlotte lately?"

"Yes, just yesterday. She's invited me to the Berkshires this summer."

Betty looked from me to her father, disgusted by our comfortable conversation.

"That sounds mighty fine. You'll need some nice shoes for the Berkshires, won't you?"

"I imagine I will."

"What are you talking about?" Betty asked her father.

He ignored her and leaned on the counter. He pointed to my arm. "That's a nice watch. Did one of your boyfriends give you that?"

I shot a look at Betty. "Patrick gave it to me for my birthday. He's so good to me." Richard Lockwell laughed. "Can I ring that book up for you, Betty?" I asked.

Mr. Lockwell took the book from Betty, saw the photo, and tossed it on the counter. "You're not getting that. That's trash."

"You would know," said Betty. She turned and stormed out of the store. Richard followed.

Lockwell shook his head. "Lilly has completely ruined that girl. Well, I'll be going. It's good to know you actually do work here." He lowered his voice. "I have a place just over on St. Peter now. You let me know if you'd ever like to . . . meet up." He grinned and left the shop.

Betty Lockwell and I actually agreed on something. I put my knuckles on the counter, signaling trash.

Cokie arrived at closing time.

"You about closed up?" he asked.

"Just about. Do me a favor and flip the sign in the window."

Cokie turned the sign to read CLOSED. He locked the door.

"Now, I got some business," said Cokie. He marched to the counter and held out his hands. "See these?"

I looked at Cokie's palms, lined deep and weathered.

"Them is some mojo hands. After Mr. Charlie's funeral, girl,

I was so blue I had to get me some fun. So I jumped into a couple games and, oooeee, I was rollin'. For three days straight, I was doublin' and winnin'. Cornbread say he ain't never seen nothin' like it. I quit just when I felt the devil himself tempting me to bet it all. I knew right then why I won that money and what I was goin' do with the pot. Josie girl, pack that thermos, you goin' to Smith College."

He pulled an envelope from his jacket and laid it on the counter.

I stared at the fat, wrinkly envelope. "Cokie, what is this?"

"Well, let's see now. It's money for the classes and money for the house you gotta live in."

"What?"

"I was a fix short, so I passed the hat with the close group. Cornbread helped. Sweety and Sadie put in too. We know Sadie ain't goin' tell nobody."

"Does Willie know?"

"No, and she don't need to know. I made sure to stay clear of Frankie so he wouldn't go sellin' secrets to her. I love Willie, but she stuck on keepin' you here in New Orleans."

I reached for the envelope and lifted the back flap with my thumb. A wad of bills fanned open from the thick stack.

"This whole thing with your momma's about to pop. She gone from bad to worse. Willie's done right by keeping you out the skittle. Massachusetts is a good distance."

I couldn't accept the money. I looked at Cokie to tell him so. His eyes were dancing, just like they were on my birthday when he brought me the thermos and the map. He wanted this just as much, maybe more, than I did. And he believed in me. I looked at the envelope.

I screamed and ran out from behind the counter and threw my arms around him. "Thank you!" We jumped up and down together, hooting and hollering.

He spun away and started to snap his fingers, "Josie girl, you goin' to Boston, so don't you jive on me."

FORTY-THREE

I hid the envelope in the floorboard and ran to Patrick's. I couldn't wait to tell him. We had discussed the issue of money, and he'd suggested selling some of Charlie's things to help. Now he didn't have to.

I knocked. There was no answer. I used my key and peeked in. "Patrick?" I said. Nothing.

"Up here," he called.

I ran up the oak stairs, leaping them two at a time. He was in Charlie's room, sitting on the floor against the bed. His face was puffy.

"It's so hard," he said. "I know I should clear all this out, but I just can't do it."

"It's too soon," I told him. "Why do you need to do it now?"

"I keep thinking the sooner I have a fresh start, the sooner I'll feel better, but now everything I look at has a memory tied to it."

I walked around the room, running my finger across

Charlie's dresser and past the framed photograph of Patrick's grandmother. I picked up the heart-shaped Valentine box and hugged it to my chest. The window over the desk was open. The page fluttered in the typewriter.

BLV

"Patrick, did you see this? There's another letter. When did he type that?"

"Yeah, I saw it. It must have been when Randolph was here. Take it if you want it. I have the manuscript."

I pulled the paper from the typewriter and sat down next to him on the floor. "I have some news that may cheer you up."

He perked a bit. "You got your acceptance?"

"No, but I got the money. Cokie had a huge streak throwing dice, and he gave it to me."

"Jo, that's great. I'm so happy for you."

But he didn't look happy. He looked completely miserable. Of course he did. He had just lost his father, and now I was talking about moving halfway across the country.

"I'm sad too. But don't worry, I'll be here to help you take care of Charlie's things. I'll come home on holidays, and you'll of course visit me out there. We'll tour Massachusetts hunting for books. It'll be so much fun." I put my hand on his leg. "I'm so happy with the way things have turned out with us. I can't believe I've been so oblivious all these years." I moved in to kiss him.

"Jo . . ." He stopped me and hung his head. His shoulders swayed. He was crying.

"What is it?" I asked.

Tears dropped from his eyes. "I'm so sorry, Jo. If I could, I would . . . choose you."

The tips of my fingers went cold. *Choose.* Verb. To decide from a range of options. I looked at him. "There's someone else?"

He was silent for a while, then nodded. "I feel so horrible. I'm awful." Patrick's crying deepened into heavy sobs. He cried so hard his entire body shook.

I sat motionless, my bruised pride battling my desire to comfort my best friend.

"I don't know how it happened. It's all such a mess. I've hurt so many people," he sobbed. He looked at me. "James," he whispered.

I searched his frantic eyes, and suddenly I understood.

I looked away from him. "Does James know how you feel?"

"I think so."

My throat pulled closed, the words wrestling with the lump in my windpipe. "I met Kitty at the funeral," I whispered. "I didn't feel a spark between them. Maybe it's okay."

Patrick's eyes met mine. "You're not upset?"

I pulled in a breath. "I feel ridiculous that you felt like you had to pretend with me. But Kitty's a gorgeous girl—I thought so when I met her. And she's smart. How can I blame you for being in love with her? But you'll have to be up front with James. Be honest. Once you do that, you'll feel so much better."

Patrick stared at me and then looked into his lap.

Embarrassed and a bit humiliated, that's how I felt, and disappointed. Patrick and I made so much sense together. We were comfortable, and he had kissed me. I had constructed the entire scenario in my head of how our relationship would grow and progress. I felt stupid for ever thinking those things. Patrick's heart belonged to someone else. Sure, Betty Lockwell was an annoying nuisance, but Kitty was a sophisticated young woman.

The conversation dissolved into awkward silence. I picked up Charlie's heart-shaped box. The red plastic flowers on the top were deformed from months of affection. I pulled off the lid.

I stared down into the box. "Where did he get them?"

Patrick shrugged.

Inside were a pair of Siamese acorns, their beret caps touching, fused at the neck, growing into and out of each other.

We sat on the hardwood floor in silence, our heads resting against Charlie's bed. The voices and claps from a children's stickball game filtered in through the open window and floated in front of us on particles of sunlit dust.

I looked at the sheet of paper in my lap. *"B-L-V,"* I read aloud, trying to stir the uncomfortable silence. "Do you think it's *Believe*?" I asked.

He turned slowly to me. "No, I know what it is."

"You do?"

Patrick nodded. "It's the title of the first chapter in the book he was working on. *Be Love*," he said quietly.

I stared at the sheet of paper and the acorns. I put my arm around Patrick and kissed his head.

And he cried.

FORTY-FOUR

Patrick wanted someone else. I wanted him to be happy, but why couldn't he be happy with me? I knew the answer. He couldn't choose me. Patrick wanted a literary life of travel, learning, and social substance. I was a scrappy girl from the Quarter, trying to make good. No matter how I parted my hair, I couldn't part from the crack I had crawled out of.

I wished I had a friend in the Quarter, someone like Charlotte. Someone I could share secrets with, collapse on her bedroom floor, and spill my guts about Patrick to. I saw so many girls walking arm in arm, laughing, an inexplicable closeness and comfort that they had a protector and confidante. They had someone they could count on.

A man leaned against a car outside the bookshop. He saw me approach and walked to meet me on the sidewalk. It was Detective Langley.

"Miss Moraine. I'm glad I waited. I was hoping I could ask you some additional questions."

I looked up and down the street, checking to see who was around to report to Frankie.

"We can step inside the shop if you like," he said.

I unlocked the door, turned on the lights, and walked to the counter. I sucked in a breath to calm my nerves. "What can I help you with, Detective?"

He mopped his wet brow and took out a tattered notepad. "The day you came to the station, you said that Mr. Hearne bought two books."

I nodded.

"Yeah, the books were found in his hotel room, and there was a receipt in one of them. His wife has told us that the check never cleared. She thought that was odd. The check is listed in the checkbook register that was found on him."

My mind raced, trying to catch up with my heart. I pointed to the sign near the register. "We don't take checks, Detective. Perhaps Mr. Hearne wrote the check before he saw the sign and then paid in cash?"

He pointed his pen to the sign. "That's gotta be it. Thank you."

"I'll show you out."

"One more thing." He rubbed his head. "I'm sure you know that your mother is being questioned. She was seen with Hearne the night of his death. Do you know where your mother was on New Year's Eve, Miss Moraine?"

I looked at Detective Langley. His story was obvious. Every Sunday he'd drive to his mother's for dinner. His mother, probably named Ethel, had meaty ankles, weary gray curls, and wore a flowered housedress. A wiry black hair sprouted from the mole on her chin. She'd shuffle around a hot kitchen all day in preparation for her son's weekly visit. She'd make something special, perhaps with frothy meringue, for dessert. He'd eat every bite. After his car pulled away, Ethel would wash the dishes, allow herself a slug of blackberry wine, and then fall asleep in the living room chair, still wearing her apron.

"Miss Moraine?" He interrupted my thoughts. "I asked if you know where your mother was on New Year's Eve."

"Have you met my mother, Detective?" I asked.

"Yes, I have."

"Then I'm sure you won't be surprised when I tell you that we have been estranged for quite some time. I've lived upstairs in this bookshop since I was twelve years old." I stared at the detective. "I've never spent New Year's Eve with my mother, and I have no idea where she was."

He put his pen in his ear to scratch an itch or dislodge some wax. "Well, the chief wanted me to come talk to you. I told him he was going to a goat's house for wool, but he's got a checklist, you know."

Coming to me was like going to a goat's house?

"So, Miss Moraine, if you weren't with your mother, where were you on New Year's Eve?"

"I was right here, upstairs in my room." I motioned toward the back stairs and regretted it the moment my hand moved.

Detective Langley looked toward the stairs at the back of the shop. What if he wanted to search my room? How would I explain thousands of dollars in Cokie's gambling money in my floorboard? He would probably think it was the cash missing from Mr. Hearne. Droplets of perspiration popped at the back of my neck.

He leaned on the counter. "Did anyone see you here on New Year's Eve?"

"Yes, Patrick Marlowe, the owner of the shop. He came by with a friend around midnight."

"Did you all go out then?"

"No, Patrick will tell you I was quite indisposed, in my nightgown and hairpins."

The detective chewed his lip in thought. I could practically see the dim lightbulb buzzing above his head. "What if I told you that someone saw you out on New Year's Eve?" he said.

"I would say they were lying, hoping to pressure me into telling you something different. I have told you the facts, Detective. I was here, all night, on New Year's Eve. You can speak to Patrick Marlowe and James from Doubleday Bookshop. They both saw me here."

I almost felt bad for the guy. He'd never stay afloat in the Quarter with such transparent methods.

He thanked me for my time and left. I locked the door, turned out the lights, and watched him drive away. Then I ran across the street to call Willie.

I recounted all the details.

"He just left?" she asked.

"Yes, he just drove away."

"They're still digging. They don't have anything," she said.

"Willie, does Mother have an alibi?"

"Trust me, you don't want what your mother has. Go back and lock your doors." She hung up the phone.

I ran across the dark street. I fumbled with my keys, trying to find the right one in the low light. I heard a noise. My hair tore from my scalp as I was yanked and slammed up against the glass door. I felt something hard in my back.

"Hey, Crazy Josie. That was a bad, bad move. You really think it's wise to go talkin' to the police?" Cincinnati's sour breath was hot in my ear.

"I wasn't talking to the police."

He shoved me into the door again. "I saw you. I stood and watched you talk to that copper." His hand was on the back of my head, shoving the side of my face into the glass.

"I wasn't talking to him. He just . . . asked me a question."

He slapped his knife on the door next to my eye. "You," he whispered, "are a liar."

My body shuddered.

I saw a couple walking toward us down Royal and opened my mouth to scream. Cincinnati jerked me off the door, slung his arm around my neck, and forced me to walk with him.

"Don't even think about screaming," he said through his teeth.

I tried to follow his paces, my face practically wrenched in a headlock. His left hand held the blade of his knife at my waistline. I felt the sting of the tip against me. We walked a block up to Bourbon Street, and he pushed me into a small bar. I saw my mother sitting at a table in the back near a window, a litter of empty glasses in front of her.

He threw me into a chair and quickly pulled one up behind.

"Look what I found," said Cincinnati.

"Hi, Jo." Mother sounded sleepy. Her blue-shadowed lids bobbed like the last flaps of a dead bird.

"I told you that was the detective who drove by. And when I looked, guess who was chatting him up?" Cincinnati lit a cigarette and blew the smoke in my face.

Mother sat up, her tone shifting slightly. "Why were you talking to the detective, Jo?"

I slid my chair away from Cincinnati and closer to my mother. "The day Mr. Hearne died, he came to the shop. He bought two books. The police found the books and the receipt in his hotel room. The detective came to ask me about them."

"Just now they came to ask you?" said Cincinnati. "Why didn't they come earlier?"

"I don't know," I said, looking at my mother. I couldn't stand to look at Cincinnati.

Mother reached for Cincinnati's hand. "See, baby? That's nothing. They just asked about books."

"Shut up, Louise. She's lyin'. The kid's slick like me, not stupid like you."

"I'm not stupid," contested Mother. "You're stupid."

"You watch your mouth."

Mother pouted. "Well, I'm no longer a suspect. They confirmed my alibi, and we'll be goin' back to Hollywood. This town's just too small for us," she told me.

"When are you leaving?" I asked.

"Tomorrow morning," said Cincinnati. "Why, you wanna come with us, Crazy Josie?" He put his hand on my thigh. I threw it off.

"I don't want to leave in the morning," whined Mother. "I

want to have dinner at Commander's Palace tomorrow. I want all those Uptown women to see me and know I'm on my way back to Hollywood."

"Shut your piehole. I told you, we have to get out of here. If you keep your mouth shut, I'll take you to the Mocambo when we get back to Hollywood."

Mother smiled, accepting the compromise. "Cinci's got in real good with some fellas in Los Angeles." Her eyes wandered like an impatient child. "Where's that pretty watch?"

"In my room. I don't wear it often. It's a bit fancy."

"You should give it to me, then. I'd wear it all the time."

"I had a nice watch comin' to me once, but your momma lost it," said Cincinnati.

"I didn't lose it!" snapped Mother. "Evangeline must have stolen it. I told you that a million times."

"Or maybe Crazy Josie found it, sold it, and bought herself a nice watch." Cincinnati stared at me.

"Mine was a gift." I looked at Mother. "For my eighteenth birthday."

"Ooh, you're legal now." Cincinnati snickered.

A uniformed police officer appeared in the doorway, greeting a friend at a nearby table.

I stood up. "Have a safe trip to California, Mother." I leaned over and kissed her cheek. "Please send me your address so I can write to you." I walked as fast as I could without jogging. As soon as I was outside, I pulled my gun from under my skirt and ran.

The heat from Cincinnati's hand hung on my thigh, and the

evening air crept in through the knife slice in my blouse. I ran past the Sans Souci and thought of Forrest Hearne, sitting dead at the table.

Whether I shall turn out to be the hero of my own life, or whether that station will be held by anybody else, these pages must show.

FORTY-FIVE

His words were stuck in my head, running on a repeat loop. *The kid's slick like me, not stupid like you.*

The fact that Cincinnati thought I resembled him in any way sickened me. It made me want to run and hide. When I was a child in Detroit and terrors chased me, I would run to my hiding spot, a crawl space under the front porch of the boardinghouse we lived in. I'd wedge my small body into the cool brown earth and lie there, escaping the ugliness that was inevitably going on above me. I'd plug my ears with my fingers and hum to block out the remnants of Mother's toxic tongue or sharp backhand. It became a habit, humming, and a decade later, I was still doing it. Life had turned cold again, the safety of the cocoon under the porch was gone, and lying in the dirt had become a metaphor for my life.

Shady Grove was my tunnel under the porch now. But it was too far to run to all the time. When I returned to the shop after running from Cincinnati, I found a piece of paper on the floor under the mail slot.

> *Is it official? Are you Massachusetts instead of Motor City?*
>
> *Jesse*

I wanted to be Massachusetts. I still wanted to believe it was possible, that my wings, no matter how thin and torn, could still somehow carry me away from a life of lies and perverted men. I wanted to use my mind for study and research instead of trickery and street hustle.

I thought about visiting Jesse, but felt guilty. Was I thinking of him only because Patrick didn't want me?

"Your mother's in way over her head," Willie said the next morning. She handed me the black book to put in the hiding box behind the mirror. "She thinks she's tying into something glamorous, that she's a gangster's moll and her boyfriend's some Al Capone. That horse's ass thinks he's big time, pulling favors. He's a flimsy pawn, too stupid to realize the hand's on his own back now."

The black hand. That's what Willie was talking about. In New Orleans, a black handprint meant you were marked, a threat for all to see unless you complied with the mob and whatever Carlos Marcello wanted. I saw one on a door once, on Esplanade. It gave me gooseflesh, knowing the person's life was in danger, wondering how someone could be so senseless as to mess with the mob.

"Mother wanted to stay and have dinner at Commander's Palace tonight," I told Willie.

"Are you kidding me? We better hope, for all our sakes, that they're halfway to California by tonight," said Willie. She settled against her pillows. "I think I'll sleep another hour. I've earned it."

I opened the door and prepared to take the coffee tray back into the kitchen. The echo of a gusty belch bounced in through the door.

"What the hell was that?" said Willie, reaching for her gun.

"It's just Dora. She's drinking soda water, says she has gas from the red beans and rice she ate after the johns left."

Willie waved the gun in the air. "I swear to you, I'm an inch from selling her to P. T. Barnum. You hear me?" She stuffed the gun back under her pillow and lay down. "Get out. Tell Dora to take her gas leak up to her room or I'll send a wagon for her."

I walked into the kitchen. "Willie says to take your gas leak up to your room."

"Well, I can't sleep, hon. I need to get this out." She waved a hand at me. "Jo," she whispered, pointing to Sadie, whose back was turned at the stove. Dora took a gulp of soda water and swallowed hard. A few seconds later a thunderous burp rattled the kitchen. Sadie nearly jumped out of her skin. She turned, furious, and started beating Dora with a wooden spoon. Dora ran from the kitchen laughing, her trail nothing but a whirl of shamrock satin.

Sadie took the tray from me. "Sadie," I whispered, "I haven't had a chance to thank you."

She looked at me with a puzzled expression.

"For your contribution, the money you gave Cokie."

She put her hand up and shook her head. That meant the conversation was over. But I caught her smiling as she put the dishes in the sink.

I walked back to the shop, watching for the postman on the way. Shouldn't I have heard from Smith by now? Patrick was behind the counter sorting a box of books when I arrived at the store. I wanted to dash to my room, avoid him altogether.

"Jo, I'm so glad you're here. I was worried that you wouldn't come."

"I live here, Patrick."

"You know what I mean," he said. "I want to apologize for everything. My mind is all over the place these days."

I moved toward the counter. "It's understandable. Your father just died."

"I just need some time. I've decided to take my mother up on her invitation, stay with her awhile."

"For how long?" I asked.

"Until Christmas."

"Christmas? That's a long time."

"I'm going to the Florida Keys first, to take some things to Charlie's friends. I'll stay a week, then sail to Havana to meet my mom and her husband for vacation. From there we'll go on to Trinidad. That's where they live now. Mom's husband has an oil deal there."

"What will you do in Trinidad?"

"Get my head together. Randolph says the US may go into Korea. Maybe I'll enlist when I come back. I don't know."

Patrick in the service? I tried to think of the goat and sheep reference Detective Langley had used. I could definitely see Jesse in the military. He'd make a good soldier. But Patrick?

"Randolph told me some of the divisions set up musical outfits during the war," said Patrick.

"Oh, so you'd go as a musician, not a soldier."

"Well, no, I'd be both." Patrick fiddled with a piece of paper on the counter in front of him. "What, sounds kinda crazy?"

Patrick in the military. Yes, it sounded completely ridiculous. "You know what?" I said. "Me at Smith and you in the military. They're both crazy." I started to laugh.

Patrick broke into laughter too. "We'll swap pictures, you in a monogrammed sweater and me in a uniform." The thought of Patrick in a uniform made me howl. A woman walked in front of the shop. We threw our hands down on the counter trying to beat each other to the signal. Patrick's knees were bent, practically in a lunge. I had dropped my purse on the floor in excitement. We both had our pinky fingers on the counter. Romance. We roared with laughter, so loud and raucous that the woman took her hand off the door and scurried away.

"Come back!" yelled Patrick. "I'll wrap them in a paper bag for you. No one will see."

"Stop, my stomach hurts," I told him. I picked my purse up off the floor.

"I'm gonna miss that," said Patrick. His face became more serious. "I've wanted to tell you something. Doubleday has offered to buy a large part of our inventory. I need to give them an answer by tomorrow. I think I'm going to do it."

"You're selling the shop?"

"Not the shop, just a lot of the books. I'll be gone, and you'll be at Smith. If I decide to stick around once I come back, I'll just buy more inventory. You know I love the buying, the hunt."

"Sure," I said. I looked around the shop, sad to think of the shelves half empty.

"Jo, I was hoping that we could keep our conversation the other day between us. I'm leaving, so what I told you doesn't really matter now anyway."

I looked at Patrick. Leaving meant he wouldn't be able to see Kitty, the girl he loved, but he also wouldn't risk betraying his friend James. It was honorable. "I won't tell," I told him.

"I have to send a telegram to my mother. Can you watch the shop?" he asked me.

"Sure. Just let me change. I'm filthy from Willie's."

I walked past the stacks of books and up the stairs, suddenly feeling a deep attachment to all of them, wondering which ones I'd have to visit on the shelves at Doubleday. My door swung open when I put the key in the lock. I stepped back. I had not forgotten to lock my door.

I kicked the door open with my foot and peered inside from the landing. The curtain lifted and swayed in the cross breeze of the cracked window over my desk. I slowly stepped into the room. My eyes immediately fastened on the green Adler's box, lying on the floor next to my desk. The hinges were popped open, the bed of white satin holding nothing but the cradle imprint where the watch used to sit. I looked toward the closet in the room. It was open a crack. I backed up toward my chest of drawers, eyes on the closet, and quietly pulled open the small top drawer. Arm behind my back, I inserted my hand. I pushed back deeper into the drawer. My pistol was gone. The closet door moved slightly. I crept toward it and grabbed the bat leaning up against my desk. Curling my fingers around the handle, I raised the barrel above my shoulder. I threw open the closet.

No one was there.

I released my breath and lowered the bat. I reached down to pick up the watch box. That's when I saw it.

My bed was moved. Just a tiny bit. Nearly undetectable. I threw down the box and dove under my bed. I was so frantic I could barely pull up the floorboard. I plunged my hand down into the floor and pulled it back up holding the wrinkled envelope.

The money was gone.

FORTY-SIX

The room lost shape. The screams erupted out of me, deep and wild, as if they were pulled from the core of the earth, up through the floor, and released through my mouth. My body shook violently as the realization of what had happened came together in front of me.

She took it. She took everything. Right now she was gliding down the highway, a red polka dot scarf around her fried hair. Her wrist, wan from Dexedrine, rested on the open window, dangling a watch with the words *Jo is 18* engraved on the back.

"Jo, you scared me to death." Patrick ran to the window and pulled it shut. "Calm down. People will think you're being murdered up here."

He put his hands on my shoulders. "Jo, stop." He shook me, hard. "Stop it."

I fought him. The frustration that was my life seared out of me in a fury so absolute I couldn't contain it. Patrick jumped away, his back against the closet door, eyes wide with panic.

My screams fell to growls, then to whimpers, ending in sobs as I sank to the floor.

He knelt beside me.

"It's all gone," I gasped between sobs. "They took the money from Cokie. All of it."

"Who took it?" asked Patrick.

I looked up at him. "Mother."

I lay on the hardwood floor all afternoon, holding the green box, staring at the ceiling.

Patrick helped customers downstairs in the shop, and I listened, hollow, the conversations entering my ears and bouncing within my corpse of a body. Jesse came by. Patrick told him I was upstairs sick. Cokie came by. He told him I was delivering an order of books. My back hurt from hours on the floor, but I didn't care. It was punishment for my stupidity. Of course my mother knew my hiding places. Ten years ago, it was a pink coin purse under my bed. Today it was thousands of dollars. How would I ever explain to Cokie that the money was gone, to Willie that the watch was gone? And now an acceptance to Smith would just be a cruel joke. I wouldn't have the money to go.

Long light from the late afternoon sun pooled across the floor. Patrick tapped on my door.

"Hey, you sure you won't come to the house with me?"

I shook my head.

He set two bags on the floor. "This one has a sandwich." He emptied the other, larger bag onto the floor. The contents made a loud clanking noise. "I went by the hardware store." He lifted up some chains. "When I leave, I want you to come downstairs and chain the doors on the inside. You'll lock them with this padlock and bring the key up to your room. That will make you feel a little safer, okay?"

I nodded but said nothing.

He walked toward the door.

"Patrick." He stopped. "I need to ask you something." I turned my head toward him at the door. "Did you kiss me out of pity?"

He opened his mouth, then looked down at his feet. "No, Jo. It's not like that at all."

I closed my eyes and turned my head from him. I wouldn't look back, even though I could feel he was standing there, wanting to elaborate or explain. He stood for a long while, waiting. Finally I heard his footsteps on the stairs, and I opened my eyes, allowing the tears to stream down onto the hardwood floor.

FORTY-SEVEN

I avoided everyone for days. My heart cracked open each time Cokie asked if I had heard from Smith. Sweety and Dora constantly asked if something was wrong. Sadie looked at me funny, and even Evangeline asked if I was sick. Willie came right out and yelled at me.

"You think you're the only one with problems, kid? I'm sick of you being a sourpuss. Is this because Patrick's going away to see his mother? Stop with the dramatics already."

I kept to myself and stayed upstairs in my room, the door of the shop chained and bolted. I was reading the latest letter from Charlotte when I heard the yell.

"Hey, Motor City!"

It was Jesse. Again. He came by every day and yelled up to my window. I never answered. Tonight my light was on, so he knew I was there. He continued to yell, "Hey, Motor City," louder and louder alternating between high voices, low voices, even singing it.

"Shut up!" someone called from a nearby window.

"Get her to come down, and I'll shut up," he yelled back. He called out again.

"Come on, girlie, get down here before we have to call the cops on this guy," someone else yelled.

"Ya hear that, Jo? They're callin' the cops," yelled Jesse.

He was so infuriating. I marched to the window and threw back the curtains. A crowd had gathered around Jesse on the street, and they all cheered when I appeared. I opened the window, and people started calling to me.

"Come on, doll, come down for the poor fella."

"Josie, please come down so he stops the racket. I gotta work in the morning."

As I removed the lock and chains from the doors, the people dispersed in the street.

Jesse laughed, smiling wide. "I'm sorry, Jo. Don't be mad."

I wouldn't look at him. He reached out as if he was punching my arm. "Are you going to invite me in?"

"No." I closed the door and sat on the step in front of the shop. Jesse dropped down next to me.

"I thought you might say that. So I came prepared." Jesse produced two bottles of soda from his jacket, popped the tops off with a key, and handed one to me. I turned the bottle in my hand. *Coca-Cola Bottling, Chattanooga, Tenn* was written on the green glass bottle. Tennessee. It made me think of Mr. Hearne—and his watch ticking under the crepe myrtle at Shady Grove.

Jesse extended his bottle toward mine for a toast. "Kicks."

"Kicks." I nodded.

We sat and drank in silence. It was something I appreciated about Jesse. He didn't feel the need to fill every moment with talk or some sort of silly exchange. We could just sit saying nothing, him reclining back against the door, his motorcycle boots crossed at the ankles and me balancing the glass bottle on my knee. It was just like on the bench in Jackson Square and on the porch at Shady Grove. And for some reason, the silence made me want to tell him everything.

"I haven't been sick."

He nodded and gestured with his bottle toward the chains near my feet.

"Pretty serious chains you got there. Saw them on the door for the past week. Everything okay?"

I shook my head. "I was robbed."

Jesse leaned forward. "You okay?"

I shrugged.

"Were you here when it happened?" he asked.

"No, it was early. I was at Willie's."

"You know the guys who did it?"

I nodded slowly and took a swallow of soda.

"Tell me." Jesse's hand balled into a fist.

I turned to him. The glow of the streetlamp threw light on his face. With the exception of the scar, his skin was flawless. The light on his hair reflected a shiny sienna.

"Tell me, Jo." His eyes, usually mischievous, were steady on mine.

It was Jesse. I could tell him. "It was my mother."

His knee bobbed, and his head dipped for a moment,

acknowledging he understood the situation. "With her boyfriend?" he asked.

"Oh, I'm sure."

He was quiet for a while. "What'd they take?" he finally asked.

I wasn't emotional anymore, just numb with disgust. "Let's see, they took the watch from Adler's that Willie gave me for my eighteenth birthday, they took my pistol, they took a cigar box with my money, and"—I looked at Jesse—"they took an envelope with two thousand dollars. Two thousand dollars that Cokie, Sadie, and Sweety had given me to pay for my first year at Smith."

The look on Jesse's face wasn't surprise or shock, just loath understanding.

"Jo, your momma's guy is up in it. People say he's part of the crew who micked that fella from Tennessee on New Year's Eve. Rolled your mom into it, too."

"Yeah, but he had never seen my watch. He didn't know that since I was a little girl, I've hidden things under my bed. That's something only my mother knew."

Jesse rolled a bottle cap between his thumb and forefinger. "I get it, you know. When I was six, my dad found my collection of baseball cards hidden in my closet. He sold them for booze."

"Exactly," I said.

A couple of cars passed by, their headlights illuminating pieces of trash in the street.

"So, you got accepted to that college?"

"No, I haven't heard yet. But what does it matter? I don't

have the money to go, and now I have to find a way to pay Cokie back."

"Well, wait a minute. Maybe you could get a scholarship," said Jesse.

"Doubtful. I didn't have any extracurricular activities for the application, my lineage is filthy, and my only recommendation came from a smutty businessman."

Jesse leaned back against the door again, his legs outstretched. We finished our sodas, not speaking.

Jesse stood up and reached his hand to me. "Come here."

I put my hand in his and let him pull me up. We stood on the street, our hands entwined.

"Remember that great day out at Shady Grove, how we threw rocks at the tree?" asked Jesse.

I nodded.

He dropped my hand, wound up, and pitched his bottle at the lamppost across the street. It shattered to a crisp. "That's your momma and her boyfriend."

I threw my bottle. It missed the lamppost and smashed against a building.

"What's goin' on down there?" someone yelled from above.

We laughed. Jesse gave me a wave and walked away. "See ya, Jo."

I stood on the step, waiting for him to turn around. He didn't.

A parked car flipped on its headlights down the street. It crept slowly past me, the windows so dark I couldn't see the driver. Once it passed the shop, it sped up and drove away.

I chained and bolted the door.

FORTY-EIGHT

James and a man from Doubleday came to get the books. Patrick said he couldn't bear to see them being carried out. I looked at the naked bookshelves. Shelves without books were lonely and just plain wrong.

James handed me a check and grabbed the last carton. "I thought Patrick would be here," he said. "We've argued over the list for months."

"I think it's hard for him. And he's busy preparing for his big trip."

"Big trip?" said James, setting the box back on the counter. "Where's he going?"

"Surely he told you. He's going to the Keys, then to Havana, and then he's planning to spend the rest of the year in Trinidad with his mother."

James stared at me. "Josie, you're joking, right?"

"No. He didn't tell you?"

James's eyes were round with shock. "No, he didn't." Suddenly he was angry. "I can't believe he's doing this to me." He yanked the box off the counter and slammed out the door.

I watched James pace the sidewalk. He was clearly emotional. What did he think Patrick was doing to him? My fingers involuntarily made a sign on the counter. I looked at my hand and then out to James in the street. Patrick wasn't in love with Kitty.

Cokie drove us to the bus station. It was raining. Patrick rattled off instructions about the house and shop. I practically had them memorized. Miss Paulsen would be checking on the house. A visiting professor from Loyola would begin a sublease next week. The piano man would come the week before Christmas to make sure the Bösendorfer was tuned and adjusted before Patrick came home. I had a list of names in the Florida Keys, the information for Hotel Nacional de Cuba, and the address in Trinidad.

"You have to keep me updated," said Patrick. "I want to know everything that's going on, especially when you hear from Smith."

Cokie unloaded Patrick's trunk at the station. He clapped Patrick on the back. "You take care, now. Next time you see Josie girl, she'll be home for Christmas from college." He beamed. "Now, I got to git. Got a pickup at the Roosevelt."

We walked into the station, out of the rain. "You still haven't told him?" Patrick asked as Cokie drove away.

"I don't know how. I think he's more excited than me. Speaking of telling, I was surprised you didn't tell James about your trip. He seemed really upset when I told him you were leaving." I eyed Patrick carefully. "Do you think he suspects your feelings . . . for Kitty?"

Patrick avoided my gaze. "Give him my address in Trinidad if you want."

We looked at Patrick's bus ticket. He had quite a few stops but just three transfers. One in Mobile, one in Jacksonville, and one in West Palm Beach. Men in suits and ties and women in pretty dresses lined up in the bus station with their suitcases, all departing for some exciting destination. Patrick's blond hair was combed neatly to the side. He looked glamorous in his tan suit and baby blue oxford.

"Thirty-two hours of luxury, and you'll be out of this rain and on the beach," I told him. "I'm jealous."

"Yeah, these buses are so nice. I wish you were coming. Thank you, for everything, Jo. You've done so much for Charlie, the shop, and me."

Patrick's bus for Mobile was announced.

"I know I've let you down," he said quickly. "You're the last person I ever wanted to hurt, I swear it." Light reflected off moisture in his eyes.

A lump bobbed in my throat.

"You're so important to me," he whispered. "Please believe me."

"Let's make sure your trunk is on," I said quickly, fighting back the tears.

We walked toward the Greyhound silverside with an illuminated placard that read MOBILE above the windshield. We stood together under the umbrella and watched as his trunk was loaded into the bay of the coach.

I looked at Patrick. "Candace Kinkaid or Agatha Christie?"

He laughed. "Definitely Candace Kinkaid. Way more fun. F. Scott Fitzgerald or Truman Capote?" he asked.

The last call rang out for Mobile.

"Oh, please. Fitzgerald. Of course Fitzgerald. Get on your bus."

Patrick handed me the umbrella. He wrapped his arms around me and planted a kiss straight on my lips, hard and long. It felt like I was watching the kiss instead of being inside of it. He ran out from underneath the umbrella to the interior shelter of the bus steps. "See you at Christmas!" he called.

I watched as he made his way down the aisle to a window seat near the waistline of the bus.

The doors hissed, then folded closed. Water rolled down the top of the bus, falling in streams over Patrick's window. He smiled and put his finger on the glass, signaling biography.

I signaled back. Poetry.

The bus rolled, taking Patrick Marlowe, and his secret, with it. I stood and watched it drive away. I thought of the line from Keats and my discussion with Mr. Hearne.

I love you the more in that I believe you have liked me for my own sake and for nothing else.

The rain plunked atop my black umbrella.

FORTY-NINE

I swept the tile floor between the shelves. Moving the books had unlocked bits of fossilized dust. Patrick had only been gone a few days, but the shop was strangely still and lifeless. I made a note to bring the radio from Patrick's house. It would keep me company.

The bell above the door jingled.

"Well, hello there. I was in the neighborhood and thought I'd pop in to see what's news," said John Lockwell.

I leaned on the broom. "You seem to be in the neighborhood a lot these days."

"Yes, did I tell you I have a place over on St. Peter?"

"Several times."

He looked around the shop. "Are you closing?"

"It's temporary. We'll reopen after Christmas. The owner passed away, and Patrick is visiting his mother in the West Indies."

"How bohemian of him. But then literary folk always are. Great for parties, always good to have a few eccentrics on hand to entertain the stuffy Uptown crowd. So, you'll be needing a job, then. Sure you won't reconsider? Some nice dresses, and you'd be a little clothes pony in the office. You'd have your own desk, typewriter, and of course cocktail privileges with the boss after hours."

"I'm fine for now, but I'll certainly keep it in mind."

"You do that. I thought I couldn't wait to get rid of you, but there's something about you, Josephine." He gave me a moist smile. "Well, I better shove. I've got an engagement."

Lockwell walked out, passing a tall man in a dark coat entering the shop. He dwarfed Lockwell, who turned around and looked up at him before walking off.

"I'm sorry, sir, we're closed. Death in the family. We'll reopen in a few months. Doubleday has acquired most of our books. They're on the six hundred block of Canal."

The man said nothing. He stood motionless in the doorway, hands in the pockets of his long black coat. His frame was enormous, at least six three, with shoulders so broad they could carry a family of four. His hat cocked slightly, and his left eye, damaged in some way, floated in toward the bridge of his flattened nose.

I moved forward with the broom. "We're—"

"Where's your mother?" he said.

"I'm sorry, do I know you?" I eyed his hands, which remained in his pockets.

"Where's your mother?" he repeated, slow and loud. His tone frightened me.

"In California," I said.

"Yeah, see, that's a problem. Your mother owes the boss money."

"I wasn't aware—"

"Her boyfriend borrowed it to buy her alibi, get them out of a murder rap. He said he'd pay the boss back, but then skipped town. The boss has a Los Angeles crew looking for them, but they're ghosts. The boss wants his money, it's already overdue, so now the marker falls to the family—boyfriend has no family, so it falls to you. That's called inheritance. The boss paid four thousand for the dame's rap. With juice, you owe five thousand. I'm here to collect."

The more he talked, the more his left eye floated. I stood there, clutching the broomstick. "There must be some mistake."

"Why people always gotta say there's a mistake? There's no mistake. Your mother was pegged for murder, she got off—pay up."

"I never made an agreement with your boss."

"You didn't have to. You owe, and you'll pay. We've been watching you and your fruitcake friends. Saw the teary good-bye at the Greyhound station, suckin' sodas with the motorcycle kid, palling around with the caramel-colored driver. Willie Woodley knows the boss. They're cordial, but she don't do no business with him. This debt's yours, see? You don't go to none of them. You flap your gums to them, we take 'em out. I personally would love to clip the old driver today, but since this is my first call, and I'm in a good mood, I'll give you seven days—that's called a courtesy. You get the money however you need to, but you don't tell no one who you owe. You only talk to me, Tangle Eye Lou. You can find me at Mosca's on Highway 90."

He turned and walked out onto the sidewalk. A black car pulled up. He got in the back. The door closed, and the car drove off.

I dropped the broom and grabbed the chains. I locked and bolted the door, my hands trembling. I turned off the lights and ran to my room. I dragged my desk in front of the door and sat huddled on my bed against the cold plaster wall, clutching the baseball bat.

I stayed that way all afternoon, into the evening, and all through the night. I didn't sleep and wasn't tired. Carlos Marcello said I owed him. Tangle Eye's words about Cokie terrified me. Not Cokie.

I waited until the sun rose. I sharpened the bookbinding knife and put it in my pocket. I crept out of the shop, chained and bolted the doors on the outside, and ran down the street.

I looked at the house. I couldn't remember which window it was, but wagered it was the one with the crankshaft on the sill. I whistled. Nothing. I found a pebble and tossed it at the window. Still nothing. I found a slightly larger stone and tossed it up. The stone catapulted through the window and the sound of breaking glass echoed across the slumbering street.

Jesse's torso appeared in the window. I waved him down.

He came out the front door, barefoot and shirtless, buttoning the fly of his jeans. He raked his sleepy hair with his fingers and squinted at me. "What gives?"

"I need your help," I whispered.

He walked down the stairs and met me on the sidewalk. "Jo, you're shaking."

"Please understand, I can't tell you everything." My voice quivered. "It's my mother. I need the shop boarded or shuttered, and it has to happen this morning. Can you do that for me?" I handed some crumpled bills in his direction.

He took my hand. "Sit down."

"I don't have time."

Jesse's grandmother appeared in the doorway.

"Go back to sleep, Granny. Everything's fine," said Jesse.

The old woman called out at us. "There's murder all around her. I can see it. Girl, you have to get the murderer to confess, to free the dead man's spirit. Put a saucer of salt on the murderer's chest while they sleep. They'll confess."

I started to cry. Jesse ran up the steps and shooed his grandmother back into the house. I turned and walked away.

"Jo, wait," said Jesse.

"I have to go to Willie's," I called over my shoulder. "Please help with the shop. I'm sorry about your window." I started to run.

The sun was up when I arrived at Willie's. I let myself in through the side door and proceeded to eat anything I could find in the kitchen. I hadn't had food or drink since Tangle Eye left the shop. The milk sloshed against the sides of the trembling glass as I raised it to my lips. I had spent all night considering the options. No one escaped a debt to Carlos Marcello, not alive anyway. Five thousand dollars was an enormous sum of money, over two years' tuition to Smith. I could raise some of it myself, but not all of it. There was no other way.

I'd have to take it from Willie and then find a way to return it. I couldn't tell her, not after Tangle Eye's threat.

Sadie knew something was wrong the moment she saw me. I told her I couldn't sleep. She kept feeling my forehead and the sides of my neck. She made me open my mouth so she could look at my tongue and throat. She brewed hot tea with lemon and fried up some eggs and thick bacon for me.

"I smell pig," said Willie as I brought the coffee into her room. "Who's Sadie cooking for?"

"It was for me. I drank too much soda yesterday and had a bad stomach all night."

Willie eyed me. "Soda, huh? Yeah, right. Give me the papers." Willie read through one of the front-page stories in the newspaper. "They're crackin' down, Jo. Says here they're hiring more cops and plan to drag the Quarter." She threw the paper across the bed. "I'm too old for raids. Used to love 'em, all the dodge and ditch was a turn-on, but I don't have the energy for it anymore. I haven't had to use the buzzer for years."

"What will you do?"

Willie thought for a moment. "I'll keep two drivers on-site every night. Sadie will sit at the window and throw the buzzer if she sees the cops. Everyone will run through the courtyard and climb through the flap door into the waiting cars. I may send a car to the bookshop—you said it's closed up, right?"

"Yes." I chose my words carefully. "I've asked Jesse to put boards or shutters up on the windows. I don't want people to see it empty."

"That's a good idea. Move the bookshelves. I'll have Elmo deliver some furniture so there's a place to sit."

"Willie, have you heard from Mother?"

"No, and we don't want to. I hope she's settled her scores here in town and won't come back. I don't need the trouble, and neither do you. I know you feel some sort of connection with her, but trust me on this, she will bring you down, Jo. She'll bring us all down."

She already has, I wanted to tell Willie.

"If I were you, I would think about changing my last name. You're eighteen. You can do it. Cut the cord."

Willie banded a stack of bills and handed them to me. "Put these in the safe."

She continued to talk about the crackdown. I stared at the stacks of cash in the safe. If I could nick two one-hundred-dollar bills, go to the bank, change them for a stack of one-dollar bills, I could fill the packs with ones. Maybe she wouldn't notice. I tried to quickly calculate how it would add up. Perspiration beaded at my hairline.

"What the hell are you doing in there?" demanded Willie.

What was I doing? *Decisions,* whispered the voice of Forrest Hearne, *they shape our destiny.*

Yes, Forrest Hearne's decisions had led to his destiny. Death.

FIFTY

"Mr. Lockwell, please," I whispered into the receiver. "This is Josephine Moraine."

I waited for several minutes. The line finally clicked. "You got your letter," said the woolly voice on the other end of the line. "You want to go celebrate?"

"Actually, I haven't received word yet. I'm calling regarding—" I paused. Could I really do this? "Regarding employment."

Lockwell was silent. I heard nothing but the wet sucking of his cigar. "Ah, reconsidered, have you?"

"I'm thinking about it. I'd like to know a bit more about the position."

"Meet me at noon at my place on St. Peter." He rattled off the address. "I look forward to discussing . . . the position." He chuckled and hung up.

When I left the shop for Lockwell's, Jesse was installing shutters on the windows and doors.

"They're castoffs from a building over on Chartres. The one for the door even has a mail slot. The fit won't be perfect, but they'll work for privacy." Jesse looked at me and smiled.

I stared at the sidewalk.

"That's what this is about, right? If it's not, tell me."

I looked at Jesse.

"Damn it, Jo. Say something."

I wanted to tell him everything. But I couldn't. I couldn't drag Jesse, Cokie, or Willie into this. So I just stood there.

Jesse dropped his hammer in frustration. "You know what? I'm tired of this. You come banging on my door or breakin' my window whenever you need something, and I jump when you say jump. But I ask a question or come by to see you, and you leave me standing out here on the street. I got school, cars to fix, and I dropped everything to do this today. I'm not some puppy. You complain about your mom being a user, but you're lookin' like one yourself these days."

I turned on my heel and walked away from him, fighting tears and the urge to run back and tell him everything, ask for his help.

The entrance to Lockwell's apartment was discreetly tucked down a deep, gated courtyard. He said the other two apartments were generally vacant, as the owners lived out of town. How convenient for him.

The apartment was small but lovely. Old oak floors ran the length of the long and narrow parlor. The high ceilings made it feel bigger. Sparsely furnished, but the pieces were tasteful, especially the desk in the corner, which had the framed picture of Lockwell on a hunting expedition. He saw me eyeing the desk.

"It's a beauty, huh? It's not all play. Sometimes I work here, too. Would you like a tour?"

The apartment was petite. There couldn't be more than the small parlor, a kitchen, and a bedroom. "No, thank you," I said, having a seat in one of the chairs.

Lockwell lit his cigar and sat down across from me. "So here we are. Quite a long way from where we started. I like how things have progressed."

I nodded, tired, slightly off my usual spar with Lockwell. The encounter with Jesse still bothered me.

"All right, let's just admit it. We've come full circle. I predicted you would come back to me for money, and here you are."

I opened my mouth to object.

Lockwell raised his hand in protest. "Now, I'll admit that you aren't the shakedown I originally thought, but I've offered you a job several times, and you've always been quick to decline. Now you're here about the job, and you're not quite yourself, Josephine." He sucked on the end of the cigar. "You need money, or you wouldn't be here. It may be for college. It may be for something else. But you need money. How much?"

I tried to calculate what I thought I could borrow from Willie's safe. "Two thousand dollars," I told him.

Lockwell's head popped back in surprise. "That's quite a hefty sum."

"That's why I'm inquiring about a job."

"It'll take you two years to make two thousand dollars as a secretary. Maybe more."

I didn't have years. I had days.

"Unless"—he leaned back in the chair—"you'd prefer a more private arrangement. I'd front you some of the money, and we'd have a weekly arrangement here."

I swallowed, hard. "And you'd front exactly how much? I'm in need of two thousand dollars."

Lockwell rolled his cigar on his lips. I was a marionette. He loved pulling the strings. The power was titillating. "A thousand."

"Fifteen hundred, cash," I countered.

He looked at me. "But you can't look like that." He pulled out his wallet and handed me a fifty-dollar bill. "Go to Maison Blanche, pick out a nice dress and some high heels. Real heels, no loafers, or whatever you call them. Get your hair and nails done, too. Buy some perfume if you want. Come back the day after tomorrow at seven o'clock. I'll have dinner brought in."

He rolled his cigar against his bottom lip and stared at me. I stared back. "Well, I've got an appointment. I'll show you out."

I could feel his eyes all over me from behind as I walked to the door. I held my pocketbook tight against my left side, trying to hide the slice in my blouse from Cincinnati's knife.

Fifteen hundred. That meant I'd have to steal over three thousand from Willie. I stepped out the door and turned around.

"See you soon, Josephine," he said with a wink.

I stared at him, and my nose wrinkled, thinking I could smell the vinegar in his veins. Could I do this? But somehow the words came right out of my mouth. "See you soon," I told him.

FIFTY-ONE

Two days passed. I still didn't have a dime. Five more days, and Marcello's men would track me down. Willie didn't ask me to put money in the safe that morning, almost as if she had read my mind and knew what was going on. I got a postcard from Patrick saying the Keys were beautiful and that he missed me. I got another letter from Charlotte, asking if I could confirm the visit to the Berkshires in August. I thought of Tangle Eye Lou showing up at the Gateses' home in the Berkshires, hunting me down for the five thousand dollars he said I owed Marcello.

The cops had raided Willie's. A car dropped Dora, Sweety, and two johns at the shop to hide. When I opened the door, they all came running in, Dora clutching a bottle of crème de menthe and Sweety holding the hand of sweaty and trembling Walter Sutherland, who wore nothing but boxer shorts and a necktie.

"Raid party!" shouted Dora. She turned on the radio, and they danced between the bookshelves. I sat on the stairs and watched beautiful, heartful Sweety with Walter Sutherland's fat pink arms around her. His eyes were closed, and his head rested on her shoulder as he drifted off into a dreamland. It nauseated me. She was so beautiful and kind, she didn't have to do this. I didn't have to do it either. I could run away, go off to Massachusetts without telling a soul.

I had just returned from Willie's and was cleaning the shop after the raid party when I heard a noise at the door. I turned and waited for a knock but none came. And then I saw it. A large brown envelope was wedged askew between Jesse's shutters and the glass door. I dusted off my hands and removed the keys from my pocket. I opened the door and the envelope fell faceup onto the tile. I saw the return address and lost my breath.

SMITH COLLEGE

I paced around the shop humming and holding the envelope. It felt like more than just a sheet of paper. That was encouraging. A rejection would be a single sheet. I used the bookbinding knife and slit the top flap. I peeked inside. There was a sealed envelope clipped to a piece of paper.

I paced some more, my hands perspiring and my heart thumping wildly. I stopped and yanked the paper out of the envelope.

The words came at me in slow motion.

Dear Miss Moraine,
  Thank you for your application to Smith College.

The Board of Admissions was pleased to have so many outstanding applications this year.

After long and careful consideration,

we regret to inform you that we cannot offer you a place in the Class of 1954.

Rejected.

Why had I allowed myself to dream that it was possible, that I could escape the smoldering cesspit of my existence in New Orleans and glide into a world of education and substance in Northampton?

The rejection went on to say that my application wasn't timely enough to be fully considered. The rest of the letter contained polite pleasantries, wishing me luck in all my future endeavors. I'd have to tell Charlotte. Even worse, I'd have to tell Cokie. Thinking about Cokie made my stomach wormy. I looked at the envelope clipped to the rejection letter. *Miss Josephine Moraine* was written in an inky script on the cream bond envelope. Inside was a letter on matching paper.

> *Dear Miss Moraine,*
>
> *I write to you at the suggestion of Barbara Paulsen, my dear friend and fellow alumna of Smith. I am a professor of literature at Smith, an author of historical fiction, and a patron of the arts in the state of Massachusetts.*
>
> *Barbara has informed me of your strengths as a clerk in the bookshop and also as a housemaid. I am a single woman, living alone, and am currently in need of such assistance. Although I cannot finance relocation expense, if you are able to travel to Northampton, I am prepared to offer you a weekly salary of eight dollars and a private bedroom with en suite bath in exchange for your duties as*

a housekeeper and administrative assistant. The position requires a five-day workweek with occasional weekend obligation.

I am hopeful for a favorable reply within the month.
Yours sincerely,
Ms. Mona Wright

The letter confirmed what I knew in my heart all along. They didn't want me. I was good enough to clean their bathrooms and dust their books, but not to join them in public. Miss Paulsen had met Mother at Charlie's funeral and probably contacted Smith. Maybe she told them to deny my application, that I was unsavory. To soften the blow and satisfy Patrick, she got in touch with some spinster and suggested I empty her ashtrays. Eight dollars per week? Sweety got twenty dollars just to dance with Walter Sutherland for an hour. I was getting fifteen hundred to . . . to what? I heaved into the trash can.

Lockwell had told me to take the fifty dollars and go to Maison Blanche. That was too risky. What if I ran into someone and they started asking questions? I went to a pawnshop and bought a small pistol, then took a bus to a store in Gentilly. I chose a sky blue cocktail dress with a bateau neckline and matching gloves. I told the saleswoman I was attending my uncle's retirement party. The dress felt tight through the chest and hips, but the saleswoman assured me that it was stylish to look shapely, even for a retirement party. She helped me pick out stockings and undergarments. She suggested shoes to match, but I opted for a pair of black pumps. Black was more practical. I could be buried in them if things didn't work out. I teetered on the high heels at first, my pale ankles rubbery. She suggested I walk in the shoes a bit to get used to the feeling. I went up to the top floor for a shampoo and wave in the beauty salon. While the beauty operator worked on my hair, another woman buffed my nails and applied makeup. She tried to get me to purchase the makeup set, claiming that I looked ravishing.

"I just need to look good tonight. For the retirement party."

"Well, all eyes will be on you, that's for sure." She propped her elbow on her hip, a menthol cigarette dangling from her fingers. "That's a compliment, honey. Most girls would kill for shiny hair and a classy chassis like yours," said the woman. "Wait till your boyfriend sees you."

I stared at my reflection in the broken mirror on my wall. The dress, gloves, shoes, makeup, hair—they looked pretty, but felt like a costume. I tilted my head. Was the mirror crooked, or was I? The new brassiere made my bosom look larger and my waist smaller. I walked around my room, trying to adjust to the heels.

Lockwell said he'd have dinner brought in. And then what? My stomach rolled. I remembered Mother talking about it in the kitchen at Willie's. She said she trained her mind. She'd smile and close her eyes and then she'd just think about something else, like eating oysters or going to the beach, and before she knew it, it was over. For fifteen hundred dollars, could I mentally eat oysters or walk along the beach?

I put the lipstick in my new purse, along with a pen and tissues. I looked at the pistol on my desk. I'd bought it to feel safer in the shop, in case Tangle Eye decided to stop by. I wouldn't need it tonight, would I?

I tried to lock the shop as quickly as I could. I didn't want anyone to see me, especially Frankie. I walked the opposite way, taking a circuitous path that would eventually lead to St. Peter. But each time I approached the street, my feet kept moving, and I ended up in the other direction. Men tipped their hats to me on the street. Others turned around and smiled. A chill draped across the back of my neck and shoulders, quickly becoming a cold sweat. Something bubbled at the back of my throat, making me think of the red beans and rice incident on Gedrick's sidewalk.

I had spent so many years trying to be invisible. The stares and smiles meant people saw me. Could makeup and a nice dress really do that? The chapters of *David Copperfield* fluttered in front of me:

I. I am born.

II. I observe.

III. I have a change.

IV. I fall into disgrace.

Light fell, and so did my confidence. I turned down another street. Three young men stood on the sidewalk in front of an auto repair shop. One of them whistled as I approached. My stomach knotted. One of the boys was Jesse.

The other two called out. Jesse didn't even look up, consumed with an engine part in his hands. Relieved, I quickened my pace, praying he wouldn't lift his gaze.

"Where ya going in such a rush, beautiful?" said one of the boys, stepping out to block my path.

Jesse glanced briefly my way and quickly returned his eyes

to the pipe in his hands. His head suddenly snapped back up. I looked down and tried to walk around his friend.

"Jo?"

I stopped and turned to him. "Yeah. Hey, Jesse. What are you doing here?" I asked, trying to turn the conversation to avoid the inevitable questions.

Jesse looked at me. His eyes didn't roam my body like his friends', and his lips didn't twitch like the men I passed on the street. He just looked at me. His hand, sleeved in grease to his elbow, loosely motioned to the auto shop behind him. "My car. This is where I work on the Merc."

One of the guys elbowed Jesse. "Show the pretty lady the Merc, Jess. Wait till you see this car."

"Maybe she'd like to go for a ride," said the other with a grin. "You got any friends for us, doll?"

At that moment, I wanted nothing more than to take a ride with Jesse Thierry, leave New Orleans, drive straight to Shady Grove, tell him everything, and ask for his help. But his face had the same confused look it did when he'd dropped the hammer in front of the bookshop. It made me feel uncomfortable, guilty.

"C'mon, Jesse, aren't you gonna ask her out?" asked the friend.

Jesse stared at me and shook his head. "Obviously someone else already has." Jesse walked into the auto shop. His friends followed, looking back at me.

Jesse was judging me. How dare he? He didn't know me. I turned around and marched straight to Lockwell's, a blister burning at the back of my heel.

FIFTY-TWO

The sky hung low and dark when I walked through the gate. Gas lamps flickered, and banana palms swayed, sifting shadows on the decrepit, trickling fountain in the center of the courtyard. A chill tightened the skin on my arms. Music floated from Lockwell's apartment in the corner. He stood leaning against the wall under the gas lamp outside his door, smoking a cigar. He watched me approach, smoke furling around his face and shoulders like gray organza. I couldn't see his eyes, but I could feel them. First the shoes, up my stockings, pausing at my groin and again at my chest, leading up to my lips, and then back down again.

He opened the screen door for me, silent. The sultry alto sax of Charlie Parker pressed at me with a swell. The lights were a low gold. I swallowed, trying to free the moth that was trapped in my throat, fluttering and making it difficult to breathe. I felt the heat of him behind me.

"Thought maybe you had changed your mind," he said quietly into my ear.

I shook my head and took a step forward to escape the cage of his presence. I put my hand on the back of the sofa to steady myself. Sweat from my palms leached through the new blue gloves. I tugged at my hand to take them off. His hands were immediately on mine.

"Slower," he said, circling around in front of me. "One by one." He walked to the table and picked up a tumbler of liquor. He watched as I removed each finger from the long blue gloves.

"Have a seat." He motioned to the sofa. "What are you drinking?"

"Nothing, thank you."

"You'll have champagne. All girls like champagne."

All girls didn't like champagne. I preferred root beer. Willie preferred anything that smelled like gasoline and burned her throat. She could hold her liquor better than any man, and I wished she was there to help me navigate John Lockwell.

I stared at Lockwell's back, his hair freshly trimmed across the neck, revealing a golf-course tan. His white shirt, once crisp with press, was now damp with humidity and anticipation. He held a linen towel to capture the cork and then poured the champagne. He sat down close to me and handed me the tall flute.

He raised his glass. "To new beginnings." He took a big swallow. I tilted the glass and let the champagne touch my closed lips. I put the glass on the table in front of me.

"You look gorgeous, Josephine. The neckline's a little high, but your modesty makes you even sexier." He slid his hand onto my thigh.

The moth flapped harder at my windpipe.

"So this is what fifty dollars does?" he said. "I like it."

I swallowed hard, hoping to force the nervous bile from the back of my throat. "Actually, I have change for you. I didn't buy any perfume, just used the tester of Chanel at the counter." I reached for my purse.

"You're serious?" he said.

"Yes. You should be more budget conscious. You gave me money for clothes, and if I didn't use it all, I need to give it back to you. I might need money, but I'm not a thief, Mr. Lockwell."

"I've told you, call me John," he said, loosening his tie at the throat. "And I think you are a thief. You're stealing my heart."

He grinned, pleased with himself. I tried desperately not to roll my eyes at the pathetic line, a line that would have melted Mother to mess. The thought of Mother brought me back to reality.

"You do remember our financial arrangement," I said.

"Look at you, getting right down to business. I like it. I'm anxious too." He hopped up, went to his desk, and pulled a banded stack of bills from his drawer. He handed it to me for inspection. I flipped through it. Fifteen hundred. Why didn't I ask for three thousand? I was a fool. He snatched it from my hands and put it in his front shirt pocket.

"Dance with me."

He pulled me off the sofa by the arm and swung my body into his. In heels we were the same height. Nose to nose. I turned my head and felt his hot breath against my cheek. Charlie Parker's sax lamented a broken heart, and Lockwell's right hand pushed into the small of my back.

He stopped moving. "Well, butter my butt and call me a biscuit, you don't know how to dance, do you, Josephine?"

I didn't know how to dance. I didn't want anything to do with his biscuit.

"Well, now, it's easy. Just move with me." He pushed my groin to his and inhaled deeply at my neck. I tried to mirror his steps. He liked that. A lot. He danced me into the sideboard and moved himself harder against me. I trembled with nausea. I looked up at the ceiling and tried what Mother had described. Eating oysters. His hand moved up toward my chest. The beach. It wasn't working. His grasp was hurting me. He slid his thumb into my mouth and told me to close my lips. I thought of the cool earth and the floorboards under the porch where I once carved my name and vowed that I would not become like my mother. He grabbed my hand and started to move it toward his waist.

I shook my head and pulled away.

"What's wrong?" he said, following me toward the couch. "Are you scared?" He looked at me, perversion fully inflamed. "God, your mouth."

"Stop it," I said.

"Now, now. Don't be a tease. Come here." He tugged at his belt.

I reached for my purse, but he grabbed my arm. "Oh, no, you don't. You don't want me to call Smith and tell them not to accept you, do you?" His mouth was on my ear. "Come on, Josephine. Earn your money. Be a good little whore now."

I heard his jaw pop as my fist connected to it. He overcame the initial shock and lunged at me with the fury of a bull, but my feet were already planted, pistol drawn. He jumped back, stunned.

"Put your hands on your head," I told him. He didn't move. I aimed over his shoulder and blew his hunting picture to pieces.

"Okay, okay!" he said, putting his hands up. I waved him into the corner.

"I'm sorry. You're right. I was moving too fast. Just put the gun down, Josephine," he pleaded. "Please, put down the gun."

"Don't tell me what to do. Sit on the floor," I commanded. "Now."

He sat in the corner. "Jesus, what did you think this was? Just leave, and we'll pretend this never happened. Go. I won't tell anyone."

I took off the black heels and hurled them at him in the corner. "Don't ever call me a whore. Ever," I said through gritted teeth. "Close your eyes."

"Oh, God, no. Josephine, please."

"I said, close your eyes!" He closed his eyes.

I ran from the apartment, my stocking feet pounding on the sidewalk. The sky was black with thunder. I opened my mouth.

A large moth flew out into the night.

FIFTY-THREE

I found it the next morning. I came downstairs from my apartment, and it was staring at me through the glass of the front door.

Wedged against the shutter. A white sheet of paper. A black hand.

Twenty-four hours. Tangle Eye would be back at the shop, demanding five thousand dollars I didn't have and had no way of getting. I owed Cokie two thousand dollars, an explanation, and an apology. I owed Forrest Hearne's wife a gold watch. But I owed Carlos Marcello, and if I didn't pay, I'd be a lot worse off than with John Lockwell.

I'd concocted a story to tell Willie. I'd say the liquor distributor had a shipment waiting at Sal's and needed payment. She'd tell me to go into the safe and get the money. I'd take the five thousand then. The thought of stealing from Willie upset my every fiber, but once I paid off Marcello, I would explain it to her, let her know that I was protecting everyone. I'd have to work it off over several years to pay the debt. She'd get what she wanted. I'd be stuck in New Orleans.

The morning was full of hiccups. The constant pressure of the police had Willie agitated. She asked me to take the black book home with me and keep it at my apartment.

"They came poking around at six last night. Six P.M.! Acted like it was some social call and stayed till one in the morning. I lost a whole night of business entertaining the chief and his cop friends. But what could I do? They played cards, and the girls stayed up in their rooms, bored as bats. The chief's eyes were on everything—I had to follow him around. I was sure he'd find the hiding spots. Take the book. From now on, I'll give you the receipt papers, and you'll make the entries at your place."

I nodded and took the book from her. She lit a cigarette and leaned back in bed.

"And you know what else? I'm too tired to play this game anymore. What do you say we cram the apple in the pig's ass and roast it."

"You're tired of the business? The police?"

"Yeah, that too. But I'm tired of this game with you. I've waited, hoped that you would come to me. At first I was angry that you thought I was so thick-headed. You're eighteen, for cripe's sake. I guess I should be happy that there's still a ridiculous innocent side to you. But sometimes it just plain pisses me off."

"I don't know what you're talking about, Willie."

"Aw, can it. I know you're upset about Charlie and Patrick, but that's not what this is about. Your mother marked Forrest

Hearne the moment she saw him, and you know it. You marked Hearne, too, just in a different way. Your mother told Cincinnati she found a target. Cinci paid the bartender to slip him a fat Mickey so Hearne would be out long enough to fleece him. Bartender slipped the Mick fat all right, and Hearne wound up dead. Even though it's obvious to every Tom, Dick, and Harry that they're guilty, they get off because they have an alibi. And who can afford to buy alibis in this town? Yeah, Carlos Marcello. So now your mother's got the black hand on her back."

I stood at the foot of Willie's bed, clutching the book. Tears pooled in my eyes.

She nodded, her hard-boiled voice lowering. "You think I don't understand what's going on, Jo? You think I don't have eyes in this town? Frankie's not my only pair of eyes. I had people pulling me aside on the street, telling me Marcello's men were on you, cars were following you all over town. And then suddenly you're acting like a lunatic. Jesse came to change Mariah's oil, and the poor kid was a mess. Said you busted his window begging for shutters and then ran off. I don't have to tell you that you've screwed that one up royal. And the whole time, I told them all that you'd come to me. I kept waiting for you to come to me."

"I couldn't," I sobbed.

"Why the hell not?" demanded Willie.

"They said they'd kill you."

"And you believed them? Jo, they want their money, and they'll threaten to high heaven to get it. I know how to handle Marcello."

"No, Willie, you can't. I don't want anything to happen to you or Cokie."

"Quit your sniveling. I'm not a fool. How much is the mark?"

I could barely look at her. "Five thousand," I said quietly.

Willie threw back the covers and started pacing, ash flying from the butt of her cigarette. A vein of anger pulsed at her temple. "Your mother should be strung up by her eyelids. Passing her daughter a mob debt? Here's what we'll do. I'll give you the money for Marcello, but you'll go to some banks and exchange it for all small notes and change. When you deliver the money to Tangle Eye, it has to look like you scrounged it up from the gutter. Pennies and nickels, even. Split it up in different bags and envelopes. If you have big bills, they'll know you had a source and they'll just keep coming back for more. Sonny will drive you out to Mosca's this afternoon. You'll go in and pay them. Make sure they tell you you're square."

"I'll pay them? I have to take five thousand dollars to Marcello's men? Won't they come and get it?"

"You don't want them to come and get it. If they have to pay a visit, then it's overdue and you owe more. You want to pay them before they come calling." The skin on Willie's chest sagged and broken capillaries crisscrossed her neck. She went into the safe in the closet and started tossing packs of money out onto her bed.

"That's four thousand." She leaned out of the closet, against the door frame. "How much did you get for screwing Lockwell last night?"

I looked at her.

"How much?" she demanded.

"Nothing."

"Nothing! What's the matter with you? You could have gotten a couple hundred."

"It was fifteen hundred." I looked up at Willie. "But I couldn't do it. He danced with me and touched me, and I couldn't stand it. I pulled my gun on him. Then I ran."

She took a long, slow drag off her cigarette and nodded. "Good girl. Good for you, Jo." She threw another thousand onto the bed.

We drove to the West Bank. I sat in the passenger seat of Sonny's car, flour sacks, paper bags, and envelopes full of small bills and coins at my feet. Five thousand dollars. Sonny rode with a shotgun between his legs. He said nothing, just smoked and listened intently to the radio soap opera *Young Widder Brown* crackling through his custom tube radio. His huge frame humped over the wheel, engrossed in the latest episode of widow Ellen Brown and her romance with Anthony Loring.

I wanted Sonny to hand over the money while I waited in the car, but Willie said that wasn't the way it was done. I thought back to the black handprint on the door on Esplanade and how I had criticized people who were foolish enough to get caught up with the mob.

Sonny rolled down a deserted stretch of road and stopped in front of a white clapboard building. He put his hand up to silence me, listening to the end of the program and the love saga in Simpsonville. He then turned off the radio and reached for the shotgun.

"Make sure they count it," he said.

I piled the bags and envelopes into my arms and shut the car door with my hip. I walked through the entrance and was instantly blinded by thick blackness, my eyes unable to adjust from the outdoors. I squinted like a watchmaker and made out a bar and a few tables. The room was nearly empty. The restaurant didn't open until five thirty. Vic Damone sang from the jukebox, and a lone skinny bartender prepped the bar.

"Can I help you?" asked the bartender.

"I'm looking for Tangle Eye."

"Against the wall in the back."

I walked past the row of tables in the dark, clutching the money. My eyes began to focus, and the room came into view. In the very back of the restaurant, three men sat at a table. As I approached, two got up and disappeared into the kitchen. I walked up and stood at the table. He stared at me with his right eye while his left floated from side to side.

"What the hell is that?" He pointed to my arms.

"It's the money." I set the load on the table and dropped an envelope. Nickels and dimes spilled out onto the table. Willie would be proud.

The effect was noted. "What do you think I am, a vending machine?" said Tangle Eye.

"It's all here. You can count it."

"I'm not touching that filthy stuff. Who knows what hole you pulled it out of. You count it out."

I sat and counted the money. He made marks on a napkin for each hundred, but quickly became impatient. He called the other two men from the kitchen to finish counting.

"You should have brought large bills," he said when the counting was finished. I was two dollars over, Willie's idea.

"I couldn't get big bills. I was busy begging to get here on time."

"Who said you were on time?" he countered.

"I am on time. And we're square."

He leaned over the table, his left eye bobbing furiously. "We're not square until the little man says we're square, understand? You better hope we don't find your mother in California. No one jumps a debt like that, see."

I stood up. "You'll have to take that up with my mother and Cincinnati. It's all here. You've noted five thousand dollars."

A man appeared and placed a plate in front of Tangle Eye. Chicken, pan-fried in garlic, white wine, and oil. It smelled delicious.

"Is she eating?" asked the man.

Tangle Eye stuffed his napkin in his collar and looked at me. "Are you eating?"

FIFTY-FOUR

My cousin Betty sent me a note with the most ludicrous tales about you.

That's what the letter from Charlotte said.

Having a swell time. Any news from Smith? Missing Charlie. Missing you.

That's what the postcard from Patrick said.

I am hopeful for a favorable reply within the month.

That's what the letter from Ms. Mona Wright had said. I still had no idea what "Ms." meant. I'd have to look it up in the practical business-writing handbook. It was obviously a title of some sort.

Sadie helped me prepare Willie's morning tray. Before going to sleep, I had resolved to tell her about Forrest Hearne's watch and also that Mother had stolen the watch she gave me from Adler's. I knew she'd be livid and call me all sorts of stupid, but I had to do it. And then I had to tell Cokie about his money being stolen. It was going to be a challenging day, to say the least.

Willie was awake, wrapped in a red satin kimono, peering out her shuttered window.

"Red, that's different. Is it new?" I asked.

"Unbelievable. It's barely breakfast, and they've already got a cop out there, sitting in his car. I'm tempted to have you take him coffee. Those cops are about as sharp as marbles, I tell ya."

"Was the chief of police by again last night?" I asked.

"No, but he sent three men around midnight. Sadie threw the buzzer, and I stalled them at the side door while everyone got out. An old attorney from Georgia didn't make it. I found the poor guy buck naked, shivering behind a banana palm in the courtyard. Had to give him all his money back. This is killing my business." She turned toward me. "What are the papers saying this morning?"

I didn't want to give them to her. The articles said the pressure on the Quarter was increasing and that more incidents of holdups and robberies were being reported. Holdups. I thought of myself, cornering Lockwell with my pistol. "Don't bother with the news, Willie."

She snapped the papers off the tray herself. I saw the heat rising in her face.

"Willie, I want to thank you again for helping me with the

debt yesterday. I can't tell you what a relief it is. Last night was the first time I really slept."

"You'll work it off. Every dime of it. Thankfully, you're not an ingrate like your mother, even if you don't wear the watch I gave you."

I started to lie about the watch. That's how easy the lies had become. But I stopped myself. I had to tell Willie about her watch and also Forrest Hearne's watch. She stood next to the bed, still reading the headlines.

"I don't wear the watch, Willie, because Mother and Cincinnati stole it."

Willie slowly looked at me over the paper.

I nodded. "They broke into my room and stole the watch and my pistol. And . . . I hadn't told you about this, but Cokie gave me two thousand dollars out of his gambling winnings so I could go to college. They took that too."

I wished I hadn't told her, that I could take it all back. Livid was an understatement. The look on her face defied description. Expressions of fury and pain blazed across her face simultaneously. Her eyes blinked rapidly.

"Willie?"

She reached out for the bed to steady herself and slid down, knocking a vase off the bedside table on the way. Her knees hit the floor.

"Willie!" I ran to grab her. Her eyes were round and protruding, and a stuttering sound came from her windpipe. She reached up and grabbed my shoulder. I screamed for Sadie.

"I'm going to call Dr. Sully. Okay, Willie?"

She motioned to the shuttered window. I understood.

"I won't let the cop in here, Willie. I promise." I screamed again for Sadie, this time louder. She came running and threw her hands to her face when she saw Willie.

"I don't know what happened. She just fell over. Let's lift her up onto the bed. Hurry, Sadie, I have to call Dr. Sully."

Willie's body was too heavy. We couldn't lift her by ourselves. Evangeline peered around the bedroom door.

"Evangeline, help us!" I shrieked. She shook her head and backed away in fear.

I wanted to beat her. "You selfish witch. Get over here and help us, or I swear I will shoot you myself. Now!"

Evangeline obeyed. She took Willie's feet, and together the three of us were able to lift her onto the bed.

"Prop her head up," I told Sadie. "She's barely breathing." I ran to the hall phone. Sweety was on the landing. Evangeline pushed by her, ran up the stairs, and slammed her door.

"Jo, what is it?" asked Sweety.

"It's Willie. I'm calling Dr. Sully. Lock all the doors. There's a cop outside in a black car."

I sat with Willie, propped up between the pillows. She was sweating and got sick over the side of the bed.

"The vultures will come. Don't let them in," she wheezed.

"Stop it, Willie. You're going to be okay. Do you hear me?"

"Don't let them in. Never let them in," she breathed.

Willie was indestructible, steel tough. Seeing her like this terrified me.

She had helped me, protected me for so much of my life,

and I was useless, unable to do anything for her. I held her in my arms. Her tremors calmed. She laid her head on my chest. I hummed "Buttons and Bows" and stroked her hair. The strewn newspapers on the floor and the untouched coffee tray at the foot of her bed stared at me, commanding me to do something more.

Willie gripped my hand. "Salted peanuts," she whispered.

Dr. Sully finally arrived and ran into the room. I looked up, tears streaming down my face.

It was too late.

FIFTY-FIVE

Cokie sat in the parlor, his face buried in his cap. His sobs pulled with a pain so deep and sorrowful it scared me. Sadie knelt at his feet with her hand on his knees. He looked up as I left Willie's room with Dr. Sully. His body quaked with sadness as he spoke.

"Is she really gone, Jo?"

I nodded. "Do you want to see her?"

"No," he protested through his tears. "I don't want to see no dead body. Willie ain't in there. She put her walkin' shoes on. She gone to see the Lord."

"Perhaps we can step into the kitchen," said Dr. Sully. "There are arrangements that have to be made."

We gathered in the kitchen, everyone except Evangeline. She wouldn't speak to anyone or open her door. Dora was inconsolable, wailing facedown on the kitchen table while Sweety rubbed her back.

"Word's gonna get out," said Sweety. "I think it's best we be organized. Willie would want that."

"Yes, she would," said Dr. Sully, whose face registered complete shock. "Jo, I assume you have Willie's papers?"

"Papers? No, she never mentioned anything," I said.

"Well, I know she has an attorney," said Dr. Sully. "I'll check with him. In the meantime, you'd best write a death notice and make funeral arrangements."

Dora sat up, her makeup from the night prior melted across her wet face. "It has to be somethin' special. Willie Woodley's gotta go out in style. She'd want that. If I have to, I'll turn tricks in the street to pay for it." She sobbed, pulling tissue after tissue out of her bosom.

"Now, Dora, Willie wouldn't want you in the street," reprimanded Cokie.

"Willie always said the Laudumiey funeral home was nice. We should have it there," said Sweety.

I had to state the obvious. "Willie would not want people coming to the house after the funeral," I said quietly. Everyone was in agreement.

"Let's have a party after the funeral, a real swank affair," said Dora. "The fellas at Galatoire's loved Willie. And the johns can just say that they're eating at Galatoire's. Oh, Willie loved their shrimp rémoulade." This small remembrance sent Dora back into a fit of sobs.

Dora was right. Willie was involved with so many people. Shopkeepers, restaurant owners, liquor suppliers, musicians, accountants, businessmen, and government officials. There was a vast array of people who would want to pay their respects but couldn't be openly associated with Willie's house. An event at a local restaurant would celebrate Willie as a member of the community, not just a brothel madam.

"I can't tell you what a very sad day this is for me," said Dr. Sully, his voice breaking up. "I've known Willie since we were children. The Quarter won't be the same without her." He cleared his throat, trying to shake off the emotion. "It sounds like we've got a plan. Josie, you'll be responsible for coordinating?"

"Me?" I said. "Why me?"

"Oh, sugar, you know it's what Willie would want," said Dora. "And y'all, I am officially in mournin'."

"I'll help you, Josie girl." Cokie sniffed. "Best I can, that is." Sadie nodded. Sweety said she would arrange for Walter Sutherland to pay for the event at Galatoire's.

Cokie got a black wreath for the door. Word flew through the Quarter. Sadie stood at the front door, Sweety at the side. Flowers began arriving. Sal brought food from the restaurant.

I sat next to Willie's bed, looking at her, hands folded across her chest. The room felt hot and airless, darkly thick. We were alone.

It was my fault. I looked at Willie's empty eyes and knew that my selfishness had made her ill. I had seen her swollen hands and ankles, noticed her fatigue, but I was too busy with my own plans to help her. Or maybe it was a desire to prove her wrong. She always warned me, predicted exactly how things would unfold, but every time life lied to me, I tried to rationalize the situation, hanging off some upside-down promise, like Forrest Hearne.

I told Willie all about Mr. Hearne, how he made me feel, and why I held on to his watch. "So I buried it out at Shady Grove," I told her. "I know he's not my father, Willie, but why can't I dream that he is? Aren't I good enough to believe that the other half of me is something wonderful, that I could be David Copperfield? If the thought that I'm part of something respectable gives me hope, why can't I hold on to that? He assumed I was in college, Willie. A fancy, smart man like that assumed I was in college, and you know what? It made me want to live up to the vision he had of me. He gave me hope. The dream is still alive in the watch."

I wanted her to swear at me, call me an idiot, something. But I didn't have to command her to speak. I could hear her voice, knew exactly what she would say and how she would say it.

"Yes, Willie, but what sort of cruel twist of fate is it that the man I dream to be my father is killed by my mother? It's almost Shakespearean."

The undertaker arrived. He seemed disturbed by my casual conversation with Willie's corpse.

"I know, Willie. I know." I turned to the undertaker. "She wants us to put the black kimono on her instead. And fresh lipstick." Sadie and I made sure everything was in the safe. All valuables were put in Willie's room, and the door was locked.

"I'm not worried about the others," I told Sadie. "Just Evangeline. She seems outside herself right now." Sadie nodded.

I walked down Conti toward Royal, not sure how my feet were even moving. My life was encased in a box and someone had picked it up, shaken it violently, and thrown it back down.

Everything was in pieces, displaced, and would never fit back together. I wouldn't make the early morning walk to Willie's each day, push through her door with her tray of coffee, explain what I'd discovered in the rooms during my cleaning. We'd never go to Shady Grove together, never shoot cans off the fence or laugh about Ray and Frieda driving from their demons at night. I'd never hear her musky voice, full of tar and gasoline, reprimanding me for being too early or too late. Willie was gone, and the gaping hole left behind was so big I felt sure I would drown in it.

By the time I approached the bookshop, I was sobbing. My face was swollen, awash with tears. The light from the streetlamp glowed, revealing Jesse sitting with his back against the door of the shop, one knee pulled up to his chest. I reached the door. He said nothing, just pulled me down into his lap and wrapped his arms around me.

FIFTY-SIX

Cokie picked me up in his cab for the funeral.

"Every time I think I'm done cried out, it comes at me all again," said Cokie. "No one ever showed me respect like Willie, 'cept you and my momma. And it scares me, Jo. Willie was stronger than a tin roof, and if she go that easily, what's that mean for the rest of us? I can't put my head around it. One day she here, and we're worried about Mr. Charlie cuttin' himself with scissors, some rich man from Tennessee dyin' in the Quarter, worried 'bout your momma and that no-good Cincinnati. Next it's all done. Gone quiet. What we all gonna do without Willie? Never gonna be the same." Cokie reached up and wiped his eyes. "Call this place 'The Big Easy,' shoot, ain't nothin' easy about it."

The funeral turnout was enormous. Bankers sat next to bootleggers. Cops conversed with prostitutes. Frankie, Cornbread, Sal, Elmo, Randolph, and Sonny all contributed to the patchwork that created the quilt of Willie's funeral. Walter Sutherland wore an ill-fitting gabardine suit covered in dandruff. Evangeline wore her hair in two braids with big black bows and an inappropriately short skirt. Jesse watched me from across the room, smiling whenever our eyes met. I had never seen him in a suit. He looked gorgeous.

Willie wanted to be cremated, but Dora insisted she first be laid out in a black coffin lined with red satin, to match Mariah. The funeral director assured us it was the Cadillac of coffins. Dora, and her bazooms, convinced him to rent it to us for the day. The sprays of flowers were enormous, including one from Carlos Marcello. Sweety sang an a cappella version of "Amazing Grace" that broke us all to pieces. Cokie wept openly and without shame, displaying the same love and respect that Willie had always shown him.

The funeral director read some sterile passages that didn't resonate to Willie. He called her Miss Woodley, which made everyone bristle. Cokie started shaking his head.

"Stop." Dora stood up and marched to the front of the funeral parlor in her forest green dress, matching glove hoisted in the air.

"Y'all, the Lord has put something on my heart, and I have to speak. First, I once stole twenty dollars from Willie and hid it in my toilet. There, I sinned against Willie that one time, and I had to cleanse myself of that. Now, Willie would not have the readin' of these depressin' psalms or passages. There was no 'Miss Woodley.' There was Willie. Willie was about life, and she grabbed it by the balls. Y'all know that. She loved a stiff drink, a stiff hundred, and she loved her business. And she didn't judge nobody. She loved everyone equal—accountants, queers, musicians, she welcomed us all, said we were all chuckleheaded just the same."

Everyone laughed. But Dora started to cry. Tears ran down

her face. "She was a good woman, and so many of us will be just lost without her. Please don't let her be put to rest in some quiet, boring way. That wasn't Willie. Cornbread, get up here and tell about the time Willie drove over your leg. Elmo, tell how Willie would test the mattresses to know if they were good enough for the game. Come on, y'all, please."

The tension in the room cracked. People stood up and told stories about Willie, about her generosity, warm heart, and cold exterior. I had so much to say but couldn't do it. Finally Sadie stood up. She looked around the room and quietly placed both hands on her heart.

I lost all composure. The woman who had never spoken a word in her life said more than any of us could.

Galatoire's buzzed like it was New Year's Eve. A large framed picture of Willie stood on a stand in the back of the restaurant. It was so noisy, so crowded, and I was so tired. Patrick had sent a telegram. His condolences left me hollow and sad. Evangeline walked through the crowd sucking a Shirley Temple through a straw. She stopped in front of me.

"So, would you ever do it?" she asked.

I shook my head. "I can't follow in my mother's footsteps."

"Not turning tricks. I mean would you ever take over for Willie? Be our madam."

I looked at Evangeline. She had to be joking. "What? No, I could never. I'm nothing like Willie."

She snorted in disgust. "You're a lot like Willie. She'd want you to take her place." Evangeline stared me down. "She loved you best, you know." She returned her lips to the straw and sauntered off in the direction of Dora's laughter, a piece of toilet paper trailing from her heel.

"Hey, Motor City."

I turned around. "Hi, Jesse. Have you been here the whole time?" I asked.

"Nah, I just came to see if you needed rescuing." He smiled. His white dress shirt was untucked at the waist. His cuffed denims and boots had replaced his funeral wear.

"It's been a long couple of days," I said.

"C'mon, let's get out of here."

FIFTY-SEVEN

We walked, silent. I was relieved to escape the din of the restaurant. Jesse handed me a stick of chewing gum. I gratefully accepted.

He stopped. "Hey, can I show you something?"

"Sure."

"Close your eyes. Keep 'em closed."

I stood with my eyes closed on the sidewalk. The sound of a door creaked and then Jesse took me by the hand.

"Now, don't open your eyes until I tell you to. Keep 'em closed." We walked a bit, and I tried not to stumble. We finally stopped, and I heard a clicking noise.

"Okay, open them."

In front of me was the most beautiful car I had ever seen. It was a deep pomegranate, like Willie's nails, with a finish so shiny I could see myself in it.

"Jesse, it's incredible."

"Do you like it?"

"I love it. It's so beautiful."

He ran around to the passenger side and opened the door. "Hop in."

The tan leather interior was smooth and flawless. Jesse got in behind the wheel.

"It took a long time, but she's almost ready to drive." He looked over at me, half of his mouth pulled up in a smile. "I'm taking you out, you know."

"You are?"

"Yeah, on a date. Once it's finished and running."

"Who cares if it's running? We can be like Ray and Frieda and pretend we're driving." I leaned back in the seat. "Where are we going on our date?"

"To Swindell Hollow," he replied without hesitation.

"Where's that?"

"It's where I'm from, in Alabama."

So we drove to Swindell Hollow. The quiet was blissful, Jesse quiet. I laid my head back and closed my eyes. I imagined the two-lane highway rolling under the tires and the breeze sliding in through the open window, lifting the ends of my hair. I felt New Orleans pass behind us, the gray net lifting, the sky becoming lighter, the trees greener.

"I owe you an apology," I finally said.

"Yeah?"

"Yeah."

I started in about the debt to Carlos Marcello. Jesse took his hands off the wheel and turned to me. "I kinda know all about it," he said. "Willie told me when I worked on her car. She was waiting for you to come to her. But you didn't."

"So you know all about it. I feel silly," I said.

"Don't feel silly. Just tell me something I don't know."

"Hmm, let's see. Did you know that the day I saw you with your friends, I was on my way to earn fifteen hundred dollars from that sleaze John Lockwell? Well, I chickened out, threw my shoes at him, and pulled a gun on him instead."

"I didn't like those shoes," said Jesse.

"Oh, and did you know that I met that Memphis tourist the day he died in the Quarter? He came into the bookshop and bought two books. He was so kind and nice I created him as my make-believe hero dad. Did you know that?"

Jesse shook his head.

"What else . . . oh, and then I found his wristwatch under my mom's bed and for some strange reason became completely attached to it. The night you saw me at the river, I wasn't there to meet Patrick. I was going to throw the watch in and sink it. But then I couldn't and broke down and cried. So I buried it out at Shady Grove, even though the police were looking for it."

I peeked at Jesse, expecting disgust or shock. He just nodded.

"Next, I bet you didn't know that I got a big fat rejection letter from Smith. And instead of inviting me to be a student, they attached a letter from some spinster writer who's asking me to come clean her house in Northampton."

Jesse perked up.

"That's humiliating, but not as humiliating as my new friend Charlotte finding out from her cousin here in New Orleans that she's invited the daughter of a prostitute to her summer home in the Berkshires."

I took a breath and looked at Jesse. "God, that felt so good."

He slid over toward me.

"Yeah? You likin' Alabama so far?"

"Loving Alabama." Thousands of pounds lifted from my shoulders and flew out the window of Jesse's car.

"Is that all you got?" asked Jesse.

"Nope. Here's one to add to the humiliation pile. Not only am I the daughter of a prostitute, I'm named after one. Josie Arlington, brothel madam, had a five-dollar house on Basin Street. For an extra fee, she offered some kind of French sex circus. And I'm named after her."

"Ding!" Jesse hit a nonexistent bell in front of us. "Ladies and gentlemen, we have a match. The two kids both have hand-me-down names of the ill repute." Jesse turned to me. "But actually, I win. You're named after a madam. I'm named after a murderer. So mine's worse."

My mouth fell open.

"Yeah, my criminal of a father named me Jesse, after Jesse James. Told me to grow up a good outlaw and live up to my name. I tell ya, I really hope that my father never meets your mother."

"Have you ever thought of changing your name?"

"Nah, Jesse Thierry is who I am."

"I want to change mine. Willie said I should change my last name."

"Last name might be a good idea, but don't change Josie," he said.

"No?"

"Nope." He fiddled with a knob on the dash. "I like the way it feels when I say it."

The cuff on Jesse's white dress shirt was open at the wrist. I reached for it and slowly began folding it back. He stared at my hands as they touched his forearm. My fingers didn't ball into a fist, just trailed lightly up and down his skin. He looked at me. I looked right back.

"Okay," I said. "Your turn. What don't I know about Jesse Thierry?"

"What don't you know?" Jesse slid his arm around my shoulders and pulled me close. "Maybe that I really wanna kiss you right now."

FIFTY-EIGHT

"We don't have a choice. Willie's attorney has requested us. He has questions," I said.

"Well, it makes me nervous," said Cokie. "I don't want to go sittin' with no lawyer rattlin' 'bout Willie. Willie never liked no one talkin' 'bout her business, and I ain't about to start now, even if she gone. So I'm not sayin' nothin'. We'll let Sadie do all the talkin'."

Sadie reached forward from the back of the cab and swatted Cokie across the side of the head. Sadie was nervous too. She and Cokie both had their church clothes on and had been bickering since we got in the cab. I was more than nervous, but not about the attorney. The law office was in the Hibernia Bank Building, one floor below John Lockwell's office. Just the thought of him brought bile to the back of my throat. I had pushed the meeting with the attorney back two weeks but couldn't delay it any longer.

We walked into the lobby, and I fished the letter out of my purse. Cokie looked over my shoulder.

"Edward Rosenblatt, Esquire. Sounds well-to-do. Willie wouldn't be messin' with no ritzy lawyer."

I shushed him, and we all got in the elevator.

Inside, I felt the same as Cokie. Willie wouldn't mess with a bank, so she certainly wouldn't do business with some rich lawyer. I had made a vow. I wasn't going to reveal anything about Willie. They could torture me, threaten me, I wouldn't do it. Don't worry, Willie, I won't let the vultures in.

We arrived on the seventh floor. Cokie pulled off his cap and began kneading it through his hands. He and Sadie stood back near the elevator. I approached the desk and told the receptionist we had arrived for our appointment. Within minutes, a woman appeared.

"Mr. Rosenblatt will see you now."

I waved Cokie and Sadie forward. We walked through a maze of typists. Sadie's eyes were as round as pancakes, taking in the upscale business environment. The woman directed us to an office. Three chairs were placed in front of a long desk.

"Mr. Rosenblatt will be right with you. Please make yourselves comfortable."

Cokie didn't want to sit down. I gave him the evil eye and pointed to a chair. The office was lovely, with oak paneling and a large wall of bookshelves with impressive sets of law volumes. Sadie nudged my arm and pointed to two pictures in sterling frames—one of an older woman, the other a photo of a large family.

"I'm sorry I kept you waiting." An elegant gentleman with gray hair entered the room and shut the door behind him. He had round spectacles and looked like the type who would smoke a pipe while watching polo matches. I thought I recognized him from the funeral.

"I'm Ed Rosenblatt. You must be Mr. Coquard?" He extended his hand to Cokie for a handshake. "And you must be Miss Moraine and Miss Vibert. A pleasure to meet you." He walked around to his desk and sat down in the tufted leather chair. He pulled a file folder in front of him. "Let's get started then, shall we?" He looked up at us and smiled. It seemed genuine, warm.

"First, Miss Vibert, I'm aware of your vocal affliction, so I'll keep our exchanges as direct as possible. I'd like to offer my condolences to all of you. I'm sure you're quite bereaved over Willie's passing."

"Yes, sir, I am," said Cokie. "So I don't mean no disrespect, but I don't want to be asked about Willie's private business. She wouldn't have it." Sadie nodded emphatically.

Mr. Rosenblatt looked from Cokie to Sadie and finally to me.

"Willie was a very private person, and we'd like to honor that," I explained.

"I think your loyalty is exactly why you're here. Let me explain something. I've known Willie since I was four years old. We came up together in the Quarter, along with Dr. Sully and a few others. In fact, when I was five, I decided that I wanted to marry Willie, but she wouldn't have any of it. She called me Rosie and said I was a fancy pants. She said instead of marriage, she'd like to be in business with me because she thought I was smart. You can imagine her at five years old, hand on her hip, finger in my face, making this business arrangement, can't you?"

I smiled. I could absolutely imagine it, the spicy little girl I saw in the photo hidden at Shady Grove.

"So there we were. Willie, Sully, and Rosie, a French Quarter version of the Three Musketeers." The attorney placed his hands on the desk. "But something happened when we were about twelve. Willie changed. She would do anything to keep from going home. Sully and I suspected her father."

I thought of Willie telling me that fathers were overrated, that mine was probably some creep.

Mr. Rosenblatt continued. "She started to run with a rough crowd. We drifted apart as we got older. Sully went off to med school, I went off to law school, and Willie opened for business. We lost touch for a while, mainly because Sully and I were frightened by the road Willie was taking. Then twenty-five years ago on New Year's Eve, Sully and I were having dinner with our wives. Willie sauntered right up to the table and asked Sully if he still had her slingshot. She said she needed to use it on some nitwit in the restaurant. It was as if we were all ten years old again." Mr. Rosenblatt smiled, reflecting. "There's something about childhood bonds, I guess. I've been working with Willie ever since."

We all stared at him.

"I'm her estate planner," he added for clarification. "I know this is a lot to digest."

"I guess . . . I just can't imagine Willie as a child," said Cokie.

Mr. Rosenblatt pulled a file folder from the bottom drawer. He handed us a tarnished photo of three kids standing in Jackson Square. Willie was in the center, making a muscle with her right arm.

Cokie whistled through his teeth. "Well, look at that. She looks like she could beat the devil outta both of you."

"She did," said the attorney. "Got the scars to prove it." He put the photo away. "As you know, Willie was a smart, organized woman. She enjoyed her money during her life and spent much of what she earned. She wasn't a saver and didn't trust banks, so it's not a large estate. I won't waste your time going through pages of legal jargon. It's quite simple. Willie appointed Miss Moraine the executor, and the assets will be distributed as follows: the house on Conti will become the joint property of Mr. Coquard and Miss Vibert—"

Sadie gasped and grabbed Cokie's arm.

"'Scuse me?" said Cokie.

Mr. Rosenblatt nodded. "I'll go through the list and then I'll answer any questions you have. As I said, the house on Conti and the furniture will become the joint property of Mr. Coquard and Miss Vibert. There is no mortgage. The house and property known as Shady Grove will become the sole property of Miss Moraine. This property is also debt free. The automobile, affectionately known as Mariah, as well as all firearms, will become the sole property of Miss Moraine. All of Willie's jewelry and personal effects will become the joint property of Miss Moraine and Miss Vibert. All of the nieces and information men currently in Willie's employ will receive one hundred dollars for each year of service. After all outstanding debts are paid, the remaining cash will be split evenly, five ways, between the three of you and the two surviving musketeers, Dr. Sully and myself."

The room was silent. Sadie sat bolt upright, her mouth hanging agape. Cokie began to cry.

"Mr. Coquard," began the attorney.

"Cokie," he corrected.

"Cokie, you worked with Willie for over twenty years. She valued your friendship and loyalty greatly. This is what she wanted," explained Mr. Rosenblatt.

Cokie spoke softly through his tears. "But none of it's no good. Don't you see? Nothing's gonna make up for Willie bein' gone."

Mr. Rosenblatt's eyes pooled. "I agree. Nothing will ever make up for Willie being gone."

He explained the next steps and the process. He made suggestions about budgets and financial-planning services. He insisted we tell absolutely no one of Willie's bequests, as she worried we would become targets for swindlers and moochers.

"Now, that's smart," said Cokie. "Josie girl here, she got a heart like an artichoke. A leaf for everyone. So don't you tell no one, Jo. You got plans, anyway." Cokie nodded and smiled at the attorney. "Josie goin' to college."

Everyone looked at me, wanting me to explain that I'd been accepted to Smith and was blowing out of New Orleans. But I wasn't.

Willie. College. Mother. Vultures. A loud fan whirred inside my head on high. At some point, I looked up and realized everyone in the room was standing.

"Is there something else, Miss Moraine?" The attorney, Cokie, and Sadie all stared.

"Yes," I said, still dazed. "Willie wanted me to change my name."

FIFTY-NINE

The sun beat down from twelve o'clock in the sky. I stretched my legs and rubbed the back of my neck.

"That's quite a car you've got there," said a man smoking a cigarette on the sidewalk.

"Thank you." The man circled the car, admiring it. I thought of Cokie and how he cried when I insisted on giving him Mariah.

"It must ride like a dream. You drive it a lot?" asked the man.

I shook my head. "It's my boyfriend's. He drives it all the time."

Jesse emerged from the post office, smiling.

"And let me guess," said the smoking man to Jesse. "You're the boyfriend."

"It's a tough job, but someone had to take her, right?" Jesse looked at me and grinned.

"You two travelin' far?" asked the man.

"Yes, sir. Takin' my girl on a trip."

The man's wife came out of the post office. He wished us safe travels.

"Well?" I asked.

Jesse slung his arm around me and whispered in my ear. "One Lord Elgin watch on its way to Mrs. Marion Hearne in Memphis. Postmark Alabama."

"Thank you." I hugged him.

He slapped his hands together. "All right, give me Cokie's map. I promised him I'd follow Cornbread's route up through Georgia."

Jesse spread the map out on the hood of the car. His car. The car he built himself from nothing but a scrap heap. Somehow he'd managed to put the pieces together, polish them up, and make them into something beautiful, completely unrecognizable from its former self.

I looked at the carton in the backseat. Charlie's Valentine box with the Siamese acorns, the page from his typewriter, a postcard from Cuba, and three pictures in sterling frames. The one of Willie as a child that I found at Shady Grove, one of Jesse and his car, and one of Cokie and Sadie in front of their house on Conti. The sadness started to seep in again. We got back in the car.

"What is it?" asked Jesse.

I shrugged. "I desperately wanted to get away from it, but somehow I'm worried that it will all evaporate, that I'll lose Cokie, the bookshop, you."

"It's a start, Jo. A safe one."

I nodded, wanting to stick to the plan.

"The hardest part is just gettin' out. Miss Paulsen got

you an interview at Smith. You have a safe place to stay in Northampton with her friend—a place where your mother and Cincinnati will never find you. Once you're there, you'll turn it into something quick. You'll get into Smith, I know it. Nothin's gonna change in New Orleans. If you ever go back, you'll find the same hustle and blow. It'll be just as you left it. And you're not losin' me."

He edged over close to me. I looked up at him.

"I'm gonna finish school and then you know what? I'm comin' for you, Josie Coquard." Jesse smiled. "Josie Mae West of the Motor City Moraine Coquard. You still owe me a window. Put that in the note to your friend."

I had been writing out a postcard to Charlotte from Alabama. At Jesse's insistence, I had sent her a twelve-page single-spaced letter. I spilled my entire history, every filthy last bit of it, including that my namesake was a madam and that Miss Paulsen had somehow pulled strings for an interview at Smith. I could barely fit all the pages in the envelope and had to tape it shut. Additional postage required, the postal clerk had said.

And then I waited, certain that no response would indeed be the response. But then a letter arrived, a single sheet of pink paper with a brief reply.

> "There is no excellent beauty that hath not some strangeness in the proportion."
> —Sir Francis Bacon

> Can't wait to see you!
> Your trusted friend, Charlotte

And so it was decided.

Josie's goin' to Northampton, so don't you jive on me.
I took a swig out of Cokie's thermos, and we pulled back onto the road.

Acknowledgments

Out of the Easy was a team effort. This book would not have been possible without the team captains—my agent Ken Wright and my editor Tamra Tuller. Ken encouraged me to pursue this story and Tamra guided every step of my writing. Their patience, wisdom, and expertise transformed this novel. I am grateful for such wonderful mentors and friends.

I am eternally indebted to author Christine Wiltz. Her book *The Last Madam: A Life in the New Orleans Underworld* inspired not only this story, but also my desire to be a writer. Earl and Lorraine Scramuzza introduced me to a historical underbelly of the French Quarter I never would have uncovered on my own. Sean Powell welcomed me into the house on Conti that was formerly the brothel of Norma Wallace and the studio of E. J. Bellocq. New Orleans historian John Magill shared his incredible knowledge and flagged my errors.

Writers of historical fiction would be lost without libraries and archives. I am grateful to the Williams Research Center in New Orleans, the Historic New Orleans Collection, the New Orleans Public Library, the Nashville Public Library, the Brentwood Library, *The Times-Picayune, The Tennessean,* Nanci A. Young in the Smith College Archives, Lori E. Schexnayder in the Tulane University Archives, Trish Nugent in the Loyola University Archives, the Vanderbilt University Archives, the Librairie Book Shop on Chartres, and the Garden District Book Shop. Writers Lyle Saxon, Robert Tallant, Ellen Gilchrist, Anne Rice, and Truman Capote brought Louisiana to life for me through their stunning prose. Thank you to the teachers, librarians, booksellers, and literacy advocates who have given me the opportunity to connect with students and readers.

My writing group sees everything first: Sharon Cameron, Amy Eytchison, Rachel Griffith, Linda Ragsdale, Howard Shirley, and Angelika Stegmann. Thank you for your dedication and friendship. I couldn't do it without you! Kristy King, Lindsay Davis, and Kristina Sepetys were all integral to the character development of Josie Moraine. Genetta Adair, Courtney Stevens Potter, Rae Ann Parker, and The Original 7 were wonderfully generous with critiques and encouragement. Fred Wilhelm and Lindsay Kee sparked the title. And SCBWI made my dreams come true.

Michael Green at Philomel, thank you for believing in me. The Philomel family—Semadar Megged, Jill Santopolo, Kiffin Steurer, and Julia Johnson. The Penguin family—Don Weisberg, Jennifer Loja, Eileen Kreit, Ashley Fedor, Scottie Bowditch, Shanta Newlin, Kristina Aven, Liz Moraz, Helen Boomer, Felicia Frazier, Emily Romero, Jackie Engel, Erin Dempsey, Anna Jarzab, Marie Kent, Linda McCarthy, Vanessa Han, and all of the incredible Penguin field reps.

Yvonne Seivertson, Niels Bye Nielsen, Gavin Mikhail, Jeroen Noordhuis, Mike Cortese, The Rockets, Steve Vai, JW Scott, Steve Malk, Carla Schooler, Jenna Shaw, Amanda Accius Williams, the Lithuanian community, the Reids, the Frosts, the Tuckers, the Smiths, the Peales and the Sepetyses all assisted or supported my efforts with this book.

Mom and Dad, you taught me to dream big and love even bigger. John and Kristina, you are my inspiration and the best friends a little sister could ask for.

And Michael, your love gives me the courage and the wings. You are my everything.

An Interview with Ruta Sepetys

How did you create Josie Moraine?

Years ago I was part of a mentoring program for young women. I met girls who were swept into the dysfunctional current that surrounded their home lives. But I also met young women who made difficult decisions and divorced themselves from a negative environment. That's incredibly hard. Those girls inspired me. They taught me that we can learn to fly, even if we're born with broken wings. The idea of that broken yet beautiful bird became Josie Moraine.

Why New Orleans?

New Orleans is unlike any city in America and such a rich backdrop for a novel. Its cultural diversity is woven into the food, the music, the architecture—even the local superstitions. It's full of secrets and dark doorways. It's a sensory experience on all levels and there's a story lurking around every corner.

Why do you enjoy writing historical fiction?

History is full of secrets. Writing historical fiction is a bit like being a detective and I love that aspect. You really have to research and dig in order to unearth information that will be interesting to readers.

How did you research the book?

I took several trips to New Orleans and spent many days at the Williams Research Center. I also combed library archives. I walked Josie's paths that I describe in the book and interviewed people who had intimate knowledge of the underbelly of the city.

My meetings were both fascinating and terrifying. I couldn't sleep at night. Scandals, murders, crooks, and crime—all beyond your wildest imagination. And as a writer, I loved it! The most incredible part of my research was being allowed into Norma Wallace's former brothel. I based Willie's house on Norma's. Standing in Norma's old bedroom, I imagined how Josie would bring Willie her coffee, where she'd count the money. I saw the girls' rooms upstairs, the hiding places, and the escape route through the courtyard for when the cops would show up. I could hear the voices of the characters in my head so clearly. I hope their personalities come across in the book.

Why 1950?

I chose the historical setting of post-war America because it's complex and often misunderstood. Following WWII, the U.S. experienced unparalleled prosperity. But the American Dream for some became the quiet nightmare for others. Societal pressures to conform were severe, and deep tensions developed across social, racial, and gender lines. People escaped these pressures in various ways, and the alluring "come hither" of New Orleans was one of them. But for some, the Big Easy was more than they could handle. People kept a lot of secrets back then. Illness and family troubles were often hidden from the public. Sometimes, what looked perfect on the outside was quietly rotting on the inside.

TURN THE PAGE FOR A LOOK INSIDE ANOTHER
NEW YORK TIMES BESTSELLING NOVEL BY
RUTA SEPETYS

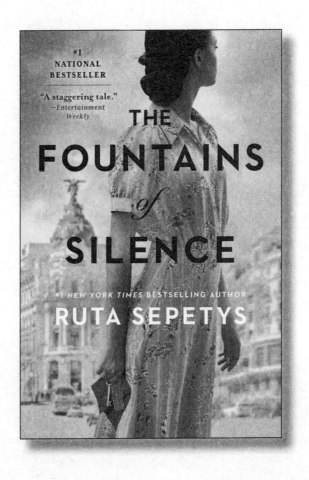

{ 1 }

They stand in line for blood.

June's early sun blooms across a string of women waiting patiently at *el matadero*. Fans snap open and flutter, replying to Madrid's warmth and the scent of open flesh wafting from the slaughterhouse.

The blood will be used for *morcilla*, blood sausage. It must be measured with care. Too much blood and the sausage is not firm. Too little and the sausage crumbles like dry earth.

Rafael wipes the blade on his apron, his mind miles from *morcilla*. He turns slowly from the line of customers and puts his face to the sky.

In his mind it is Sunday. The hands of the clock touch six.

It is time.

The trumpet sounds and the march of the *pasodoble* rolls through the arena.

Rafael steps onto the sand, into the sun.

He is ready to meet Fear.

In the center box of the bullring sits Spain's dictator, Generalísimo Francisco Franco. They call him *El Caudillo*—leader of armies, hero by the grace of God. Franco looks down to the ring. Their eyes meet.

You don't know me, Generalísimo, but I know you.

I am Rafael Torres Moreno, and today, I am not afraid.

"Rafa!"

The supervisor swats the back of Rafael's damp neck. "Are you blind? There's a line. Stop daydreaming. The blood, Rafa. Give them their blood."

Rafa nods, walking toward the patrons. His visions of the bullring quickly disappear.

Give them their blood.

Memories of war tap at his brain. The small, taunting voice returns, choking daydreams into nightmares. *You do remember, don't you, Rafa?*

He does.

The silhouette is unmistakable.

Patent-leather men with patent-leather souls.

The Guardia Civil. He secretly calls them the Crows. They are servants of Generalísimo Franco and they have appeared on the street.

"Please. Not here," whispers Rafael from his hiding spot beneath the trees.

The wail of a toddler echoes above. He looks up and sees Julia at the open window, holding their youngest sister, Ana.

Their father's voice booms from inside. "Julia, close the window! Lock the door and wait for your mother. Where is Rafa?"

"Here, Papá," whispers Rafael, his small legs folded in hiding. "I'm right here."

His father appears at the door. The Crows appear at the curb.

The shot rings out. A flash explodes. Julia screams from above.

Rafa's body freezes. No breath. No air.

No.

   No.

      No.

They drag his father's limp corpse by an arm.

"*¡Papá!*"

It's too late. As the cry leaves his throat, Rafa realizes. He's given himself away.

A pair of eyes dart. "His boy's behind the tree. Grab him."

Rafa blinks, blocking the painful memories, hiding his collapsed heart beneath a smile.

"*Buenos días, señora.* How may I help you?" he asks the customer.

"Blood."

"*Sí, señora.*"

Give them their blood.

For more than twenty years, Spain has given blood. And sometimes Rafa wonders—what is left to give?

{ 2 }

It's a lie.
   It has to be.

I know what you've done.

Ana Torres Moreno stands two levels belowground, in the second servants' basement. She rips the small note to pieces, shoves them in her mouth, and swallows.

A voice calls from the hall. "Hurry, Ana. They're waiting."

Dashing through the windowless maze of stone walls, Ana wills herself to move faster. Wills herself to smile.

A weak glow from a bare bulb whispers light onto the supply shelf. Ana spots the tiny sewing kit and throws it into her basket. She runs to the stairs and falls in step with Lorenza, who balances an assortment of cigarettes on a tray.

"You look pale," whispers Lorenza. *"¿Estás bien?"*

"I'm fine," replies Ana.

Always say you're fine, especially when you're not, she reminds herself.

The mouth of the stairway appears. Light from a crystal chandelier twinkles and beckons from the glittering hall.

Their steps slow, synchronize, and in perfect unison they emerge onto the marble floor of the hotel lobby, faces full of smile. Ana scrolls her mental list. The man from New York will want a newspaper and matches. The woman from Pennsylvania will need more ice.

Americans love ice. Some claim to have trays of cubed ice in their own kitchens. Maybe it's possible. Ana sees advertisements for appliances in glossy magazines that hotel guests leave behind.

Frigidaire! Rustproof aluminum shelving, controlled butter-ready.

Whatever that means. Beyond Spain, all is a mystery.

Ana hears every word, but guests would never know it. She scurries, filling requests quickly so visitors have no time to glance out of their world and into hers.

Julia, the matriarch of their fractured family, issues constant reminders. "You trust too easily, Ana. You reveal too much. Stay silent."

Ana is tired of silence, tired of unanswered questions, and tired of secrets. A girl of patched pieces, she dreams of new beginnings. She dreams of leaving Spain. But her sister is right. Her dreams have proven dangerous.

I know what you've done.

"For once, follow the rules instead of your heart," pleads her sister.

Follow the rules. To be invisible in plain view and paid handsomely for it—five *pesetas* per hour—this is the plan. Her older brother, Rafael, works at both the slaughterhouse and the cemetery. Between two jobs he makes only twelve *pesetas*, twenty cents according to the hotel's exchange desk, for an entire day's work.

Ana hands the sewing kit to the concierge and heads quickly for the staff elevator. The morning is gone, but her task list is growing. Summer season has officially arrived at the hotel, pouring thousands of new visitors into Spain. The elevator doors open to the seventh floor. Ana shifts the basket to her hip and hurries down the long corridor.

"Towels for 760," whispers a supervisor who shuttles past.

"Towels for 760," she confirms.

Four years old, but to Ana, the American hotel smells new. Tucked into her basket is a stack of hotel brochures featuring a handsome bullfighter, a matador, holding a red cape. In fancy script across the cape is written:

Castellana Hilton Madrid. Your Castle in Spain.

Castles. She saw old postcards as a child. The haunting newsreel rolls behind her eyes:

The tree-lined avenue of Paseo de la Castellana—home to Spanish royalty and grand palaces. And then, the bright images fade. 1936. Civil war erupts in Spain. War drains color from the cheeks of Madrid. The grand palaces become gray ghosts. Gardens and fountains disappear. So do Ana's parents. Hunger and isolation cast a filter of darkness over the country. Spain is curtained off from the world.

And now, after twenty years of nationwide atrophy, Generalísimo Franco is finally allowing tourists into Spain. Banks and hotels wrap new exteriors over old palace interiors. The tourists don't know the difference. What lies beneath is now hidden, like the note disintegrating in her stomach.

Ana reads the newspapers and magazines that guests discard. She memorizes the brochure to recite on cue.

> *Formerly a palace, Castellana is the first Hilton property in Europe. Over three hundred rooms, each with a three-channel radio, and even a telephone.*

"If you are assigned to a guest in a suite, you will see to their every request," lectures her supervisor. "Remember, Americans are less formal than Spaniards. They're accustomed to conversation. You will be warm, helpful, and conversational."

"*Ay*, I'm always warm and conversational," Lorenza whispers with a wink.

Ana wants to be conversational, but her sister's call for silence contradicts hotel instruction. The constant tug in opposite directions makes her feel like a rag doll, destined to lose an arm.

A man in a crisp white shirt emerges from a door into the hallway. Ana stops and gives a small bob. *"Buenos días, señor."*

"Hiya, doll."

Doll. Dame. Kitten. Baby. American men have many terms for women. Just when Ana thinks she has learned them all, a new one appears. In her English class at the hotel, these words are called terms of endearment.

After what happened last year, Ana knows better.

American diplomats, actors, and musicians arrive amidst the swirling dust of Barajas Airport. They socialize and mingle into the pale hours of morning. Ana secretly notes their preferences. Starlets have favorite suites. Politicians have favorite starlets. Many are unaware of what transpired in Spain decades earlier. They sip cava, romanticizing Hemingway and flamenco. On rare occasion someone asks Ana about Spain's war. She politely changes the subject. It's not only hotel policy, but also the promise she made.

She will look to the future. The past must be forgotten.

Her father executed. Her mother imprisoned. Their crime was not an action, but an ambition—teachers who hoped to develop a Montessori school with methods based on child development rather than religion. But Generalísimo Franco commands that all schools in Spain shall be controlled by the Catholic Church. Republican sympathizers must be eradicated.

Her parents' offense has left Ana rowing dark waters of dead secrets. Born into a long shadow of shame, she must never speak publicly of her parents. She must live in silence. But sometimes, from the hidden corners of her heart, calls the haunting question:

What can be built through silence?

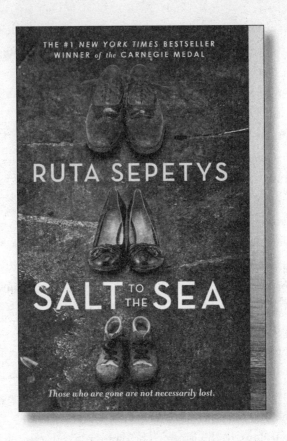

A #1 *NEW YORK TIMES* BESTSELLER
AND CARNEGIE MEDAL WINNER!

"Ruta Sepetys acts as champion of the interstitial people so often ignored—whole populations lost in the cracks of history."
—*The New York Times Book Review*

"Superlative . . . masterfully crafted . . . [a] powerful work of historical fiction." —*The Wall Street Journal*

★ "This visceral novel proves a memorable testament to strength and resilience in the face of war and cruelty."
—*Publishers Weekly*, STARRED REVIEW

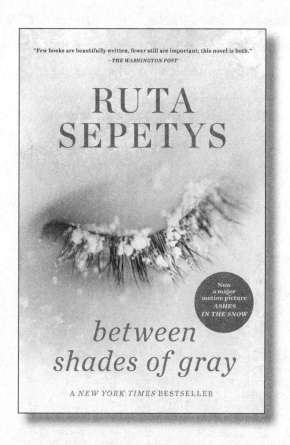

A #1 *NEW YORK TIMES* BESTSELLER
AND WILLIAM C. MORRIS AWARD FINALIST!

"Few books are beautifully written, fewer still are important; this novel is both." —*The Washington Post*

"At once a suspenseful, drama-packed survival story, a romance, and an intricately researched work of historical fiction." —*The Wall Street Journal*

★ "Beautifully written and deeply felt . . . An important book that deserves the widest possible readership." —*Booklist*, STARRED REVIEW

Look for *Ashes in the Snow*, the movie tie-in edition of *Between Shades of Gray*, featuring a behind-the-scenes look at the making of the film!

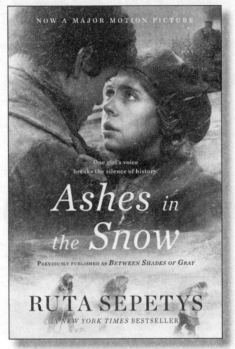

Movie tie-in edition

Now available on DVD!